H.H. Laura

Ryeth

Sensate Nine Moon Saga

Ryeth

Sensate Nine Moon Saga

by H. H. Laura

1st Edition

Published by RNL Associates
April 2016

Cover art copyright by Cora Graphics, Inc.
April 2016

ISBN No.: 978-0-9846678-4-0

Sensates.com

License Notes

This book is licensed for your enjoyment only. If you are reading this book and it has no cover, then this book was obtained or sold illegally. Please destroy the book.

Thank you for respecting the hard work of the author.

Dedication

To Mathew and Gregory:
May your hearts always be filled with love.
-Ma

Preface

Ryeth is the second book in the Sensate Nine Moon Saga series and although it can be read as a stand-alone book, I believe you will derive much more pleasure if you read the series in order beginning with *Larkspur.*

In all three books you will find that I adhere to certain principles: true love is pure, it harbors no guile or pretense, and it endures an eternity. I believe in what lurks between the lines and the process of 'fade to black,' and finally, that good shall always prevail over evil.

Please enjoy my Sensates and have as much fun reading about them as I did creating them.

Table of Contents

Prologue

1513 - The Caribbean, near La Florida

Thunderous waves crashed against the sides of the Spanish galleon and spat the chilling sea onboard. Men, cargo, and sails, held tight by casings or bloodless fingers, braved the mighty sea. Two young men huddled against the cold beneath a tattered oilcloth.

Juan looked into the eyes of his companion and read no deceit. "Eh, amigo, Captain de Leon is a mean one," he said cautiously.

"Aye. I got the scars on my back to prove it." Esteban shifted against a brace of wind as it whipped through their protective oilcloth and sucked away the little warmth they had.

Unsure of his friend's loyalty, Juan was careful to choose his next words. "The quest for the Fountain of Youth sounded good, but the Captain's use of the cat o' nine tails is a different matter."

Images of the island natives' flashed in Juan's mind. Peaceful and kindhearted, the Taino Indians greeted the Captain with welcoming gifts and friendship. It didn't take long for the Captain to repay that kindness. The brutal whippings and torture that brought near extinction to the tribe would be hard, if not impossible, for Juan to ever forget.

Esteban shook his head and said, "The Tainos on Boriquen did not even fight back."

Juan nodded. His stomach soured. "He lusts for savagery."

Esteban shook his head. "I will not be whipped again."

The fierceness of Esteban's words mimicked Juan's own convictions. His desire to be out from under the sadistic thumb of their captain spurred the conversation onward.

"Be careful, my friend," said Juan. He peered from beneath the tarp to see if they were alone. "Choose your words and friends wisely."

Esteban nodded. "I can trust you, Juan; you have honor."

Juan relaxed his guard. "Listen, as soon as we land, I plan to get as far away from that mean son-of-a-dog as I can."

Esteban jerked, visibly shaken. He whispered as his eyes furtively searched the deck. "If he catches you, he'll whip you to death."

Juan straightened his shoulders. "I owe no loyalty to a man who treats good men as dogs," Juan said as his lip curled. "Too many eyes stopped my escape on Boriquen, but I can handle no more of his barbarism. Less conquistadors on this trip means less men searching when I slip away."

A strong gale wind blew, slapping the make-shift tarp against their bodies. Chills wracked deep into his core as he held tight to the oilcloth. It was a few minutes before their bodies regained the lost warmth.

"My bones ache." Esteban pressed his back against the wall. "This blow from the north will take us off course."

"Nay, for all his meanness, the Captain's a good

sailor," said Juan. "We will land in two days, as he said."

Juan forced his thoughts away from his misfortunes to the promise of a new beginning. Though the cold cut through his fingers and legs threatening to deplete what warmth he had lost, his mind was elsewhere. His path was set. He would build, create, and thrive. The desire to marry, beget children and establish a family grew within his chest. He would recoup the life lost.

Esteban's voice stirred him from his thoughts. "May I go with you?" he asked.

His words were barely audible, yet they filled Juan with hope. "It will not be easy," he said. "I had no wish to start alone." He placed his hand on Esteban's shoulder and said, "I'd be glad of your company."

The wind whistled as the night turned even blacker. The two, brought together by loathing, wiled away the night formulating their escape.

***

The storm subsided and the sun welcomed them to a new day. Juan and Esteban emerged from the tarp to begin the day's work.

"I'm back to the galley," said Esteban as he headed toward the hatch.

"Stay out of trouble," he said.

Juan began clearing the deck of the ropes that had loosened during the storm. He caught his image in the porthole glass. At eighteen, he possessed his father's broad-shouldered frame and dashing good looks. He sniffed and gave a cockeyed expression at his reflection. If it hadn't been for his greedy uncle, he would have entered a life at court, stealing kisses from young senoritas, and testing his mettle against military swordsmen of his caliber. Instead, his uncle caused the death of his parents, stole their property and forced him to flee Spain. Soldados hot on his heels, he had slipped aboard the first ship out of port to save his hide and put distance between himself and his powerful uncle.

He looked around at his comrades. The ship's crew consisted of life-hardened young men trying to break free from the bondage of their misfortunes. Most were assigned as crew in lieu of a life-sentence in prison. Such was the case of Esteban Sosa, who had made the mistake of poaching on royal grounds and now paid heavily for his oversight. They all met with the same unsavory existence no matter the reason for coming aboard.

By happenstance, he ended up destined for the new world under the machinations of one of the cruelest captains to lay hands on a crew. Juan Ponce de Leon, well-known conquistador and Captain of the San Cristobal, wasted no love on his crew, his soldados, or on the unfortunate native inhabitants of the new worlds he claimed for Spain. Juan was aware the King favored Ponce de Leon, hungered for gold, and cared not how it got in his coffers.

Due to his change in circumstances, Juan decided to forge a new existence in a land untainted by the worldliness of court activities. His months at sea honed the body of a child into that of a man. Juan learned to read the moodiness of the captain and his first mate and rarely caught the lashes of the whip. Esteban wasn't as lucky.

It was well known that the punishment for desertion was a hundred lashes. It was rare for anyone to survive such beatings. Over the past months, Juan had witnessed several whippings for drunkenness. The brute that wielded the whip in lieu of the captain rivaled the captain's brutality with every strike. Juan knew the punishment he might incur, but the need for freedom was strong within him. Fear of the unknown paled against his current plight.

Within two days, land loomed ahead. Juan and Esteban were among those selected to go ashore to set up camp while soldados explored the surrounding area. As they unloaded the ship stores, they secreted away portions of the supplies. Hours later, they had a small cache of dried meats, beans, and flour - enough to support them until they acquired shelter and distance from the soldados. A stockpile of weaponry to be cleaned and serviced would come later, just before the full complement of two hundred men disembarked.

Juan had confidence in their plan. Between the two, they possessed various skills and knowledge. Esteban's skill with trapping and curing, and Juan's talents with sword and bow complemented each other. Their plan was to track the coastline northward and follow the first large river inland, but all was contingent on escaping the soldados. It was rare for a sailor, even a forced one, to leave the protection of the soldados, who ensured their safety from native inhabitants and vicious animals. Juan and Esteban were counting on luck and perseverance to see them through.

***

A squabble broke out over which soldado was in

charge. Juan watched the commotion through hooded eyes as Esteban snuck to the cache and disappeared from view. He scanned the group to see if anyone noticed Esteban's escape. Luck was on their side; he'd gotten away clean. Juan tucked his head low and continued the work at hand and waited for a similar opportunity to join Esteban on their trek north as planned.

Hours slipped by with no chance for Juan to break away from the group when a loud voice caught his attention. The burly, slobbering sailor who blustered his way among the crew chose, once again, to assert himself with another less-fortunate sailor. Instead of cowering to the much larger man, the wiry mate fought back. Juan cringed. In another time and place, he would have rushed to defend the small mate's honor the blade of his thin epee sparkling as it caught the rays of the sun. As it was, the ruckus created a circle of on-lookers which was quickly dispelled by the soldados. While the crew and soldados focused on the punishment, Juan made his way to their cache, grabbed what remained, and hid from view of the soldados.

He glanced to the opposite side of the rough camp where a horde of weapons beckoned. A young, anxious, Spanish heart hammered in his chest as he snuck around to the stash and sequestered two broadswords, a knife, and one fine epee. His steps were swift and deft as he made his way around the camp and crept northward. Juan kept his ears peeled for sounds of pursuit and followed a worn game trail away from the beach into the woods.

So intent was he on his mission of what he left behind, that he failed to notice what was ahead. While skirting the encampment, Juan ran smack dab into two large natives of La Florida. The red men stood before him, a stark wall of reality that prevented him from moving forward. He was at a distinct disadvantage with his arms filled with plunder from the ship. At a dead stop, his heart skipped a beat. His eyes widened and his mouth went dry. He turned to flee, and in doing so, he realized, from their vantage point, the natives had observed their landing, unloading, the punishment about to take place, and his escape.

Turning back to the natives, he met their eyes in the semi-darkness of the forest. He nodded. One native nodded in return. The other turned to leave, and motioned for him to follow. The three stole away into the night.

The natives were dressed in hides that clung to their bodies like a second skin and wore soft leather shoes, which molded to their feet. Although Juan's steps were quiet, the natives' steps made no sound at all. Soon, they met up with four others of their kind. A smile broke on his face as he spied Esteban among them.

Esteban stepped forward and clasped him on the shoulder, grinning from ear to ear. "Juan, I thought you would not make it. They found me; I would have become lost."

Juan glanced around at their six new comrades, who were talking and gesturing. One, who seemed to be the leader of the group shook his head and motioned toward Esteban and him.

"We might be alright for a while, but we don't know their intentions," Juan said, keeping one eye on the group as he spoke.

"They are friendly. I waited with them. They wanted to go but I would not leave. The leader sent two off, and they returned with you."

"At least we ended up together." Juan checked the woods and listened for any indications of pursuit.

The Indians motioned for them to follow. They walked at a swift pace the remainder of the night and into the next day, only stopping to rest twice before they came upon a village.

Rounded huts covered with grasses and skins dotted the clearing. Near each hut was a fire pit. Some of the women, dressed in tanned hides, were busy making pottery, a few were tanning hides, and some chased scantily-clad youngsters around with a stick. By their clothing, he could tell their native escorts were not of the same tribe as the village. Alert braves greeted their party and guided them to the chief. As they led Esteban and him through the tiny village, the inhabitants gathered to watch their procession.

He could do no more than watch as the chief studied them and listened to their new friends. After what seemed like the ending of an inquisition, they were allowed to continue their journey through the chief's land.

The lead Indian held the respect of the others. Oftentimes they looked to him for decisions and heeded his instructions without question. Each wore leather pants with no middle section, held up by a belt and caught up at the hip. Their breach cloths had two flaps, one in front, and one in the back, which covered their nether regions. The tanned chests were bare except for the highly decorated necklaces they each wore. From the back, they all looked the same, tanned red by the sun and well formed. The lead Indian had a feather on the side of his necklace and had much more muscle mass.

The natives always positioned Esteban and him between them as they walked. Juan kept up a continuing conversation with Esteban that made the miles go faster.

"They make no noise with their feet," Esteban noted.

Juan looked at the Indians' feet. Their boots had been fashioned from some kind of soft leather that was sewn to fit their feet perfectly. Compared to his own boots, which did not bend easily and chafed his legs, they looked lightweight and comfortable. "We sound like a pair of oxen next to them. Their footwear is more accustomed to comfort and walking quietly."

"Where do they take us?" asked Esteban.

Juan shrugged. "Right now, I only care that we are moving away from Captain DeLeon."

The lead Indian motioned for them to stop. Juan dropped to the ground and removed his boot. His stocking had dropped down and he had walked on the bump for hours. As he straightened his stocking and replaced his boot, his stomach growled.

He looked up to see the Indians staring at him with a comical look on their faces.

"Cmokman e'bkite'wat." It was the first time the leader had spoken distinctly. He pointed to Juan.

Two of the six Indians broke away from the group and slipped soundlessly into the forest. Juan's pulse raced. He looked quickly at Esteban, noted his panic-stricken eyes, and then into the emotionless eyes of Featherman. The Indian had come to some sort of decision.

Featherman walked over to Juan. Juan jumped to his feet and faced him.

Featherman pointed to his stomach and said,

"Bukte' manIn," and gestured as if he had something in his fingers and put it in his mouth. He pretended to chew, then smiled and rubbed his stomach.

Juan broke out in a broad smile. "Yes," he said, nodding. "Yes, I am hungry." He rubbed his stomach.

Featherman pointed to his chest. "Taima."

Juan nodded. "Taima," he repeated.

Taima smiled.

Juan pointed to himself and said, "Juan," and pointed to Esteban and said, "Esteban."

Taima nodded and repeated, "Juan, 'Teban."

Esteban grinned. "Teban is good." He nodded with great exaggeration.

The introductions behind them, the three exchanged a few words, each repeating the name clearly, so the other could hear the inflections. Within a half an hour, each had a basic concept of the others' language. Juan learned about fifteen words and two which he considered of great importance, "I'm starving."

Juan and Esteban offered their meager stores to their friends, who declined. Taima motioned for Juan to put his food aside. After the Indians made a small fire and cooked the freshly killed and gutted squirrels, Juan understood why. The natural seasonings pulled from small sacks the natives carried around their mid-section imparted such flavor to the succulent meat that Juan couldn't contain his pleasure.

Taima watched his expression and smiled at Juan.

"Good," he said to Taima and nodded.

***

Taima's tribe greeted them with curiosity and friendship. Though Juan's past afforded him the luxury of experiencing people of various colored skin, it was apparent the natives of this new land found their skin color and speech a novelty. The tribe fingered their clothing, rubbed their skin, and marveled at the curly hair on his and Esteban's heads.

The tribe took them into their fold, shared their farming, hunting and fishing techniques, and taught them how to endure the harshness of their new land's winter season.

The following spring, after the leaves budded and snow melted, Juan and Esteban took their leave from the Algonquin Indians and headed inland, up the mouth of a wide river. Their first year challenged their survival skills during the harshness of the winter, but they managed to survive through hunting and trapping. The early spring ushered forth as the two became accustomed to a new way of life.

Meat stores depleted during the long winter made it necessary for them to hunt for larger game to smoke and dry. Crisp air filled their lungs as the two crept around an outcropping of rocks. Shock halted them in their tracks. Two small brown bear cubs frolicked in front of them not twenty feet away. Fear gripped Juan as he remained still and scanned the area for the mother he knew would not be far away.

Chills ran down his neck as Juan heard a low growl above and behind them. Esteban turned around just as the beast sprung from the overhead boulder and landed on him full force. The action was so quick, Juan had no time to deflect the weight of the animal from his friend.

Though Juan and Esteban had matured and blossomed into manhood, Esteban was no match for the bear and lay pinned beneath its massive hulk. Juan pulled a knife from his belt and rushed to Esteban's aid. The bear's paw pressed on Esteban's chest as the animal let out a roar, baring its teeth. Juan jumped on the back of the bear and plunged his knife into its neck, pushing it into the hilt. He pulled upward to slice its neck, but was thrown as it bucked him off.

Esteban lay motionless as the animal turned from him and centered its attack on Juan. Still stunned from the landing, Juan failed to get to his feet before the bear was upon him. His knife entered the bear once again, this time in the chest. The animal's attacked ceased.

He pushed the body from him and rushed to Esteban's side. A pool of blood poured from his companion's head. A quick glance confirmed Esteban's skull had been crushed on impact. Emptiness washed over the life-hardened young man of twenty. The last connection to the world of his youth disappeared beneath rock and soil.

Now, completely alone, but clothed in a warm fur, Juan stood atop the rocky peak, breathed the crisp mountain air and mourned the loss of his friend. He nodded, giving a grudging respect for the country that threatened to engulf him. Juan scanned the visage. Thick forests and lush valleys lay like a blanket before him. The scent of new growth and rich fertile land called to his farming roots. He took one last glance, shifted his pack on his shoulder, and began the descent into the valley below.

Following mostly game trails, his path rounded the crest and made its way down the rocky and boulder-laden slope until it reached a stream where ice still clung to the edges. He knelt down and hand-cupped the cold water to his lips. As he dried his mouth on his sleeve, he noticed fresh deer tracks on the opposite side. Chirping above were small black-eyed birds with white tufted breasts. The warm air loosened insects from their homes to hunt their first taste of life. The valley awoke from its slumber.

The water twisted downward as it picked up other smaller offerings and grew larger. The land flattened out and the rocks lessened. The stream became sizable and now contained fish instead of minnows. Intent on finding the perfect spot to make his home, Juan continued his search downstream.

The noise from the rushing water grew loud in his ears. Breaking through the forest canopy, the stream flowed into a small lake, perfectly situated in a wide valley surrounded by glorious mountain peaks and lightly forested lowlands. Reflected in the smooth glassy surface were the mountain peaks and blue sky. The scene warmed his heart. He said in the language of his homeland, "Este es un lugar que un hombre puede llamar su casa." - This is a place a man can call home.

Chapter 1

About 1545 - Somewhere in the hills of the north near the great waters

"He means nothing to me." Onatah sighed.

Juan caressed her face in his calloused hands. "Ona, I am not questioning your loyalty; I am concerned he will misinterpret your kindness."

"Am I not to be kind?" Her dark eyes rose to meet his.

"I've watched how he looks at you."

She was aware of Juan's protective nature. Not possessing a jealous nature, Juan cared only for her safety.

"I cannot help the stars in his eyes," she noted softly. "Surely he can see I have eyes for only you."

"My sweet Ona, you are so very good to everyone. He does not know the difference and is mistaking your kindness for interest. It is no wonder the young brave is enamored with you; after twenty years, even I am still flattered that you chose me as your husband. It is hard to believe our son is sixteen and yet you are as fresh and beautiful as the day we met."

Juan kissed her soft lips and then smiled. She lowered her eyes, unwilling to let Juan see her resignation. Her time with him neared its end.

Carving out an existence in the New World was not an easy task and made old men quickly from the young stalwart ones who set out to tame the land. At forty-three Juan looked closer to his sixties. His hair had long since grayed and his face, though still handsome with his high cheekbones and kind eyes, was a map of the hardships he had endured.

Onatah, young, fresh, and untouched by the years or the harshness of the land, appeared closer to the age of her son.

Over the many years she had lost count of her many husbands. She could visit them in her dreams, but the pain of separation from her many husbands and children gripped her chest and threatened to squeeze the air from her lungs.

Her mind wandered into regret. If she could choose, of all her husbands and all her children, she would choose this man who came from afar and their son as her one lifetime. Juan was not an Algonquin like Onatah. Where her skin blushed as if kissed by the sun, his tanned brown warmed by the earth. Juan told her his birth home was far across the great water. Onatah could not imagine a place like Española, even when she saw it through her husband's dreams and knew it to be a wondrous place. Her land, the land of the Iroquois, although vast, was slowly shrinking with the migration of the 'white man.'

"Promise me you will stay away from Nootau." Her wonderful husband spoke firmly.

Nootau, a young brave from a nearby tribe had become captivated with her. Although she quickly told him she had a mate, it was too late. If only the young brave had not happened upon her while Onatah gathered mushrooms in the forest... "I will try, my husband. He waits until I am alone doing my chores and only shows himself when you are away."

"I fear he is completely besotted with you, Ona, as am I." He ran his calloused finger down her soft cheek.

Onatah smiled at her husband. He never failed to let her know how much he loved her. While she carried the burden of mating with many men over many lifetimes, she had never rested her heart with anyone until she met Juan.

She owed him an explanation; she could not keep her secret one day longer. Although she failed to share her story since her first lifetime, she sensed this special man would understand. She waited until after the evening meal, and once their son was asleep, she took her husband's hands in hers and began her tale.

"My dear husband, I have a tale to tell you that will cause you to not believe your ears. But you must believe me, Juan, for as the great wind blows, the mighty sun shines, and the forever moon looks upon our faces, I speak the truth."

His eyes grew wide and she sensed his protective shield.

"What is it that scares you so?" he asked.

"I am afraid, if I tell you my story, I will no longer see love in your eyes."

His face softened and she sensed his great love for her. "That will never happen," he said, "for as long as I live, my heart can love no other."

Ona took a deep breath, let it out slowly, and continued, "I was born like no maid before me. For fifteen hundred of your years, and so many moons I have lost count, I have been known as Mother Earth."

Juan's brow furrowed. "You are speaking of strange things." He felt her forehead and looked deeply into her eyes.

"The tale is stranger still. One hundred forty-six like me have lived longer than the normal span of moons for one lifetime. The earth speaks to us and we can speak to the earth. We can also talk to each other across the mountains and meadows without a word being spoken."

Juan rose and began pacing the room. Onatah watched as many emotions passed over his face. As she sat comfortably in a chair, she listened to her husband's mind as it raced through all the possibilities.

She has been working too hard in the sun. He looked at his wife. *She's not speaking randomly, she seems to have full rein over her faculties. Ona isn't ranting or raving, she has distinct composure.*

He ran his hands through his hair. *Did she say she was 'Mother Earth' for FIFTEEN HUNDRED YEARS?*

"Juan, I do not have sun sickness. Yes, I said 'fifteen hundred years.'"

Juan spun around at her words and looked at her intently, his eyes wide. *You know what I am thinking?*

"Yes, I know what you are thinking."

He grabbed her by the shoulders and stared at her with widened eyes. "Ona, by the stars in the heavens, whatever you are doing, stop it now. Only demons, warlocks, and witches can cast spells."

She heard the rapid beating of his heart and knew he feared for her. She spoke with softness and conviction. "I am no demon, warlock or witch. I am, and always have been, Onatah."

Juan dropped his hands from her shoulders and looked at her intently.

She continued. "First, I was called Daughter of

the Earth by our medicine man. He used me to make his medicine stronger. When the braves grew afraid of my powers, the tribe cast me out. The ones like me, who are my children, now call me Mother Earth. I did not cast a spell on you, my dear husband. I have always been able to hear your thoughts."

Gazing at Ona and trying to reconcile his conflicting emotions, she heard, *Is it really so? Ona looks just as she did twenty years ago.*

"Do you not age?" he asked, her truth beginning to settle inside him.

"Not like you do."

"Where did you come from?"

"I have always been Algonquin, an Iroquois, and I have always lived on this land."

"Do you not die?" He sat next to her and grasped her hands in his.

"We can die, but we are blessed with very good health. If we are not killed, we live a long time. None has lived as long as I, since I am 'mother.' Only one other is as strong, and that is Genotah, my daughter. She has the mark on her shoulder as do I."

"I thought that was a tribal tattoo."

"No, it came on my skin when I was but twenty winters." Onatah watched her husband waiting for the inevitable question about her previous mates.

His shoulders sagged. "Why did you tell me this, Ona? Do you plan to leave me to find a new mate?"

She took his face in her hands and brought up his eyes to meet hers. "I can love no other. Since you, there can be no other. You are in my heart forever."

Her hands fell from his face. She held them in her lap, watching his reaction to her words.

Onatah spoke in Juan's mind, *I love you, my husband. Now and forevermore.*

Juan's eyes displayed the shock of hearing the words without Onatah speaking. She sensed his heart beating rapidly like a bird's. His eyes darted about the cabin as his mind played through many scenarios before he finally reached a place where he could rationalize his thoughts.

"I'm beginning to understand," he said. "My heart aches for you. For when I die, and die I must, I don't wish for you to be alone."

Her heart ached at his words. Only Juan would be concerned for her happiness above his own.

"Please understand," she said. "I can give my heart no longer. It is no longer mine to give. You stole it from me twenty of your years ago. I have rested in your arms in peace like never before."

Looking into Ona's eyes, he said, "Why have I not seen the antiquity and wisdom in your eyes before? I now see years of selfless acts, one on top of the other, interlaced with the vastness of time." He pulled her into his arms and held her.

She felt his intake of breath as she sensed his next thought.

"Our son?" Juan hesitated; he was almost sure of her answer. "Is he…"

"Ryeth is strong like Genotah and me. He does not know yet. I have told the others of my group about him. They do not know I am 'Mother Earth,' the mother of them all. Genotah and I have kept that secret from them. Soon, they will contact our son to join the group." A smile spread over her lips. "He will be stronger than any other."

Ona began seeding Juan's mind with her timeless memories. She held nothing back wanting and trusting him to be a haven where she could find respite within his love. All that night and into the wee hours of the morning, Onatah shared. Juan never asked questions, for Ona felt them rising and answered all queries before being asked. They fell asleep wrapped in each other's arms.

The dawn brought forth a new understanding between them. Their love grew deeper than ever. Ona listened to Juan's thoughts to make sure he was comfortable with her confession and was humbled by his admiration for her.

Life continued unhampered for Juan and his lovely Onatah over the next few months. Some from Onatah's group would contact their son. The process to make him part of their special world would begin as soon as his powers emerged. Juan and Onatah watched their son with pride knowing the unbelievable future that would unfold as part of his mother's heritage.

"Ona, when will you tell our son you are Mother Earth?"

"As soon as he finds the place in his mind where his inner eye sleeps."

"Do you know when that will happen?"

"It is different for each, maybe tomorrow, maybe in five winter's time. There is no way to tell."

"He will be so proud of you, Ona."

Smiling at that thought, she used her senses to warm Juan's heart in appreciation of the love they shared.

Chapter 2

Eastern North America mid 1500's

Ryeth couldn't shake the notion that something bad was going to happen. A prickly feeling crept up the back of his neck upon rising, and persisted throughout the day.

He straightened to scan the surrounding area. Their farmland was fertile and though it took to the hoe easily, the task of maintaining the half-acre vegetable garden was daunting. His mother worked at the edge of the field near the house on the items that required careful tending, carrots, turnips, and onions. His father, on the opposite side near the forest, hoed the corn and beans.

He reached down, grabbed a clump of dirt, stood to stretch his back, and crumbled the rich soil in his hand. A slow smile crept across his lips; their hard work would taste good when the cold winds blew in from the north and painted the ground white.

Well-formed at sixteen, his bone structure promised growth into a formidable-sized man. His tanned skin glistened with sweat. The hair on his arms, bleached golden brown by the sun, stood out in contrast to the pitch-black hair on his head. Slung low on his hips were a pair of breaches tied up carelessly with a piece of rope.

He bent over the row intent on finishing it before the sun set, and concentrated on cutting the weeds and hoeing up a mound around the base of the potatoes.

A shrill Indian war cry broke through the peaceful air.

Ryeth spun to see an Indian brave standing over his father wielding a knife. He saw the knife slice through the air and sink into his father's torso. His mother's piercing scream echoed through the valley as he ran across the field toward his father. Seething with anger, he had one thought - to save his father from a second blow. His giant strides consumed the distance quickly, and as he reached the brave, his mother ran between them.

Ryeth and the brave locked eyes. The brave's eyes grew wide as he shoved his mother away, and with a horrified wild look in his eyes, turned and fled into the woods.

His mother slid down, her knees buckling.

"Ma!" he cried, his heart clamoring. As he caught her from falling, he saw the brave's knife sticking out of her chest.

He gently lowered her to the ground, holding her close to his chest. His father lay lifeless at his feet.

Terror filled every pore of his being. His father's lifeblood spilled from his body, coloring his sweat-laden shirt in crimson red. The tale of his death was told by the lack of movement.

Ryeth turned to his mother laying limp in his arms, blood oozing from the wound in her chest.

"Oh Ma, stay with me!" he sobbed.

She spoke softly, "Ryeth. Remember..."

He watched in horror as she grabbed the hilt of the knife with both hands and pulled the blade out. Blood flowed like a river. He put his hand over the wound to stop the flow. She slumped to the ground, her strength all but gone. Her breath was labored. She held up the knife and whispered something so softly he couldn't make out the words.

"Ryeth." She gasped. "A great future awaits you."

"Don't talk, Ma. You'll be all right." His dad was dead, he was sure, and his mother's life ebbed. Panic gripped the man-child.

"Listen." She took several short breaths. Her eyes held his as she spoke. "When all is threatened, give this knife to one whose heart is pure." Her breathing grew shallow; her words were barely audible.

He leaned closer. She lowered her lids. As her chest rose slowly, he heard her whisper, "Do not forget."

Ryeth choked, his eyes blurred with tears. "Ma, I'll do whatever you want."

She closed her eyes. He clutched her nearer still, tears streaming down his cheeks. His mother's body went limp. She opened her eyes with one last effort and gazed at her son. Their eyes held until her eyes grew dim and lifeless. As she faded from the world, he heard her words in his mind, *All is as it should be.*

The once vibrant life was gone. Tears flowed as he rocked back and forth cradling her body. The pain in his chest became unbearable. Images of their life together filled his mind. He re-lived every memory in great detail, as he held his mother close in death.

Chills from the cool evening air made his body spasm and shook him from his reverie. Spent from grief he realized hours had passed. He laid his mother's body on the ground next to his father with great care, and with a finger, moved a lock of hair from her cheek.

Ryeth stood, and then remembered the knife. He bent low to take it from her lifeless hand, then straightened, as hatred of the thing that killed his parents welled up inside. As the rage grew, he glared at the blade in his hand. His breath came in rapid bursts as he clenched his jaw and his lip curled.

"Hey, what's going on there?" A gruff male voice sliced through the air.

Ryeth jerked around with all the loathing he felt displayed on his face. He recognized the tinker, Mr. Pritchard, who mended their pots.

"What have you done, boy?" Mr. Pritchard ran at him, screaming and shaking a hatchet in the air. "What have you done?"

Fearing for his life, and not knowing if he'd be believed or not, Ryeth took one last look at his parents and then ran off into the woods as fast as his feet could carry him.

Pritchard's feet thundered after him. "Get back here, heathen! You'll pay for the sin you've committed this day! We'll find you, and stretch your neck at the gallows."

Hiding behind the thick trunk of a tree, he could hear the man's panting. Afraid to breathe, Ryeth stilled himself to prevent detection. Soon, Pritchard turned away from his search and went back to the farm.

Creeping close and hiding behind a bush, his intent black eyes watched as the tinker looked over the scene, shook his head, and hurried back to his cart. As soon as the tinker's cart passed the bend in the road, Ryeth went back to the cabin and packed up supplies.

Time was short. Pritchard would soon return

with folks from the nearby town to witness the aftermath and decide his fate. The town folk would receive Pritchard's account of the incident and have a predisposition of his guilt.

Bitterness spread throughout his body and turned his heart cold as he leaned over his parents' bodies one last time. Just as the Indian had ripped his parents from his life, the town folk would take the interment of his parents from him as well.

Ryeth moved his father close to his mother and placed her hand in his. Tears fell from his cheeks onto his father's dirt-ridden shirt. The moisture spread into a blot that mixed with his father's sweat.

He wrenched his eyes away and pressed the horror of his parents' deaths into the far reaches of his heart by turning away and putting one foot in front of the other until miles separated him from their cabin.

Steps that started out strong and sure now wandered aimlessly as Ryeth's mind sought to pacify his loss with survival. Legs that would no longer continue dropped the lad next to a large tree. Close to exhaustion, he pulled a biscuit from his pack and stared at it as he rolled it around in his hand. The need to glean every memory of his parents from the little he had left hit him full force.

His mother took exceptional pride in her biscuits as she did in all she prepared. She was exquisite in every detail. All who met her fell prey to her kindness and beauty. His father was no different. Smitten for twenty years, he displayed his love for her in every task. Ryeth was privy to the proper way to cherish another.

As the day neared its end, he stood and looked around. The sky was clear, so shelter could wait, but he lacked water. A quick search of the area turned up a game trail. Years of hunting with his father had taught him to follow it to water. Within half an hour, he came to an outcropping of rocks where a clear mountain spring trickled from the base. He scooped out a basin-sized hole and, while waiting for the water to clear, made his camp and gathered wood and kindling for a fire.

In the low brush, he found an old bird's nest that would catch fire to the kindling once he struck flint to steel. His father would have been proud of the way the fire caught on the first spark. He fed the small flames until larger pieces were consumed in the flame. Lost in the orange flickering colors, his mind flashed a picture of his father smiling. It was more than he could bear. A lump formed in his throat and brought on physical pain. Unshed tears glistened in his eyes, so he closed them against the emotion that welled up inside.

He banked the fire, opened his bedroll, and settled down for the night. Mental and physical exertion took its toll and he fell into a deep, troubled sleep.

Images from the murders filled his subconscious mind. He dreamt the scene over and over, each time reliving the horror, but in the last dream, he gained a reprieve. He got to his father much earlier and he was able to deflect the Indian's knife, which buried into his forearm instead, saving both his father and mother. His injured hurt much more than from the stab of a knife.

Ryeth woke in a panic. His arm was in the mouth of a wild boar that threatened to tear it from his body. The angry animal thrashed his arm back and forth wildly, and drug him toward the woods. Ryeth yelled and screamed at the bristle-skinned boar as he pounded his fist on its head. Nothing deterred the animal from its goal. It had him tight and fought violently to acquire its meal.

Helpless against such determination, Ryeth tried to break the hold on his arm by kneeing the boar in the stomach, but that only resulted in tossing it over his head and twisting his arm backward to the boar's advantage. He spun around on the ground and managed to get alongside the beast. Throwing a leg up, he kicked the creature off its feet and quickly wrapped his leg over it. He pulled it close enough to lock both legs around its middle. His clenched arm and the boar's ugly snout were directly below. With his weight holding the wild boar down, he slipped the knife from his boot with his left hand and plunged it into the heart of the beast.

The boar breathed twice and then no more. Still full of adrenalin from the fight, Ryeth punched the offending animal with all his might in the snout with his free fist.

"Let go, you dirty beast," he yelled at the unresponsive animal.

Using his bad arm to press the jaw down, he held the jaw in place with his knee, and then gripped the snout and pulled it up enough to slide his arm out sideways, away from the tusks.

He sat next to the boar and clutched his arm close to his body, and listened for sounds of more savage beasts in the area. Luck was on his side. The boar was a young rogue and apparently hunted alone. Ryeth, though battered, felt relief. A passel of boars could have torn him to shreds, and a fully grown one could have bitten clean through his arm. In the darkness, crickets and cicadas sang their songs, unaffected by the discord.

The boar became his first concern. He tied its hind feet together and threw the remainder of the rope over a branch of a tree several yards from the campsite. Hoisting it shoulder high, he slit the abdomen, and cleaned the carcass. Although the pain in his arm thumped, he pressed on and pulled the carcass high up into the tree to let the blood drain, and then buried the entrails.

Blood soaked the arm of his shirt. Half-afraid of what he'd find, he pulled up his sleeve to view the damage. His stomach lurched. Both the top and underside of his arm suffered tears from the animal's teeth. He shuddered when he spied a flap of skin and muscle hanging loose and bleeding.

He shuddered. A deep, cleansing breath helped to settle his nerves. He stoked the fire back to life and threw on heaps of additional wood until it burned large and bright. Grabbing a branch, he seared the end until it glowed red hot, and then pressed the ember to the wound. The stench of his burning flesh almost caused him to retch. Beads of perspiration formed on his upper lip as he held pressure on the stick. His eyes rolled back into his head, he dropped the stick and fell to the ground unconscious.

Chapter 3

Rays from the early morning sun filtered through the canopy and flickered on Ryeth's face. As his eyes opened and he took in his surroundings, he cursed. He'd lived through the night only to face the emptiness of the following day.

He made a poultice using herbs he'd located nearby, and then wrapped his arm with a strip of cloth torn from the tail of his shirt.

Before he left to scout the immediate area, he lowered the boar, laid it on a piece of burlap, salted it, wrapped it tight in the burlap, and secured it high in a tree. He filled his flask from the spring basin he'd hollowed out the night before, tied it to his pack, and started off, following the trickle from the spring.

Soon, the trickle joined a stream, and the stream grew wider. An area thick with briars that overlooked the water by a height of twelve feet or more now blocked his path. As he attempted to go around the thicket, he flushed a rabbit out of its hiding place. It scurried under the briars in an instant. The thicket took on new meaning and gave him an idea.

Hours later, and after many pricks to his arms, he'd chopped, carried, and built a thick briar fence to surround his camp at the spring. The briars would deter wild boars, bobcats, fox, and he hoped, bears from gnawing on him while he slept. There were no openings to his makeshift fort, so he had to hang from a large branch to drop inside, and jump up to grab the same branch and walk hand-over-hand to exit. The rudimentary shelter would have to suffice until he built a cabin or lean-to.

The weather co-operated, so he made a fire and roasted a huge boar flank. As he chewed on the tasty meat, he felt strength return to his body. He skewered the remaining meat on branches high above the fire. By morning, he would be able to pack the smoked meat into his pouch.

Flames from the fire flickered in his dark eyes as dangerous black thoughts crept into his mind. Why had the Indian attacked his father? They had been friendly since their arrival over twelve years ago. His mother was part of the matrilineal descent of her people, the Iroquois, who held her in high regard. She even told him how she nominated sachems, their chiefs, and ensured they held up their responsibilities to the people. Unlike the white man, whose lines traced the fathers' lineage, the Iroquois women defined the political, social and economic values of the tribe.

The knife that entered her body had done so by accident; the Indian had aimed for him. But why did the Indian want both his father and him dead? Anger mounted in his chest. The Indian should pay for their deaths. As the events of the past few days played over and over, he fell into a troubled sleep with his parents' loss weighing heavily on his mind.

***

He woke early the following day and remembered the special people his mother told him about a few weeks past. They would believe him. He would tell him he could call fish from the water. He doubted the possibilities of any other special powers, but considered, since they were his mother's friends they would help him understand. If only he knew how to contact them or where they lived. Ryeth concentrated his thoughts trying to remember if his mother said anything that could help him in his search.

A loud voice resonated, *Do not contact us again! You are not worthy.*

Ryeth jumped up and hurriedly scanned the area, his knife drawn.

"Who's there?" he yelled. "Come, show yourself!"

The forest came alive in his senses. Carefully picking through each sound, he found nothing to indicate another presence. He shook his head to clear it, positive he'd heard a voice.

At once, he realized the voice came into his head and was for him, alone. They, the people with the special powers, could hear his thoughts, and he heard their response loud and clear. They, without knowing the full story, judged him guilty and deemed him unworthy.

They believed the tinker's side of the story and never once gave him a chance to speak the truth. If they believed him a murderer, soon everyone else would believe the same. They would all assume his guilt.

Anger built from deep within. With his nostrils flaring, he sucked in deep gulps of air as the pain and hurt of his parent's deaths became a greater emotion. Blood coursed through his veins giving a deep red glow to his skin. Every muscle flexed taut as they became engorged with the excess pressure. His eyes narrowed, his face contorted, and for the first time in sixteen years, Ryeth experienced rage. They had judged him guilty for a crime he did not commit.

With all the force of his will he bellowed to the sky, "What right do you have to judge me?"

His words echoed off the hills causing birds and animals to take flight. He could not deny the influx of wrath and hatred his words contained. At the zenith of his rage, he concentrated his thoughts on those with powers and shot them a message full force, *Keep your knowledge! I will never be like you!*

His emotions grew to seething. Realizing he could not contain the explosive rage within, he jumped up, grabbed his exit branch and flipped himself over the briar hedge. He ran down the animal trail with wild abandon as branches whipped his chest and face. When he reached the stream, his steps never faltered once as he plunged head first into the cold water; he only broke the surface when his lungs screamed for air.

Shock from the chilling waters dropped his rage to a level he could manage. He pulled himself onto the bank and rolled onto his back. The only sound in his ears was the rapid pounding of his heart. His breathing slowly returned to normal as he focused on the cloud-free sky and the new growth of buds on the trees.

Gradually, he became aware of his body, and felt welts rising on his face and arms from his careless race through the woods. His left shoulder seared red hot as if it had been branded by the smithy's heated iron. As he reached to rub it, he realized it was more than a simple welt from a branch. He pulled down his shirt to see a round circle blazed on his skin, located in the same spot as his mother's Indian tattoo.

It was identical to her marking. Voices in his

head? People who could hear his thoughts? A branding coming from nowhere?

A piercing ache entered his chest as remorse filled him once again. The loss of his parents created a void too great to measure. Inching into that void swelled a multitude of questions that proved too much for the man-child to grasp.

As tears rolled down his cheeks, he spoke in a voice no greater than a whisper. "Ma, what am I?"

Chapter 4

Special people with powers like his refused to have anything to do with him. Hah, who needed them? Holding his hefty fish in one hand, Ryeth made his way back to his camp. His first taste of self-assurance filled his chest and made him smile. He would never want for food again.

As his foot falls traced the trail, the air felt different. Ryeth stopped dead in his tracks. Someone was near. He stepped off the path, slid behind a large tree, and concentrated on listening. Muffled at first, the voices cleared and then became so loud he thought the men might be staring him in the face.

Although he could not see them, he was certain three men headed his way. A knowledge of the scene entered his mind. Two Indians spoke the same dialect as his mother's tribe, and a third spoke his mother's language, but he was not one of her people. They were talking about him!

"It was his camp. He travels this path," the outsider said.

"You will know him, Nootau?" said the old Indian.

"Yes, I saw him kill the man and woman," Nootau replied.

Ryeth's eyes narrowed as his anger rose. Without seeing his face, Ryeth was certain Nootau, the young Indian, was the one that killed his parents.

The older tribesman spoke. "The woman was

Mother Earth. Her loss weighs heavy in our hearts."

Ryeth felt the sincere remorse of his words, and also Nootau's uneasiness.

"I did not know she was Mother Earth," Nootau said.

"Genotah, my woman, told me this was so," the old Indian said. "She felt when Mother Earth's heart stopped beating. Mother Earth told her something before she took her last breath."

Nootau's heart pounded fast and loud in Ryeth's ears. He sensed Nootau's fear as the scene unfolded in Ryeth's mind.

The old Indian turned to Nootau and challenged him. "Genotah said you, Nootau, killed Mother Earth and her man. Genotah saw it in her mind."

Nootau turned to run, but the outsider stopped him with one burly hand. The older Indian spun around, and came up behind Nootau, shoved his knife deep into his lower back, and ended his life.

The old Indian raised his voice to the sky and yelled. "Son of Mother Earth, know that her death and your father's are avenged. Daughter of Mother Earth, hear my words. The one who took Mother Earth from us has paid for his deed."

Ryeth sank to the ground. He felt the life go out of Nootau, and knew the Iroquois had settled the score. He listened as the men constructed a travois, mounted Nootau on it, and carried him away. Still shaken, he leaned against the tree, unable to believe what had just happened.

Daylight filtered through the leaves and left a patchwork of light and dark dancing across his face. Although the men had been several hundred yards from him, he had heard and witnessed everything. They had created the scene for his benefit. But who was Genotah? According to the older tribesman, he and Genotah were 'daughter' and 'son' of Mother Earth. The Indian and his woman, Genotah, knew he was innocent. They could clear his name and he could return home.

The thought was bittersweet. It would never be 'home' again without his parents. He could make fish jump from a stream, yell at those with powers in their minds, and watch a scene in his mind even though he wasn't there. But he could never truly go 'home' again.

Once the men were far enough away, Ryeth made his way back to his camp, where his existence and place in the world plagued his every waking thought.

Chapter 5

Ryeth rose the following day, placed items into a pouch and headed for the nearest Indian village. His mother had spoken freely of her time with the Algonquin people, and he had lived within their hunting grounds all his life. The Algonquin village was not far, perhaps a four-day journey if no unforeseen events occurred. The Algonquin typically stayed in the same place until their fields lacked nutrients, and only then moved their village.

Ryeth carved his existence from the forest. He set traps for beaver and otter to check on his return trip, and hunted deer and elk.

On the second day of his trek, he stood next to a stream anticipating the fish he wanted for supper. A particular fish eluded his spear four times, so he waited for the perfect moment to strike again. As he focused on the fish and awaited the ideal opportunity, he smiled as a childish thought passed through his mind. What he really wanted was for the fish to jump out of the stream and land at his feet. He watched as the fish slowed, and just as he raised his spear to strike, the fish leapt from the water and flopped on the bank at his feet.

"What?" He jumped back, startled. He looked around expecting to see some sort of magic net vanish into thin air, but found he was alone. Fear and astonishment made his heart race. Did he do this? Did he have the power to pull fish from a stream? He bent to retrieve the fish. Was this what his mother's meant when she told him he was special? If so, getting fish to jump from a stream would come in quite handy.

Although he was eager to test his special action again, he put it off, realizing that to pull another fish would be a waste.

The following day he crossed a large stream and scanned the water. A large fish swam by, and as he concentrated on making it jump to the ground, he said, "Come here."

It landed at his feet. Elation surged from within. He picked up his wiggling supper in both hands and held it high over his head as he danced around. A smile beamed on his face, for as he headed back to his camp, he could no longer deny his special power.

***

Two days later, when he came upon the Iroquois camp site, he was surprised at the length of the long house. Its length signified the matriarchal lineage was strong.

A brave met Ryeth and led him to the sachem, who sat comfortably on the soft furs of many skins in his wigwam. The sachem kept his hair in two long braids and wore a necklace with tiny brightly colored feathers interspersed among many beads. Large, more ornate feathers stuck out from the top of his braids, one on each side. He wore a beautiful woven wrap over his shoulders.

Ryeth spied assorted carved jugs made from dried squash and familiar bulrush mats which hung from the walls of the wigwam. A pang of remorse pinched in his chest as he remembered his mother's expertise at weaving. He strengthened his resolve by pushing the pain of loss to the deep recesses of his heart.

Though Ryeth knew many Algonquin phrases, he was surprised when the sachem greeted him in Spanish.

"Welcome, son of Onatah," said the chief, who motioned for him to sit.

Ryeth sat down on the right hand of the chief, which was proper. "Thank you for your hospitality," he said.

"We were sorry to hear of your father's death and Mother Earth's passing. We did not know the Spirit of the Earth lived among us."

The phrase 'Mother Earth' in reference to his mother confused him. It was apparent she was revered among her people who seemed to know of her but not who she was in particular.

"Thank you, sachem," said Ryeth, his heart full. "I knew her only as mother." The ache in his chest reappeared and threatened to consume him, but he pressed forward, almost choking. "I have a sister?"

The sachem lowered his eyes. His voice carried great sadness. "Genotah has left the earth to follow Onatah's spirit. You have a sister no more."

Ryeth's shoulders sagged. Just when he thought he could have learned more of his mother and regained a partial family, his hopes crumbled. His sister was also gone. How could she have been this close and why had his mother never mentioned her or brought her into their home. And if he had a sister, was not his father his sister's father as well?

His head spun with unanswered questions, but he reached for hope one last time. He raised his eyes to the chief as his hope wavered. "Her mate?" he asked.

"Black Wolf seeks answers in Spirit Quest."

His own quest floundering, Ryeth continued. "Are there no others like Onatah and Genotah?"

The sachem shook his head. "We know of no others who walk with the Spirits. I am sorry I can tell you no more."

Ryeth's fear turned into reality as he realized his solitary state in the world. He had no people, no family, and he had no idea where the ones with special powers were located.

"Many thanks to you, sachem, for speaking with me," Ryeth said and then rose to leave.

The chief stood and patted him on the shoulder. "May the Great Spirit always walk with you, my son."

Ryeth turned to make the trip back to his camp. His last shreds of hope vanished in a whimper.

***

The arduous trek back to camp took on a path of its own, mostly due to his unsettled mind. Rather than adhering to the proper course, Ryeth drifted aimlessly and wandered. When he finally came upon his stream, he realized he was several miles from his intended crossing point. The mental struggle left him spent, so he unstrapped his pack and proceeded to make camp for the night.

After starting the fire, he went to the stream to obtain a fish. He smiled knowing his powers would make the catch an easy one. As soon as he spied a nice one for supper, he motioned for it to come forward. It landed, flopping at his feet.

Ryeth was so engrossed in his immediate satisfaction and his lingering mental turmoil that he missed the intake of breath from those hiding in the bushes.

They were on him in a flash. Though he fought gallantly, four against one-not-fully-grown man were odds he couldn't win. They smothered his fire, tied his hands behind his back and roughly pulled him along with another rope tied around his neck.

Ryeth tried to make out the words they spoke as they dragged him to an unknown destination, but he did not understand their language. Their clothing and beards marked them as fur traders from the north. His father had spoken of them. They were from France, a country that bordered his father's Española.

The further they walked, the more his hands swelled from the tight bindings on his wrists. Without his arms to balance, he stumbled and fell. Each time he fell, which was numerous, the man following him jerked him up roughly by the collar of his shirt, choking him in the effort, and sat him on his feet once more.

When they stopped for the night, they gave him a sip of water and tied him to a tree. The four carried on a lively conversation as they made camp and ate. Ryeth tried to listen for words that represented a motion or action so he could figure out why they captured him. Instinctively, he knew when the conversation settled on him.

One of the four sitting around the fire stood, beckoned with his hand in a 'come here' fashion, and said, "Venir ici!" Then he wiggled his hand back and forth like the fish flopping on the ground.

Ryeth's heart sank. They had seen him calling the fish from the stream. All four turned to stare at him.

"Daemon!" Another spat in his direction.

Fear consumed him, but only for a mere second. A stirring began in the pit of his stomach as his soul quickened with rage. Once again he found himself condemned without any say in the matter. The feeling turned to bile, and the bile to acid. Injustice burned deep in his core. His eyes narrowed to slits as he mentally spat the acid from his stomach into the fire.

His eyes widened as the fire popped loudly and thousands of sparks blew out showering his capturers. Their gaze ripped from Ryeth as they jumped away from the fire and patted the hot sparks from their lit clothing and beards. The unintended result, though shocking, gave him distinct pleasure.

"Mon Dieu!" the large Frenchman screamed and then yelled commands to the others. He rummaged hurriedly through his pack, found what he was looking for, and then quickly ran at Ryeth.

Ryeth bobbed his head and swerved his body to avoid the man's hands until the large Frenchman succeeded in placing a filthy cloth bag over his head.

Seething beneath the confines of the canvas bag, Ryeth's anger built to a climax. His body shook with unrelenting emotion that became too large for its container. Tears flowed like those from a tumultuous storm. His stomach twisted with spasms and his breath came in stringent gasps. Muscles in his legs tightened and released. Ryeth tried to control the emotions that surged through every pore of his body, but was unable to appease the onslaught. It was several hours before his fury subsided. His drained body collapsed into a motionless heap, completely spent.

***

He awoke groggy with rough hands pulling him to his feet. Last night's emotional surge left him weak. Before he was able to regain any semblance of his situation, he was pushed and prodded to move forward, guided by the tug of the rope around his neck and for all purposes, blind. Two days of traveling in this manner led to numerous tumbles and spills. They would yank him by the arm to a standing position so he could, once again, trip and fall. Not one inch of skin failed to hit the earth at one time or the other.

Each time he was ruthlessly tugged forward the rope cut into his neck. Blood dripping from the wound stuck to the coarse threads of the sack tied around his neck. The coppery odor of blood mixed with sweat hung in his nostrils, blocking the sweet smell of the forest he knew so well.

Ryeth's trips and falls lessened as the path became smoother beneath his feet. He had little time to appreciate the brief break and focus on a means of escape before it dawned on him that a well-worn path meant he neared civilization. Soon they reached their destination.

His captors yelled to their mates. He sensed their anger and fear as he was paraded through the center of the village. Voices were gruff and loud. Ryeth was grabbed by the arms, led away from the group and tossed down on the ground.

A gate slammed. It was not the heavy gate of a large paddock, but something weaker, maybe that of a pen for a large animal.

Ryeth slumped to the ground, parched and weak from lack of food. He sighed as he rolled to a more comfortable position. Though his hands were still secured together, he was unable to untie the rope around his neck, but he did shift it to a less painful position. Drained, his body went limp.

A vision of Pritchard, the tinker, bearing down on him with an axe flashed through his mind. He sniffed. If resentment was edible, he would have a full stomach. Would people never cease their judgement of him? How in Hades had his life taken such a wrong turn? He shook his head to clear it; self-pity would not loosen the ropes that bound him.

He brought his hands up to his face and pushed the side of the bag into his mouth. The cloth was firm and well-woven. He tasted his own dried blood and sweat as he chewed through the bag. So lost in his attempt to chew a peep hole in the bag, he did not hear the approach of the riotous voices of men, women and children until they were on top of him.

***

He could make no sense of the words of the riotous townsfolk, but their hate permeated his senses loud and clear. Something struck him on the leg, then he suffered another harder strike in the chest. Rocks hit him from all angles. He rolled into a ball to protect his face and eyes.

A soft-speaking man reproached the crowd and the pelting stopped. The man threw a liquid on him and spoke at length in a monotone voice. The man then spoke aloud to the crowd. Ryeth heard the word, "daemon." The man moved away and soon the pelting of rocks resumed.

The group of people grew larger, louder, and more vicious. A deep voice commanded attention. The rocks ceased. A man entered his cage and grabbed him by the arm, pulled him with ease to stand and escorted him through the yelling mob. Ryeth fell against him. The man felt to be as large as a mountain, for he never swayed nor missed a step as he lifted Ryeth upright.

After the small trek to what he thought might be the village square, ropes were wrapped around him, securing him to an upright pole. Strapped at the neck, chest, knees, and feet, he could do nothing to escape.

Ryeth's heart leapt from his chest as he heard them pile brush and logs at his feet. The crowd continued to jeer and hurl objects. At last, someone jerked the cloth from his head. He squinted at the bright light, threw his black hair from his face and then opened his large black eyes to see the mob before him. He could not suppress the snarl that came to his lips.

The crowd gasped and stepped back.

Men bearing torches came toward him and touched them to the kindling. Perspiration formed on his upper lip and spread to his forehead. He yelled his innocence, but even to his own ears, his voice mimicked the sound of a wounded animal's croak instead of anything human. Ryeth swallowed hard; the lack of moisture caused him to wince. He ran his dry tongue over cracked lips and awaited the inevitable. Blood rushed through his veins and pounded in his ears.

The loathing of the crowd hit him full force. Their faces contorted in fear. His senses felt every emotion that passed through their superstitious minds. To them, he was an unknown, something to be feared and ostracized, and in his case, exterminated. He felt their hatred, but as much as they hated him, he hated them more.

The fire took hold in the brush and quickly crept close. Heat grazed his lower legs. Smoke burned his lungs and nostrils. The wind shifted and brought fresh cool air to revive him only seconds before engulfing him once more in the acrid smoke. Ryeth gritted his teeth, silently vowing not to scream. Death would take him with nary a sound.

The crowd continued to jeer and pelt him with stones. A large rock hit him squarely on the temple. Dizziness swirled the scene before him as he relinquished himself to blackness. Noise from the crowd faded into the background as he no longer felt objects hitting him. A smile formed on his lips; a merciful god had intervened to spare him the pain of death.

Slowly the crackling of the fire entered his ears once more. People cheered. The rock to the temple had merely stunned him as he opened his eyes to the horrific ordeal once more. His inner strength began to ebb, realizing there would be no gratifying darkness before the flames consumed him. Once again, he stiffened his resolve to endure his fate.

The flames licked his legs and grew hotter. He could feel the skin grow taut on his legs. His time on the earth would soon end. Focusing on the edge of the woods a few hundred yards behind the crowd, he imagined the coolness of the shade. The darkness of the forest had no yelling crowd, no flames, and no anger - just peace and the moist dark earth. He remembered the feel of the earth on his bare feet and wiggled his toes. Summer was in full splendor yet he knew the forest offered cool springs and a respite from the heat. He closed his eyes and pictured himself walking in the forest, and hoped, in death, he would meet his parents soon.

It worked. His mind took over. The smoke no longer burned his nose. The sound from the townspeople became a distant memory. His legs were no longer consumed in flames. He smiled and relished the cool moist ground; he was at peace. He opened his eyes for one last look before departing the earth.

What? A quick glance confirmed that he now stood in the forest, yards away from the town. Free of his bonds, he quickly spun around to see the crowd violently yelling at the fire before them, the stake completely engulfed in flames. Ryeth didn't know which god set him free, but he was thankful just the same. Run.

As fast as he could go, Ryeth put one foot in front of the other. The smell of his singed clothing mingled with the earthiness of the forest as he fled away from the French, away from mean-hearted people, and away from the north - to freedom.

Chapter 6

Ryeth headed south. Without a bag over his head he was able to travel quickly. He grunted at the reminder. People sickened him. They judged, were filled with superstitions, and had caged him like an animal.

Looking back to assure he wasn't followed he ran as fast as he could. Miles went by before he slowed his pace and stopped to catch his breath. Muscles in his legs turned rubbery and refused to hold his weight. Slouching to the ground, he coughed, his mouth dry from lack of water.

He closed his eyes to block out his other senses and listened. The forest, filled with birds chirping and leaves rustling in the wind, grew quiet. The welcome stillness brought peace to his mind, and then he heard it - the trickling of a small stream. A game trail led him in the direction of the trickle and within half an hour, he was able to quench his thirst. The first gulp hurt from lack of moisture for so long, so he took him time and sipped smaller amounts.

The cool water refreshed his body as well as his spirit. Sated, he scanned his surroundings. Bone weary, the days to his camp loomed ahead and presented a burden too large to consider in the diminishing light of dusk. He spied a giant elm, climbed high into its inviting arms, and fell fast asleep.

Birds chirping with the dawn of a new day

sounded in his ears. As his eyes fluttered open, enough questions to topple a cart filled his mind. What made him leap from the fire to the woods? Could he really be a demon as the French called him? Wouldn't he know if he were?

A heavy heart sought answers. "Ma, I need you and Pa," he said quietly. His breathing slowed. Tightness constricted his chest and threatened to overwhelm him. A lump formed in his throat that no amount of swallowing could remove. He could not control the tears that fell. Ryeth lost himself to the pain of loss. His sobs, caught by the forest, stilled the natural activity and echoed his sorrow.

Wiping his eyes on his shirt, he pushed the weakness aside and forced his thoughts in another direction.

How wonderful it would be if he could get from one place to another as quickly as he had gotten away from that fire.

"How did I do that?" A touch of anger entered his mind. His eyes narrowed. "What good are powers if I don't know how to use them?" He clenched his teeth.

Was it fear? Or was it his desire to distance himself from the situation that caused it to happen?

Desire, want, need. Were they all the same? Desire had more depth than a simple want or need. He scoffed at the idea. If he had any desire at all, it would involve reversing time to get his parents back. Once again to have their love surround him; a love he would relish as never before. Blasted Indian! Blasted Frenchmen! Blast them all. If he could, he would make them all go away.

He shifted his weight and winced as his body's stiffness reminded him to go easy. He patted the old tree. "Thank you for a good night's rest, old girl. You kept me safe."

Just a short time ago he had taken for granted the comfort of his bed. It was certainly more suitable than the nook of a tree for sleeping. His mother taught him how to stuff a mattress from soft grasses, and to add just a touch of wild honeysuckle to keep it fresh. His real bed was warm and cozy, not like the hard bark that pressed into his back, and on cold nights beneath tanned hides, he had nestled there in comfort and love. Ryeth closed his eyes and could almost smell the sweet honeysuckle. Just once more, to feel the pleasure of his own bed.

He rolled over and rested beneath the warmth and felt the soft fur on his cheek. His eyes shot open wide. By all that was holy! No longer in the crook of a tree, he was now snuggled beneath the hides in their cabin. Lips forming a half-smile, he stilled himself and lay there, barely moving and half afraid he was dreaming, listening for the telltale sounds of people. He could sense no one near.

He propped himself up on one elbow. The small joy of his new found trick ended abruptly. As his eyes scanned the interior of the cabin, they glistened with unshed tears. Unable to push it down, anger crept up and rage boiled inside. He threw the hides to the side and leapt from the bed as if catapulted. People had taken his life away. He would take it back. He would take all he could get and then take more.

Ryeth burst from the door and surveyed the farm. The area surrounding his home was too visible. People looking for him might easily see him from afar. A wooden cross beneath the giant oak caught his eye and caused him to gasp. Leaded feet carried him slowly to his parents' graves; he fell to his knees between them.

"I miss you more than words can say." The words caught in his throat. "Walk with the Great Spirit until our paths cross again."

He stiffened as his heart grew cold against the anguish. Senseless deaths. Anger welled up inside as he rose and stalked back to the cabin.

Throwing the door open, he gazed at the contents of the one room cabin and sleeping loft. The early morning sun cast a ray inside and magnified the swirling dust particles as his eyes adjusted to the dim light. The rough-hewn cabin was now devoid of the love that once made it a home. He fingered each memento as he placed them in his pouch. Memories flooded the unsuspecting boy. The anger subsided, replaced by the love that lingered within the four walls.

As a plan slowly formed, he took one last look before he said his farewell. He returned to his camp, where he filled his stomach, grabbed dried meat and hides, and then moved by his new found travel method to the southernmost hunting camp he could remember sharing with his father. The camp was overgrown, but by late afternoon he scanned the day's work and smiled at the rabbit roasting on a spit. Its aroma filled the small glen and made his mouth water.

***

Without any formal plan in mind, the hardened young man traveled across the country using his powers. The process required a bit of refinement, but he quickly learned to focus on a point in the distance and end up there. The landings tended to be the most difficult, since he could not actually see his landing spot with any level of detail. Trial and error landed him in the tops of trees precariously clinging to limbs that threatened to snap under his weight. He slammed into several rock faces, and splashed down in more than one body of water.

The going was tough and bumpy until he learned to combine the power that allowed him to see Nootau's death with his ability to move from place to place. He figured out to use the sounds of the forest to see into a potential landing place before he made the jump.

Ryeth never stayed in one place too long, nor did he spend time with other people. Instead, he oftentimes frequented their camps from a distance. He listened in on conversations, and in doing so, found out that by 'close listening' he could hear people's thoughts before they spoke.

The discovery of his powers by the French and the disastrous results kept Ryeth to a singular life style. He made camp at the far reaches of the woods and only visited settlements to trade for supplies he could not get on his own.

***

For the next several years, Ryeth kept his lifestyle and perfected his powers. Without intricate knowledge of his powers or the full extent of them, steering away from potential misconceptions and groups of superstitious people became a way of life for the young pioneer. Ryeth relished his time in the forest. He settled in remote areas and uncovered the boundless beauty it afforded. He slept in trees hundreds of feet high, stood on precipices that overlooked great valleys, and followed bats into subterranean passages which led to breath-taking underground caves. With the untamed regions of a whole continent to explore, Ryeth had little time to suffer from any form of isolation.

***

As Ryeth walked down a game trail, he stopped at a cool spring coming from an out cropping of limestone. The water was cool and refreshing as it passed his lips. He wiped his mouth on his doeskin sleeve and glanced at his reflection in the clear pool.

Gone was the innocence of youth. Staring back at him was the hardened face of a man fully grown. The roundness of his cheeks was no longer evident in the chiseled features that stared back at him. A rough beard gave him the appearance of a much older man than his actual twenty-five years. His eyes narrowed to slits as he plunged his fist into the water and splashed the reflection from view.

As he rose and stretched his large frame, he placed his hands on his hips and scanned the woods. Instantly, he sensed something awry. An internal surge began in his stomach. Dropping his pack, he grabbed his mid-section; his breath came in rapid pants. He fell to his knees as the rumbling within radiated outward from his core. It was as if he had swallowed a giant bee and the buzzing sought every part of his body. He shook from head to toe, and as he held his arms out wide, blue flashes sparked at the tips of his fingers. The hair on his head felt like it was on fire. He clenched his teeth to stop them from chattering, and balled his large hands into fists. His muscles flexed and his veins stood out, pulsating. After what seemed like hours, but had only been minutes, the shaking subsided. Ryeth fell to the ground, physically exhausted from the strain.

The feeling in his limbs returned to his fingers first. He sucked in a huge breath, opened his eyes, and rolled over onto his back. His legs were weak and leaden, but grew stronger with each breath. A stinging sensation began in his legs and arms, then seemed to radiate to his chest, back, and head.

Jumping up, he frantically slapped and rubbed his body to stop the stinging. It escalated instead. Looking down, he was horrified to see the skin on his arms move. He blinked and looked again, only to discover his arms and legs were covered in hundreds of biting red ants.

In a flash, he moved himself to splash down in the stream where he bathed, and remained underwater, brushing the nasty insects from his limbs until his lungs threatened to explode. He removed his clothing piece by piece and tossed them on the bank, but remained in the water until he was certain the ants had floated away.

Anger flared within as he thought of the ones who ostracized him and left him alone with his powers. Yelling full force he screamed, "You will rue the day you turned your backs on me!"

***

Since the ant episode, Ryeth's powers grew in strength daily. The special things he could do became easier and had more force. He discovered he could make a sound in the mind of animals and scare them. Once, when he shouted too loud, he killed a buffalo.

It was too much meat for him to eat alone, so he shared it with a tribe of Iroquois.

Maintaining his many well-stocked camps throughout the continent kept his body lean and muscular. Wiping the sweat from his brow, Ryeth leaned his axe against the log to survey the pile of wood.

Visions of the buffalo's unintended death entered his mind. He looked to the sky. "You 'teachers' left me to fend on my own," he said. "Who gave you the right to be judge and executioner?" Ryeth picked up a log and threw it into the pile with such force it splintered. "Who gives dangerous powers and then turns his back? What kind of people are you?" The tendons in his jaw flexed as he clenched his teeth. His eyes narrowed and his fingers curled into fists. "The day will come when I will not only ask questions; I'll demand answers."

He stacked the wood and hung the axe in the shed, all the while questioning the upside-down fate that governed his life. His steps took him down the path to the lake. He ran the last few yards and sliced the water with nary a sound. The water was cool against his bronzed, sun-heated skin. His form broke the surface and swam to the far side of a narrow inlet. Pulling himself up onto the bank, he took a few steps and then dropped down onto the soft grasses.

As he gazed into the sky, a sense of peace made him smile. His eyes fluttered once as he fell into a deep sleep.

Hours later he awoke with a start. People were near. He scanned the area with his senses and determined three traders were two miles due east. From their conversations he was able to recognize two of them from the past. The other one was new to the area, but an experienced trader. The three were headed his way, probably for the lake's abundance of beaver.

He pulled six fish from the stream, moved himself to his camp, stoked the fire, cleaned the fish, and when he heard the men a hundred yards away, placed the fillets in a skillet with a bit of boar fat.

"Ho there in camp!" yelled Potter.

Ryeth looked up and waved. He'd recognized his voice when he first heard the men stomping in the woods. Potter showed up about once a year with his cohort Red. They dealt mostly in beaver pelts, but hunted bear as well.

Red sniffed the air and caught the aroma. "How'd ya know we were a commin?" he asked.

"You tromp through the woods like a wild boar," said Ryeth, "and the smell of you carries through the wind for miles. With that much warning I wonder you catch anything at all."

"Aw, we do alright," said Potter.

Red dropped his large pack. "This here's Dugger Johnson," he said nodding to the newest member of their group. "We picked him up down the river a ways. Says he's looking for gold."

Ryeth nodded. "Welcome, Dugger."

Potter pulled a log closer to the fire and sat on it to monitor the cooking process. "I tole ol' Dugger that if we was lucky enough to catch Solly home, we'd have a feast."

Ryeth smiled at the nickname the traders had given him. They chose 'Solly' because he was always alone - solitary, 'Solly', for short. Since Ryeth chose to keep his name to himself due to his parents' deaths, he accepted Solly as a proper name.

"The trout is ready, serve yourself," said Ryeth.

After all stomachs were full, the small group gathered around the fire in the dim light of the evening. Potter shared his small horde of raisin scones he'd kept tightly wrapped in a scrap of canvas. Though they were weeks old and dry, the men thanked Potter and enjoyed every crumb.

Ryeth traded salt-cured wild boar with them for items he needed. Even though he could readily access anything at his whim, he kept up appearances of needing certain items.

The conversation turned back to the gold that Dugger sought. The item piqued Ryeth's interest. Dugger passed a nugget around. When Ryeth held it in his hand, he memorized the composition. It was heavier than a normal rock and softer. He learned from the men that the yellow rock was very valuable.

The men stayed only one night, and when they left, Ryeth set out to look for this gold with his mind. The finding of it turned out to be easy; the digging for it, not so easy. He found it in streams, mountain caves, and in ribbons in the ground. The amount he gathered became so great that he stored it in several places throughout the continent.

In a deep cave in the far recesses of the northwest, Ryeth stood looking at the many barrels of gold as a slow smile spread across his lips...

Chapter 7

"A dreamer is one who can only find his way by moonlight, and his punishment is that he sees the dawn before the rest of the world." -Oscar Wilde

Current day - somewhere in the mountain forests of Pennsylvania

Introspection occupied all but the tiniest corner of Ryeth's mind as he sat leaning against the massive trunk of a great hickory tree. Bewilderment, disbelief, acknowledgement of wasted years, and flat-out confusion consumed what remained. Since his sixteenth year, he had endured life on his own without entanglements from other humans.

If he didn't know better, he would call Alexandra a witch, albeit a good one. That woman had the uncanny knack of compelling him to be honorable and, like a blasted boy scout, do good deeds. The thought alone soured his stomach. She could no more be a witch than he could be a warlock, if such things even existed. Hell, for all he knew, the Salem witch trials were the direct result of not concealing their abilities.

They were Sensates, at least that's what they called themselves. He had no idea what possessed him to become involved with the very group he'd cursed and sworn vengeance on for nearly five hundred years. Over those years, his greatest focus was learning about those who had deemed him unworthy of his powers. Those who had left him to fend for himself, and those who were like his mother and like him.

He'd developed his powers to a high level and used them to locate and listen to new Sensates. Years of observing them and some trial-and-error tactics on his part proved their powers and his originated from their five senses. Not all Sensates had the same level of powers as he did; some had a single power developed from one sense. Some had many talents, but their strength was weak, and others had powers he had yet to obtain.

He'd spied on them for centuries; listening in on their conversations until 'new' Sensates learned to block their minds. He had grasped many, but not all, of their secrets.

Thinking back, he cursed the day he discovered the Prophecy, for it had ignited a flame of desire deep within his core he could not quench. He couldn't stop the pull to be near those of his kind. Though he had put thousands of miles between their collective and himself, the desire to be near them, and even part of them, would not cease.

Blast that Alexandra woman, and blast the whole group of Sensates. They'd ignored and shunned him for nearly half a millennia.

No one had been there to tell him he would not age like other people. No one taught him to use his powers. No one saved him from evil, or guided him to success in life. They did not come to his rescue when the town called him a murderer, nor had they saved him from the quick trial that sentenced him to burn at the stake. Instead of insight from others, he foraged on his own, always cautious of discovery and the danger it presented.

He sneered as the train of thought neared the same dead-end he had reached numerous times. For the first time in nearly five hundred years, Ryeth ached for the companionship of his own kind, and if the thought of 'being good' soured his stomach, this desire for his own kind spun him completely out of control. The need was strong and against his nature. It gripped him at the scruff of the neck and bade him go forth like a puppet.

As Ryeth felt the bark against his back of the age-old shagbark hickory, he compared himself to the tree. It had grown and broadened with the passing of years, yet he had not. Looking back, and being honest, he sensed the revenge that fueled his existence also caused him to waste seven or eight lifetimes. Caught in the powerful maelstrom of hate and revenge for hundreds of years, he had literally stalled at one stage of development. The singular five-century path of revenge had left little room to deviate into a normal lifestyle.

So how could saving a girl from a lunatic alter his life so significantly? In securing her rescue, the bile of hatred had formed in his throat and, although he aided in her captor's 'boiling over,' he stopped his interference shortly before causing his death. All his life he never caused the death of another human being. Ryeth had no clue why Alexandra's captor brought forth such loathing in him.

***

The bark of the tree felt secure against his back. Ryeth closed his eyes and took a deep, calming breath. "Wise old pawcohiccora," he asked, "where do I begin?"

"Tell me you weren't just talking to yourself," said a soft melodious voice.

Startled from his reverie, Ryeth looked up to see a female jogger on the path next to his tree. Consumed by his thoughts, he had not heard her arrival. The sun shone over her shoulder and blinded his vision.

He squinted up at her and quelled his first instinct to cloud her vision and seek escape, a ruse he had used numerous times in the past to keep his wall of isolation intact. Instead, he gritted his teeth, let out a sigh, and decided to suffer through the inquisition.

"Forgive me. What did you say?" he asked.

"Sorry, I didn't mean to intrude. Just catching my breath. That hill was steeper than I thought."

She looked around and stepped closer so that her shadow blocked the sun from his eyes. "Were you talking to yourself, or is there someone else here?" she asked.

"Are you always so blunt?" he said. His eyes took in the outline of her form in spandex running pants. He looked up just in time to catch the stiffening of her shoulders from his remark.

"Just trying to figure out whether or not I need to fear a pack of wolves, or just one," she said, inclining her head.

"You certainly have a high opinion of yourself," he said, looking at her from beneath partially hooded eyes.

She appeared undaunted by his short quips, and shot back immediately. "I am what I appear to be, a jogger out for a run. You, on the other hand, are leisurely propped against a tree with no backpack or hiking gear in sight and miles from the nearest parking lot. You're wearing tasseled loafers with not a speck of dust on them, so you haven't been hiking." She paused, and then resumed pointedly. "Care to fill in the blanks?"

"No," he replied. She certainly was an observant intruder; he'd give her that. Dark hair, almost black, was pulled up into a ponytail that exited through the back of a baseball cap. Her cheeks glowed rosy from exertion as her red lips pressed firm. With her eyes hidden beneath designer sunglasses, she posed a slight mystery. When she spoke, she tossed her head in an I-don't-care-attitude, which caused his mouth to draw up into a barely perceptible smile.

"You would rather be an enigma?" she said.

"Why not?" He shrugged. "No one likes to give away the ending at the beginning of a book."

"Touché," she said. "Of course that statement assumes someone is intrigued enough to read the book."

She bent over to inspect a shoe and retied the lacing. As she stood, she reached for her ponytail, separated the two halves, pulled it tight, and glanced at the 'book' in front of her.

"Have a good day, mystery-man." She turned to start the descent.

"You as well, lady jogger. Beware of wolves."

She smiled. "Always," she said over her shoulder as she took off at a nice pace.

Ryeth grinned and congratulated himself regarding the exchange. He had done well, in his estimation, almost as if he had been carrying on conversations for years instead of merely listening to them.

"Pawcohiccora," he said while resuming his relaxed state next to the huge shagbark hickory, "we have a lot of catching up to do."

He closed his eyes and opened his mind to the great tree. New buds unfurled, the slight wind rustled through the leaves and the branches swayed in response. The lifeblood sap flowed from the very tips of the leaves, down through the many branches, where each drop combined in the hundred foot trunk and ran like a river into the ground. At first, he sensed the warmth of the ground. The deeper the roots sank into the earth, the cooler it became. The flow lessened as the sap branched into smaller and tinier roots, until it entered the fibrous roots at the very tips stretching and growing, pushing the lifeblood of the great pawcohiccora deep into the earth and at the same time, high into the sky.

The tree was age-old, as was he. It had bent to great winds, stood tall to find the sun, and dug deep to plant roots; it had weathered life, and grown in the experience. The thought brought sadness.

He disconnected his mind from the pawcohiccora, as a vision from long ago played through his mind: Dressed in the garb of the Iroquois, his mother's peaceful countenance and spirit filled his senses. Her soft doeskin dress, decorated with dyes from plants she found in the woods, had removable sleeves, which she varied depending on the season. Hand-sewn moccasins covered her tiny feet. She never altered her dress, oftentimes making a new one so similar to the last, she remained unchanged throughout the years.

As a toddler, they had walked through the woods, hand-in-hand. She told stories of the Iroquois and their relationship with the shagbark hickory or pawcohiccora, the name given to the tree by her people, the Algonquin. A menagerie of forest creatures always appeared and played a short distance away. Nature opened up for her. Ryeth sensed his 'gift' probably came from her.

As he grew older, he remembered teasing his mother, for he towered over her five-foot frame. He told her she needed to stitch bigger pockets in her next dress and load them with stones so the wind wouldn't blow her away. Thoughts of his mother always eased the ache.

Ryeth rose and took in his surroundings. Over the years, urban sprawl had shrunk his private domain. He came to this spot to reminisce and mull over options many times throughout his lifetime. The last two times the isolation he desired had eluded him. Since Alexandra's rescue, he'd found it impossible to suppress the unfamiliar emotions emerging in his character. A wall had cracked, and despite all attempts to reinforce it, life continued to seep in. Jediah, Alexandra's husband, encroached first, but he could hardly hold that against him. Under similar circumstances, Ryeth would have moved Heaven and Earth to get his mate back. The jogger interruption proved a distraction he could get used to, maybe even enjoy. He didn't recall seeing her around before. After today, it would seem he needed to either seek another place for solitude, or learn to accept intrusion into his space.

He took a deep breath, not knowing if it would work or not, and reached out to touch Alexandra's mind.

Chapter 8

He was surprised she hadn't blocked him.

Alexandra? He sensed her quickened breathing.

Who is it? Her telepathic voice wavered.

Ryeth, he said. He waited for her response, and could sense her apprehension. When none came, he continued. *If you don't wish to speak to me...*

Please forgive my hesitation. I do wish to speak to you. I was startled, nothing more. She relaxed a little, but he still sensed caution.

You and Jediah are now married?

Yes. We have taken up residence on the mountain where...

He sensed her reservations and finished her thought. *Where I tried to take the key from you?*

Yes. You scared me.

I understand your caution. I was a bit heavy-handed.

Heavy-handed? she said. *You looked like the messenger of death in that get-up, with the wind whipping that long black coat. You know, when you have black hair and black eyes, maybe you should switch to pastels.*

He felt her nervousness, and her attempt to mask it with humor. He had to give her credit; she faced challenges like a tiger. *Pastels don't really suit me, but I could give red a chance.*

Red? She flashed an image of a terrifying devil into his mind that made him laugh.

If I promise to work on my wardrobe, would you consider forgiving me? he asked.

I'll try. She hesitated before continuing. *I went by your house to thank you for helping me, but you were gone. So, 'thank you' for getting me off that boat and out of Tom Magis' clutches.*

You're welcome, he said.

Are you all right?

He smiled at her concern. *Yes.*

I sense a change in you, she said.

Was it possible she could sense his indecision? He strengthened the bars around his mind. He wanted to talk, not share his mind.

She must have sensed his reluctance, for she was now guarded. *You contacted me, remember? Ryeth, a lot has been happening. Are you aware of Nancy Jane's passing?*

Ryeth thought back to a month ago. *Yes, I sensed the power transfer. It was a sizable rupture in space. I am sorry for your loss.*

He sensed her awe. *You could sense that?* she said.

Yes. He could feel her resolve strengthen.

She paused before continuing. *Do you have a mark on your shoulder?*

Ryeth hesitated. *Yes.*

Are you aware of the Prophecy? He sensed her great caution.

Ryeth's mind swung between disclosure and hedging the truth, but as before, he didn't seem to be able to withhold information from her when asked. He replied, guarded. *Yes.*

Her tension eased a bit before she continued. *Jediah gave me a translation of the Prophecy. I thought the other with the mark might be you.*

Ryeth sensed her uneasiness as she asked, *Do I have anything to fear from you?*

No, he said.

He could almost see her indignation as she said, *If that's so, why did you try to take the key?*

I wanted the power. He struggled to release answers, but hid nothing.

You don't want it anymore?

He sensed her confusion and sighed. *It wasn't meant for me, I know that now. Beside, I've come to realize I have enough power.*

Ryeth sensed she relaxed a bit. He felt her hesitation before she continued. *Do you know of any immediate danger?*

No, he said.

How much do you know about the Prophecy?

Ryeth tore down his wall of protection and, without giving it a second thought, flooded Alexandra's mind with his knowledge of the Prophecy and how he obtained it. Her unguarded reaction of relief passed to him.

You listened in on new Sensates? she said.

Only until they were taught to block others. My best resource turned out to be Jonathan, who, for some reason, never learned to block, said Ryeth.

Alexandra's warmth and smile passed to Ryeth. *I was told they discovered the lapse in his education after you rescued me.*

Ryeth began cautiously. *One question, if I may?*

Yes?

Does Jediah know we are in contact? Her hesitation and anxiety transferred into his senses.

No.

It was Ryeth's turn to relax. For a reason he could not explain, he trusted Alexandra without question, but for now, that trust extended no further. *I know you trust him completely, but the Prophecy makes me think we should protect ourselves somehow.*

I know. Alexandra was confident, he sensed. *I feel the same way, but it bothers me to keep anything from him.*

I understand. Ryeth knew she'd made her decision.

There's something else, she said. *I have been hearing a soft voice crying out. I hear it mostly in the mornings. Have you heard it?*

No. What did it say? He sensed a bit of fear and continued. *Are you afraid of something?*

No, the voice was afraid. It asked if I could hear it.

I sometimes hear new Sensates before they are taught to block their thoughts, like Jonathan, but I have heard nothing lately. To be honest, concentration on a personal task may have left no room for it to penetrate. I will make an effort to listen.

Thanks, Ryeth, she said. *This may be important.*

You are welcome. I will be in touch. He ended the connection.

Ryeth closed his eyes and began to listen to the minds of others. Thousands of voices assaulted him creating a whirlwind in his mind. He quickly refined the mechanism to remove those who had no telepathic abilities and immediately the voices stopped. Adding more power broadened the search. At the peak of his powers, he heard nothing. By closing off the other areas of his mind, Ryeth allowed the portal to remain open at all times without compromising his own thoughts. If the voice spoke again, he would hear it.

He chastised himself for wasting valuable time. The Prophecy should be his main concern, not yearning for lost lifetimes. He had taken the first step to connect with other Sensates by contacting Alexandra. According to his interpretation of the Prophecy, he must combine his powers with the strongest of the Sensates. His relationship with Alexandra was vital. The clock had begun counting down with Nancy Jane's transfer of power to Alexandra. If the Prophecy came true, a battle to decide the fate of humanity hung in the near future. As far as he was concerned, the fates must have selected him at random for such a task, for he certainly didn't fit the typical Sensate mold. Until Alexandra trusted him, there was little he could do.

He took one last look around his forest sanctuary to make sure he wasn't seen, smiled, and then moved himself back home.

***

Thinking over the morning's events, Ryeth considered he would have to be more careful in the future. The enticing jogger had observed his state of dress in the forest and had posed disturbing questions he was forced to evade; he would not make the same mistake again. Joining the human race might require a bit more effort than he initially surmised. He stepped from the shower, towel-dried his hair, slung the towel low around his hips and tucked the end to secure it. Glancing up, his reflection in the mirror neither pleased nor displeased him. As far as bodies went, he supposed his was well-formed and muscular. He considered it proportional to his height and since it had served him well over many years, he truly had no right to complain. With high cheekbones, a dark countenance, and a straight frame, he looked like a larger version of his father. He remembered the way his father used to look at his mother and how she had adored him. A similar relationship to the one of his parents had eluded Ryeth for centuries. He had no sharing of one's life with another, and until now, had never realized he missed anything. The familiar lump in his throat formed as his throat constricted. If his mother could see him now, she would say he was woefully inept in social skills.

There had been three intimate liaisons in Ryeth's life. The first had been a wench who latched onto him as soon as he entered a tavern for the first time. It had been a year of firsts. He had escaped a town's attempt to burn him at the stake by his first shift in location. A few months later, he gave into loneliness and stumbled into a tavern on the outskirts of a desolate town. There, he had his first drink, and bedded his first woman. The exchange was not what he had envisioned, and did nothing to quell the ache inside.

Not until many years had passed, did Ryeth have occasion to have a romantic liaison with the second woman to cross his path. He remembered more details of their short time together because his head wasn't clouded from drink at the time. He still recognized it for the transient connection it had been: two people brought together by circumstance; each needing to hold someone close for a little while.

The third woman was a grasp at humanity when he had none, and left a bitter taste in his mouth. The revulsion had haunted him for decades.

All three had left him with a greater emptiness

than he had felt before; after the third attempt, which was about three hundred years ago, there had been no other. Revenge and hate left no room for attachments so he closed off the longing he carried in his heart.

Chapter 9

Ryeth raised his chin, stared in the mirror at his black eyes, and set his resolve; he was ready for the challenge. As he covered his chin with shaving gel, he wondered if the lady jogger might be staying at the lodge. Half an hour later, he donned suitable attire in anticipation of an 'accidental' meeting.

The lodge was half an hour away. The drive gave him time to collect his thoughts and bolster his ego. Since he knew the roads intimately, he allowed his mind to wander. As he pictured the lady jogger, he discovered the thought made him nervous, so he switched on the satellite radio and let the sounds of James Galway's flute calm his inner churnings.

Once he arrived at the lodge, he parked the car, and entered the lobby. He positioned himself in one of the leather chairs facing the window wall, which overlooked the valley below and mountains in the distance. He could discern the tops of five mountain peaks and knew there were four more hidden in the mist. This was his land, and he knew it intimately. He sensed the changing of the seasons through the whisper of the leaves, the migrating birds by their song, and the slow evolution of the earth by its moaning deep within. He gave a snort at the irony - he knew much about the earth and the forest inhabitants, and so very little about humans. With a bit of trepidation, he braced himself to enter the next phase of his life.

Using his heightened hearing ability, he listened in on a few conversations, while attempting to grasp the flavor of the room and their tone in general. He was slightly dismayed that the majority of conversations lacked substance, and soon realized he could obtain no pointers, so he opened his well-worn first edition of John Grisham's *A Painted House* and pretended to read.

Luckily, it wasn't long before the object of his attention came into the large seating area. Slung over her shoulder was a large Valentino bag, which suited her. She took a seat three chairs down from his, placed her bag on the floor, and withdrew an e-Reader. She relaxed back into the chair, flipped open the leather case, turned on the device and began to read. Her black hair was loose about her shoulders with soft waves that fell about her face. Her hair caught the light and reflected a midnight blue, rich in depth and allure.

He watched her out of his peripheral vision, not wanting to stare at her directly, and pretended to be lost in the view of the mountains. He located her reflection in the glass and continued to absorb every curve of her face.

The intricacies of entering into a conversation with her eluded him. The earlier episode had been a fluke, so he concentrated his efforts on formulating his initial approach. Discounting numerous strategies, he eventually arrived at one he thought might not seem contrived. He would close his book, stand, take a last look at the valley below, and when glancing her way he just might catch her eye. He would then say, 'Ah, a jogger no more?'

It seemed a good plan, but would it work? Would she look up at the precise moment? What if she did not? Maybe he needed to put more thought into it. He glared into the pages of the book and tried to work up a fool-proof plan, one with an outcome he could predict with greater certainty. Anger rose within. He was unprepared. This would never work.

A melodious voice interrupted his thoughts.

"I'm sorry?" he said, still glaring when he turned in response.

"I said, 'If you are so angry at the book, why read it'?"

There she was, the object of his attention, speaking, and catching him mid-growl. Not knowing how to handle the awkwardness, he had no recourse but to shake his head and laugh. "Are you intentionally trying to catch me at my worst?" he asked.

"You set yourself up easily enough. Consider my observations: You talk to trees and growl at books."

She lowered herself into the vacant seat next to him. He looked into mesmerizing green eyes with flecks of gold encompassed in black whisper-soft, feathery lashes. "Guilty as charged," he replied.

"One could have cause for concern if those two traits got out of hand," she said.

"Believe me, those two are the least of my concern," he said, being quite honest.

She smiled and offered her hand, "Kimberly Koza, recent transplant from Florida."

Taking it, he replied, "Ryeth Garmendia, firmly planted, present locale."

He noticed her well-manicured hands and exquisite taste in jewelry. She wore a single gold pinky ring with vines and tiny flowers on her left hand, and a gold band on her right that displayed a beautifully cut amethyst. Simple, yet elegant, just like the girl herself.

"You are staying at the lodge?" he asked.

"Yes, until I find something more suitable. I wanted to be away from the hustle and bustle, but near enough to have a bit of social activity. I assume you have a home here?"

"Yes, it's a bit out-of-the-way, so when I feel the need talk to something other than trees, I stop by the lodge."

"Does this happen often?" she replied smiling at his candor.

"To be quite frank, no. I don't make a habit of frequenting places that harbor so many people."

"What finally pushed you over the edge and away from your trees?"

Ryeth shifted his weight in the chair, a bit uncomfortable with the question. "Do you always ask so many questions?"

"No, only when something or someone is interesting."

His smile drew up on one side as he asked, "You find me interesting?"

"Somewhat. I still can't figure out how or why you managed to be miles away from civilization in the clothing you were wearing."

"Maybe someday I'll tell you," he eluded.

"But not today."

Ignoring the rhetorical question, he pushed forward. "Do you have plans for dinner?"

She smiled. "No, I was planning to eat in my room."

"Would you care to join me?"

"Where? Here, in the lodge dining room?" she asked.

"Yes." He could sense she was being cautious, and was glad she didn't trust him completely.

She looked around then returned her eyes to his gaze. "I'd love to join you."

Feeling a bit satisfied he confirmed the date. "Eight o'clock, here in the waiting area?"

"That sounds perfect."

He stood and said, "Until then, Ms. Koza." Ryeth bowed slightly, and then took his leave. It was a few minutes before his heart rate dropped to normal. He only breathed a sigh of relief once he sat in the front seat of his car.

Well. It was easier than he had expected. At the point where his skin felt prickly and he thought he might jump out of it, he'd taken his leave. He was too old to feel giddy, and hoped it hadn't shown. Everything he felt was new to him. Kimberly was the first woman he had interacted with that *he* had chosen. The others had just happened. She was his choice, and it felt considerably different.

Ryeth grinned and rubbed his chin thoughtfully. He hadn't been this much on edge since the flames licked his boots almost five hundred years ago.

Chapter 10

Alexandra loved being back in Waynesburg with Jediah. The weeks spent jumping from estate to estate and country to country was the most amazing honeymoon she could have ever imagined.

Unknown to Alexandra and prior to their wedding, Jediah had spoken with her contractor to double or triple workers as needed to complete construction by the time they returned from their honeymoon. After two weeks of furniture shopping and accepting deliveries, the newlyweds were ready to move out of the Larkspur bungalow and into Heartseed on top of Alexandra's mountain.

"Jediah, it's hard to believe so much has happened since I came to live at Larkspur."

"Are you having any regrets?" he said while brushing a wayward strand of hair from her cheek.

"I wish Tom Magis wasn't facing years in prison," she said with just a tad of hesitation.

"I'm on the fence on that one." Jediah ran his fingers through his hair while shaking his head. "Your abduction took a toll on all of us. You are much more forgiving of your captor than I am at the moment."

Memories of reading about her ordeal in the paper flooded her mind. She'd been missing for almost six weeks before she woke up in Ryeth's bed and promptly teleported back to the bungalow. "It's probably because I don't remember anything. I wasn't even aware that time was passing, or that I was being abused by Magis."

Jediah turned and pulled Alexandra into his arms. "Alexandra," he whispered into her hair, "I was painfully aware of every second you were absent from my senses. It was an emptiness I never wish to feel again."

The impact of his statement reverberated through her senses, bringing to attention the anguish others had suffered during her ordeal.

It was hard to believe that just six months ago she had been a graduate student wondering what life held in store. Listing what had passed within those six months made her head whirl. Nearly trapped forever in a cistern, she had begun a journey set in motion by her great-great-grandfather, Teater Higgins. The journey had taken a turn for the worse when a member of her high school graduating class had abducted, abused, and forced her to consume mind-altering drugs. Ryeth, whom she feared, had pulled her out of that loathsome place and dealt with Tom Magis. In between everything, she had fallen deeply in love, married Jediah Saffle, and developed powers to become the newest Sensate.

Although she had tremendous powers and possessed amplified abilities, she seldom used her gifts, primarily because she feared discovery. She had no wish to be the cause of any hardship for the benevolent Sensates. Although she knew there were many Sensates, she had met only five. She still found it hard to believe she was 'one of them' despite the evidence to the contrary.

"Jediah, when will I meet the other Sensates?" she asked.

"I can set things in motion for this coming

weekend, if you'd like," he said smiling.

"Oh, that sounds wonderful. What will it be like?"

"The introductions will take place at Balisier, and, for some odd reason, Sensates have always made a big production of bringing another into the fold, so it's quite the gala affair."

"Is there time to get it together by then?"

Jediah held his wife at arm's length and looked at her with just a bit of incredulity. She caught his thought pattern and cuffed herself mentally for lack of forethought.

"Forget I asked," she said. "You guys can accomplish amazing things at the wink of an eye. I'm still getting used to your world of Sensates."

"Our world," he corrected.

She wrapped her arms around her new husband, breathing in his scent. Her fingers brushed against his soft linen shirt and came to rest on the hardened muscles of his chest. Much like his shirt, his gentle exterior masked the un-tapped power held beneath. She could sense it - a raging volcano with a well-maintained, finely honed pressure valve keeping it all in check.

"I look forward to meeting them," she said. "It's hard to believe they have connections in so many areas."

"We have been at it for a while, you know," he said as he brushed a lock of golden hair from her cheek.

She lowered her eyes and pressed her chest to his. As she breathed in she felt his gift of serenity wash over her. Alexandra smiled, knowing she would always be safe in his arms. She leaned back and gazed upon her handsome, broad-shouldered husband. "I'm slowly beginning to realize our footprint. We carry massive responsibility for our concealed powers."

"Yes we do. Economic, social, political… all of them and more, globally."

A chill ran through her. "If everyone knew of our powers, the ramifications would be greatly destructive. The world would drastically change and we would all be at tremendous risk."

"It's a hard truth, my love," he said, running a finger down her neck, "and a danger we live with daily."

She strengthened her resolve to protect the Sensates at all costs. "The most tedious task I have encountered in my life before this was weeding carrots," she said.

"What?" He pushed her to arm's length and stared at her.

"Have you ever weeded carrots?" she asked indignantly.

Jediah scratched his head and said, "Can't say that I have."

"Well, carrot seeds are as tiny as a grain of sand. In fact, you have to mix them with sand to plant them or they grow too close together. Even with mixing them with sand, they still grow too thick and you have to thin them. Imagine a row a hundred feet long and filled with millions of tiny carrots. You have to sit on the ground and thin those millions to a thousand. Do you have any idea how long that takes? And how careful you have to be so as to not disturb the remaining thousand?"

"I'm beginning to get the picture…," he said.

"Well, take the mind-numbing attention to detail that task commands, and multiply that by, what?

Infinity?"

Jediah shrugged.

"That's the depth of commitment required to safeguard the Sensates' secret."

Jediah broke out in a dazzling grin, "Oh, I see. It's similar to herding cats?"

She couldn't suppress the giggle that escaped her lips as her mind formed an image of Jediah high upon his black stallion attempting to herd cats.

He continued. "Or catching a dozen Slinkies coming down the steps at you all at once?"

Laughter came full force as she pictured him jumping back and forth catching Slinkies.

Adding to his list he exclaimed, "Ah, I've got it: being responsible for four machines of Whack-a-Mole with only one whacker."

That image, plus his use of the term 'whacker' put her over the edge. Her sides ached and she was close to hiccupping. She doubled over and slid to the floor, immersed in her thoughts.

Her unabashed laughter was contagious. Jediah sat next to her and joined in. As their joy subsided, he leaned close and brushed the hair from her damp cheeks. "It is a tough job, but we've managed our secret for over two thousand years. You'll find, after a century or so, it'll come naturally."

She sighed. "A century or so, huh?"

"It depends on your strength of character. Could take as long as two." He glanced at her with one eyebrow raised.

"I won't fall for your teasing. If everyone else can manage to contain and guard our secret, I can do it too."

"Never doubted you for a minute," Jediah said. "Oh by the way, you'll need to don your finest for the introductions."

"My finest? I don't have a 'finest'."

"You soon shall, for before the weekend, we'll take a wee shopping trip. Are you up for it?"

She straightened her shoulders and said, "I am woman. I can do anything."

Jediah leaned close and brushed his lips to hers. She knew he would lead her through the new life that waited before her. If she faltered, he would be there. Decades of mastering his powers and leading the group had perfected his character. She would pattern her life after his.

WishkIs, echoed in her mind.

WishkIs? What was that? She searched her mind; did she know what it meant? Yes! It meant 'I am strong.'

She leaned back to look into his face. "Are you familiar with the word 'wishkIs'?"

"No, I've never heard it before. What does it mean?"

"I think it means 'I am strong,' but I'm not sure."

"Where did you hear it?"

"It just came to me. It wasn't a voice, it was more like an echo."

Jediah's brows knit together and he spoke solemnly. "The abilities you acquired by being an Ultra Sensate are unbelievable in themselves and could be staggering to someone newly indoctrinated into our world. Mom gave you her powers, which were considerable in their own right. Coupled with the ones you were born with, the total is mesmerizing, to say the least. Adding the full powers you received on our wedding night - something a typical Sensate would have had years to become accustomed to - by all rights, you should be overwhelmed. No other in our history has ever had so many abilities or as much power as you have at this very minute."

As his words sunk in, she became aware of the rapid beating of her heart. Her breathing quickened. "Oh, this is too much to get my mind around."

Jediah rushed to calm her. "I only recapped the events to illustrate the implications, sweet girl. Not only will you travel where footsteps have taken the rest of us, you may also cover new ground. I can only offer my support; I may not be able to explain all that happens to you."

"You think understanding another language and not knowing how, might be normal?" she asked.

"Maybe, for you. It has never happened to me."

His eyes carried such trust and compassion her fear of the unknown dissipated. "I'm just glad you're here with me. It'd be easy to misinterpret the oddities of our abilities as figments of my imagination, or worse yet, the beginning of a psychosis."

Jediah smiled at her concerns. "You are mentally strong, more so than anyone I know."

"Thank you for easing my mind." She smiled at the glint in his eyes and sensed a forthcoming adventure.

"How about donning your hiking boots and exploring the far reaches of Heartseed?" he asked.

There were still spots on her two thousand acres she'd not seen. "I'd love it!" she said

***

"Hey there, you with the long legs, hold up a minute," she yelled at Jediah.

Alexandra dropped down onto a fallen log, her breath coming in gasps.

Jediah looked at his watch. "For a city gal you hung in there for a little over and hour before you hollered 'uncle'." He winked as he sat down next to her. They settled into a mutual place where no conversation or words were required.

The voice in her head began as softly as a sigh... *No, this is wrong.*

Alexandra opened her mind to Jediah so he might hear too. The voice repeated, *This is wrong.*

Jediah spun to face his wife, his eyes intent with unasked questions. He pressed his finger to his lips to let her know not to respond.

She reinforced the impenetrable bars over her mind to protect herself from the unknown as Jediah closed the distance between them.

Not again, I can't stop them.

Alexandra probed the girl's mind to take in her surroundings. The room was cold, well-lit, and it echoed, as if empty. The girl was unable to move. Her only view was that of the ceiling, which had institutional lighting with ceiling grids.

They felt the girl's fear coupled with a growing sense of hopelessness as the girl turned her head. Two people entered her room.

Alexandra sensed the girl's desperation sink even lower.

If you can hear me, please help me. I can't be the only one...Please. The girl's strength dwindled. *No. Not again...*

The voice receded to a whisper, faded, and was gone.

"Alexandra, who was that?" Jediah asked. His eyes were wide with unanswered questions.

"I don't know. I've heard a faint voice before, but since it didn't make sense, I didn't make much of it. This time her voice was distinct. I heard her cries for help and wanted you to hear too. It seemed like a beacon to anyone who would listen."

"Did you stop the connection?" he asked.

"No, it just faded away. She's hunting for us, hoping we exist, afraid she might be totally alone."

"Yeah." Jediah rubbed his chin, "I don't know how you tapped into her, or she into you, but before we take any action we must gather more information. Since you shared the imprint of her mind with me, I can share it with the Ultras. We need to listen for her thoughts constantly. Let's see if they can pick up anything."

"Good," she said, "I'm worried for her. Something's terribly wrong."

"I think so too. I'm going to Balisier; I'll be back in a few minutes."

After kissing her cheek, he was gone from sight.

Alexandra thought for only a few seconds, and then contacted Ryeth.

Ryeth? she said telepathically.

I heard her too, Alexandra.

She's being held against her will.

Sounds like it, he said.

When I felt her presence, I let Jediah hear too.

Ah, smart girl. I wondered how you would work out that bump in the road. He paused. *Does he know we chat sometimes?*

I don't believe so, she said. *Even if he sensed anything, he would probably let me work things out on my own.*

Good. What's the deal with the girl?

Alexandra sensed Ryeth's intrigue. She collected her thoughts before she began. *I can't tell,* she said. *Everything seemed a bit dreamlike in her mind and didn't take solid form. She's afraid, and hopes there is another like her who can hear her cries for help.*

She could feel Ryeth's indecision. *Then she doesn't know about us,* he said.

He was being cautious, which probably wasn't a bad idea. *No, she hopes, but isn't certain. We have to help her. Jediah's gone to alert the others.*

It could be a trap, Ryeth said.

A trap! Alexandra felt Ryeth's caution. So that's why Jediah didn't want her to respond. *Oh, I never thought of that. My only thought was to help her. I almost locked onto her and went to her aid.* She sensed Ryeth's patience and supposed it came from years of dealing with naïve innocents.

After a few seconds he said, *Let's keep monitoring her and see what we can find out. Keep me posted.*

I will, she said.

Alexandra walked back to the house and listened for the girl constantly but was unable to make contact. Almost an hour later Jediah returned home.

"The Ultras are going to work in shifts listening for the girl. I think that's all we can do until we know more."

"What do you suppose is going on?"

"I'm always wary of a trap," Jediah said while stroking his chin.

Him too? Was she the only one who took it for face value? She needed to remember the importance of their secret. "Who would do such a thing?" she asked.

"I don't know who, but I can guess why. 'Who' could be almost anyone, especially if one of us let down his or her guard. The 'why' concerns me more. Someone following up on a normal déjà vu occurrence wouldn't bother me as much as someone hoping to infiltrate our ranks to use our abilities."

Alexandra's heart skipped a beat. That someone or a group of someones might seek the Sensates to use against others wasn't a foreign thought, but to realize it in the present, not in some far off future hit her smack between the eyes.

"I'm sorry," she said. "I have to keep reminding myself of what's at stake." She shifted the barriers in her mind. "There. I've placed Nancy Jane's steel trap around my mind and left a tiny window open for this voice at all times."

"I've done the same," Jediah smiled at his wife. "We seem to be thinking as one."

"Aren't we?" The thought made her smile.

"Mom was quite adept at blocking intrusion into her mind." Jediah's voice seemed far away as he spoke. "She left us with a very precise instrument for protection."

Her eyes clouded over. "I miss her, Jediah."

"Me too. After having her by my side for so long, I often forget she's gone. I catch myself beginning a conversation, and then remember she can no longer answer."

"I'm so sorry," she said.

"I am too." He hugged her close. "But all is as it should be," Jediah replied.

"Your Mom used to say that all the time."

"So did Teater," he said.

"They must have had a wonderful friendship."

"Ah," he said, "that they did."

Chapter 11

Slamming the folder shut, Detective Richard Mokros of the Waynesburg Police Department, turned to Officer Johnson. "I don't like it when outsiders stick their collective noses in our investigations."

"We don't have much choice." Officer Johnson shuffled through the papers on his desk, trying to make them appear more orderly.

Detective Mokros stood and began to pace the floor of the ten by ten foot office they shared. "I refuse to have them dictate my actions on a daily basis."

Trying to cool Mokros down was taking more effort than he cared to give. Serious stuff just hit the fan and all his partner could focus on was a testosterone competition. "Homeland Security is carving a niche in our local law enforcement, and whether we like it or not, they're the ones calling the shots."

Mokros was unaffected by his attempt to keep things calm. "It just grates on my last nerve that they have that kind of authority over us," said Mokros. "It's bad enough we have to bow down to the Feds, now we have Homeland to cater to as well?" Mokros picked up the folder, and slammed it down once more.

Johnson sighed, he was getting nowhere. "It would seem so. I wonder what triggered their interest?" said Johnson trying a re-direct.

"Harrumph, for all we know it could be as trite as a hangnail or something we missed in our investigation."

"Na, we didn't miss anything," said Johnson. "We were extremely thorough with that girl's abduction. I can't imagine it has anything to do with her or with Saffle."

Mokros' lip curled. "They both have money out the whazoo; maybe it's ill-gotten-gains."

"That's the most likely area to consider, but there wasn't even a hint of anything off-color when we researched their finances. The Higgins girl..., Hell, I'd better quit calling her that, *Alexandra* only had two sources of income: the coal company, and her recent inheritance from that long lost ancestor. Saffle's money, on the other hand, goes back generations and from what we could tell, he's as squeaky clean as a new born babe." Johnson shook his head.

"There has to be something," said Mokros, "but darned if I know what it is. How are we supposed to keep eyes on them when they're sitting atop a mountain? The best we can do is to monitor their internet traffic and phone calls until they decide to grace our fair city with their presence."

Mokros stood, sending his chair backward and grating on the old wood plank floor. "Let's call it a day and pick up early tomorrow before the pain-in-our-butts get here."

Johnson nodded to his partner, shifted his sidearm to a more comfortable position, and slung his jacket over his arm. With a practiced nonchalant air, he made his way out of the building and crossed the distance to his car in the parking lot.

He needed to talk to Jediah, and he needed to do it *now*. It took what remained of his composure to exit the parking lot with a leisurely speed and point the car toward home. Finally able to concentrate, he hailed the leader of the Sensates.

Jediah, it's Gabriel.

Yes?

Gabriel Johnson plunged head-first into his news. *A small group within Homeland Security is interested in Alexandra's case. They plan to arrive here tomorrow and go over our files.*

Is this normal? He sensed Jediah's immediate concern.

No, said Johnson, *not by any stretch of the imagination. I'm worried.*

How soon can you meet at Balisier?

Gabriel glanced at his watch. *Half an hour, tops.*

See you then.

As Gabriel disconnected from Jediah, he felt part of the load ease from his shoulders. Jediah was a source of strength for all of them. Their leader would see to their safety. Raking through his mind for any red flag, Gabriel could think of no apparent reason for Homeland's intervention.

***

Busy in Heartseed's kitchen sorting through her collection of teas, Alexandra detected concern on Jediah's face as he arrived home.

"Something happen at Balisier?" she inquired.

The concern eased, replaced by a knowing smile and one raised eyebrow. "Yes, as a matter of fact. I was just considering how to broach the subject."

Alexandra stepped back from the counter and

crossed her arms. "Well, you've got a few centuries on me concerning proper etiquette. I'm certain you'll figure it out." She waited patiently as she watched varied emotions pass over his face.

Finally, he looked up at her with a wry smile. "Not going to make it easy on me, are you?"

"No." She smiled at her beautiful husband. "If you're having that much trouble, maybe you should just spit it out."

He took a breath, looked her directly in the eyes and blurted, "Homeland Security is looking into your abduction case. They will arrive tomorrow to go over the files at the Waynesburg Police Station."

Whomp! There it was - that dratted other shoe dropping. She knew her good luck couldn't hold out forever. At some point, someone would try to tie up the loose ends of her abduction. In an attempt to remain cool and collected, she said, "What are the ramifications?"

"Right now, we have to wait and see what they uncover. It bothers me that the visit from Homeland Security is happening at the same time you are hearing a voice seeking help."

How quickly his mind worked. She hadn't even begun to make any connection. It was no wonder he was selected to be in charge of their group. "Oh, it does seem more of a trap if you consider both at the same time," she said. "I wish I knew more so I could help. What should we do?"

"Well, until we have more to go on, I think we should go shopping."

"Shopping?" He was incredulous. Danger of discovery from Homeland Security, coupled with a potential trap, and he thought they should go shopping? "Are you sure?"

"Yes, change your clothes, wife, we're going to Paris."

"I'll never get used to this lifestyle," she said. "Shouldn't we be worried about being compromised?"

"Most assuredly, however, we still have an affair to attend this weekend, and you have no gown. We'll discuss the fallout if and when it happens. Nothing good ever came of worrying; it's the single-most waste of time and energy."

He had a way with words, and he always eased her mind. If a man who lived on this Earth for two hundred-fifty years said they were going to Paris, then Paris it was.

"Who am I to argue? I'm a newbie," she said, smiling.

She hurriedly gathered the teas, put them into cans, placed them back in the cupboard, and then hollered over her shoulder as she ran up the stairs, "Ten minutes should do it."

Jediah yelled, "I'll grab a drink and wait for you in the arbor."

As she changed, she shared the new information.

Ryeth?

Yes, Alexandra.

Homeland Security is looking into the police files of my abduction. They are to arrive on Monday.

What are they looking for? he asked.

Alexandra had no wish to alarm Ryeth, but was short of time so she blurted out the information just as Jediah had done. *Their final conversation with me involved tying up loose ends. They wanted to know how I escaped from Magis and how I got back home.*

Of course, I didn't have answers...

I'm sorry, Alexandra, said Ryeth. *I was worried my actions might cause repercussions.*

She felt Ryeth's remorse, if that's what it could be called. She sensed something deeper, something he felt to the core. *No, it was all Tom Magis' doing,* she said, *he's the one that opened Pandora's Box. I didn't contact you to make you feel bad, I just wanted you to know what was happening.*

Ryeth was quiet, then he spoke slowly. *If I hadn't been so bent on revenge, perhaps I could have saved you that horror.*

She spoke quickly to dispel his regrets. *It's all water under the bridge, Ryeth. We can't go back.*

What she sensed now from Ryeth was tempered rage. *Alexandra, surely you've guessed that I don't cling to all your Sensate ethics crap. I cross lines your group would never consider honorable.* His voice became soft and controlled. *I could have done more.*

His words stung as they cut through her. *Ryeth, we are who we are. You were exactly what I needed at the time.*

She sensed his bitterness as he spoke. *I have not lived with the same sense of security as those within your fold. I had to do things to survive that you wouldn't deem 'proper.' Your level of ethics is beyond my reach.*

I understand. Left to her own devices as he had been, she would have probably had to stretch or break boundaries to survive. There was protection within their fold. He hadn't had that luxury.

Ryeth's voice was firm. *I will do whatever it takes to ensure our safety, Alexandra. My interference caused the breach.*

You rescued me. I'll never forget that. Who's to say what would have happened if you hadn't acted as you did?

She felt Ryeth's conflict as he withdrew from the connection. Though she didn't know why, she sensed the struggle between his past and present contained centuries of anger and regret. Her dark and brooding rescuer was fighting a major internal battle.

The Sensate moral code and honor guidelines ensured each adhered without question. No one would peer into her mind to discover that she communicated with Ryeth, not even her husband.

By the time she met Jediah in the arbor, she had compartmentalized extraneous thoughts of her conversation with Ryeth and prepared herself for the trip.

"Oui, oui, monsieur, I am ready," she said to Jediah as she curtsied.

"Ma petite femme, j'ai eu la chance de l'amour à vos yeux. Irons-nous?"

"Jediah! You speak French?"

"Yes, and a few others. I can share the language with you, if you'd like."

"You mean teach me?" she asked.

"No. I would give you that knowledge, and you would be able to speak it fluently."

"Oh," she said thoughtfully. "When your mother taught me to read minds, I never made the connection that we could read and store that knowledge. She told me things would seep into my mind, things I hadn't considered. This is one of them, isn't it?"

Jediah picked her up and spun her around until she was dizzy and giggling. As he steadied her in his arms, he said, "Let's call it shared resources. Open your mind and I will share with you."

It began as a tiny tickle. As it grew, so did her understanding of the French language. In two minutes' time, she was fluent. During the transfer, his orb appeared and whisked them off to Paris.

Within three hours, they were sitting in a quaint French café sharing a croissant with a pile of packages at their feet. It had been a wonderful experience. Using her new language, she had conversed, joked, and made purchases. No longer would she be an outsider in a place of a different language. She could speak fluently without a trace of her American accent. Jediah had given her a fantastic gift.

Even with the excitement of being in Paris for the first time, she was unable to stop the threat to their very existence from entering her subconscious.

"What do you suppose Homeland Security is hoping to uncover, Jediah?"

He sighed. "I knew I couldn't stop your mind from wondering too long." He winked, and said, "Answers to the inconsistencies. The Sensate within the police department is concerned enough to bring it to the attention of the High Counsel. We take any threat to our security very seriously."

She toyed with a croissant crumb. "Do you think they'll uncover a breach?" If it were humanly possible she would kick herself. The newest Sensate threatened to compromise the security they had maintained for over two thousand years. It was all her fault.

"We can only wait and see," he said. It's better to be watchful than have our heads stuck in the ground assuming we're untouchable."

She could bear the guilt no longer. "Oh Jediah, I'm so sorry."

"Sweet Alexandra, there's no reason to be sorry. Circumstances were beyond your control. You couldn't possibly have known Tom Magis would abduct you, hold you captive and try to brainwash you." Taking her hand in his, he continued. "Darling, you're completely innocent of any wrongdoing."

"But I flashed myself home and in doing so, left a question mark as to how."

He shrugged. "Where else were you to go when you finally woke from a drugged state?"

"You're just trying to make me feel better. It's causing concern, isn't it? Tell me the truth, and don't sugar-coat it."

Jediah looked deeply into her eyes and held the stare for a while. "Yes, it is causing concern, that and exactly how you escaped. Along with those, there's Magis' incapacitation to be considered."

She let out a breath and could feel her shoulders slumping. "I thought this was all in the past."

He slipped a finger beneath her chin and raised her face to meet his. "It soon will be, for aren't our lives just a snippet in time?"

She grimaced. "I can do without this particular snippet."

"All snippets are important, dear wife, even this one. If you could see through Time's eyes, you would find a finely woven tapestry where no thread is more important than any other."

As she looked into the depth of her husband's eyes, she caught a glimpse of the vast wisdom and serenity that resided there. His peaceful nature surrounded her. Soon her anxiety disappeared.

"I'm so glad you're mine," she said as she slipped her arms around his neck.

"I'm the lucky one," he replied, kissing the tip of her nose. "Ready to go home, Mrs. Saffle?"

"Yes. I can tread any path, as long as you're beside me."

Chapter 12

Only her wedding gown surpassed the grandeur of the ivory and moss green chiffon gown Alexandra saw reflected as she twirled happily in front of the mirror. As the folds rocked back and forth like waves then finally settled, knowing arms wrapped around her from behind. The mirror image now held that of Jediah gazing over her shoulder to meet her eyes.

Jediah was a veritable hunk when dressed in his jeans and shirt, but when he dressed in his finest, he became Alexandra's slice of heaven. "Umm, if you were not my husband, I would seek a gypsy's love potion to put in your drink tonight."

"If you were not my wife, I'd..." He spun her in his arms. The intensity in his eyes left no room to doubt his feelings. "I don't know what I would do. I have already waited two hundred thirty years, and once engaged, allowed only four days for you to change your mind before spiriting you away for an extended honeymoon. I'd say I came close to using every trick in my arsenal to assure you ended up exactly where you are. However, it is nice to know you would go to similar lengths to assure the same."

She smiled and snuggled in his arms. "You wear a tux well," she whispered.

His arms tightened then his brow furrowed ever so slightly. "Smile, we have company."

She heard a beep from the driveway alarm. From the console screen, they noted Alice Jane had arrived and was waiting for admittance at the gate located at the base of their mountain home. Jediah punched the release code and watched as the gate opened.

"You've got about ten minutes before the world as you know it ceases to exist. Any last thoughts, dear wife?"

Alexandra paused. "I can't tell if you are being overly dramatic or poking fun at me."

"To tell you the truth, it's a little of both," he said. "All Sensate doors will open to you tonight at Balisier. I'm not certain how many Sensates will remain hidden from your view. Even so, the evening will be one you will remember for an eternity."

Jediah placed a whisper of a kiss on her cheek, and then slipped from the room leaving her alone to contemplate the upcoming festivities.

Shoving the false bravado aside, disbelief poised on the threshold of her thoughts. Who would have thought falling into a cistern could turn into such an adventure?

Her mind broke apart and whirled into several directions at once. One thread led to her parents who died three years ago; she felt the ache clench her throat. Then, along came this Sensate thing which brought about necessary subterfuge from a lifetime of camaraderie with her best friend. Regret formed a knot in the pit of her stomach. The inability to share her newfound abilities with Cassie created an empty hole inside. The excitement, thrill, and wonder of being a Sensate ended up a crippled victory due to the need for secrecy.

"I miss you, Cassandra Hudson. As happy as I am with Jediah, and as unbelievable as my life is, I have reservations about being a Sensate. It wasn't enough to lose Mom and Dad, did I have to lose you too?"

Her eyes filled with unshed tears. Without thinking, her senses filled with thoughts of Cassie, and as her heart warmed, she realized she had transported herself to Cassie's bedroom, directly behind Cassie! Luckily, Cassie was rummaging through her closet looking for shoes, frantically tossing them left and right and didn't notice the intrusion. Alexandra flashed back to her own bedroom, her heart beating so fast it rushed in her ears.

She raised her hands up and said, "See? I'm not the right person for the job. Too much rests on my shoulders and I'm dumber than a box of rocks. I don't have the wisdom or experience to keep my head above water. Whoever decided my fate should seriously reconsider their actions because I'm completely wrong for this."

An even bigger mistake came to mind. "Just think of the trouble I caused by flashing myself home after the Magis incident. Because of that a freaky group from Homeland Security has put us under surveillance. How is a person supposed to deal with this stuff?"

Ane'mot.

Alexandra jerked. She was talking aloud but didn't expect anyone to answer. The touch seemed familiar, yet she couldn't place it. She reinforced the barriers around her mind.

Ane'mot, she heard again. The woman said 'breathe.'

As her heart raced, Alexandra asked, *Who are you?*

All in good time, memiki.

Memiki. She called her 'butterfly.' The

woman's touch felt soft and motherly, similar to Nancy Jane's, but all-encompassing and ethereal at the same time. How had this woman gotten through the block Nancy Jane had taught her? Was her mind to be Grand Central Station; open against the strongest mental walls known?

She took a deep breath to calm her thoughts. The touch to her mind was gone.

Walking to the banister that overlooked the foyer, she saw Jediah embracing his sister, Alice Jane.

"It's good to see you again, Alice," Alexandra yelled over the banister. "I'll be right down."

"What a great color on you! That gown is perfect!" Alice said. "Get down here so I can take pictures before we go."

"Thanks, I'll be down in a sec. Jediah, show your sister around while I finish up."

"Sure thing," he replied.

Alexandra wiped her eyes, took one last glance in the mirror, and headed down the stairs.

Before they left for Balisier, Jediah took his wife aside and shared a mechanism.

He said, "What I just gave you is the ability to sense other Sensates. This is one power that has to be given, not acquired. When we were just one, and then the two, Onatah passed this to her daughter. This one gift comes from Onatah herself, passed down from Sensate to Sensate. You will never feel alone again."

A warmth flowed through her body. She was keenly aware of Jediah and Alice, but also of many others. It was like a chorus to her song, something that filled, yet did not consume.

"Oh, I had no idea... it's wondrous. Thank you,

Jediah." She reached up to kiss his soft lips.

"I only shared," he said. "Thank Onatah."

***

Jediah's orb took them to a high overhang in Balisier where the entire village was displayed before them. The vision stole her breath away. Tiny shivers ran up her back. She still found it unbelievable that this space had been carved out of a mountain of solid stone - her mountain.

It was massive, perhaps the size of four football fields. The sides were dark and had texture. As high up as she could see, there didn't appear to be a top. There were no stars or moon, and the ceiling exhibited no visible means of support. The buildings of the exquisite village were constructed from solid limestone, each stained a different hue from the same pallet - sand, taupe, ivory, brown, and embellished with burnished red-brown accents.

She knew from Jediah that a giant waterfall located in a chasm far below generated enough hydroelectric power to supply the village with electricity, power the ultraviolet rays for plant growth, and run the plant that produced filtered breathable air and maintained its temperature.

There were no streets in this small village; instead, it had wide walkways carved with the same beautiful vine and floral pattern as the floor of her arbor. A bluish glow from lanterns hanging from intricately wrought iron poles lined the walkways and rendered a dream-like appearance to the village. Lights on a timer simulated outside conditions. The village square, lit with thousands of tiny lights, gave a fanciful air to the festivities held in her honor.

Jediah's hand on her waist brought a smile to her lips as he guided her down the winding stone staircase to the village below.

She couldn't believe her eyes as James Dawson and his wife, Sarah came forward to greet her. James had managed all the paperwork regarding her great grandfather's will. He and Sarah had attended their wedding.

Sarah hugged her and whispered in her ear. "I can sense you are pleasantly surprised."

"Sarah, what an understatement; I had no idea that you and James were Sensates. It seems highly unfair that all this time you knew and I didn't." She stepped away from Sarah and hugged James.

"I'm so glad this event is finally taking place," James said. "Sarah and I wanted to tell you, but we think it's much more fun to see the surprise when we all get together."

"I never thought people I already knew might be Sensates," said Alexandra. "This is unbelievable."

Jediah touched her elbow. She followed his eyes and scanned the crowd. A huge grin broke across her face when she recognized several other Sensates. Walking toward her was William Snyder, the goldsmith who crafted her wedding gift to Jediah.

He leaned forward, took her hands in his and kissed her on the cheek. "You have just been kissed by the oldest living Sensate. I am six hundred and twenty-seven years young, and a member of the High Counsel. Welcome to our village and to being a Sensate."

"Thank you, William. I should have guessed…"

"If you had, then shame on me," he said with a twinkle in his eyes. "I also need to welcome you as a member of our High Counsel."

She reached over to squeeze Jediah's hand as nervous energy flowed through her body. "I - I don't know what to say. I'm so new, and unworthy... and ..." She faltered. Her eyes met Jediah's as his calming presence washed over her. He was her Gibraltar, her foundation. "I am honored, William. Thank you."

William bowed ever so slightly and, with a nod of his head, moved away into the crowd.

Turning to her husband, Alexandra said, "You told me some members might hide themselves from me. Have any done so?"

Jediah looked around and then said, "Not a one. This has never happened before. It could be because of your hardship in getting to us. They had a long time to get to know *of* you before your actual arrival here this evening."

The most handsome man in the village, the one whose arm was linked with hers, looked lovingly at her. "Jediah, it's you. You're the reason they opened up to me. I've watched their reaction to you. They trust, respect, and hold you in very high esteem. I'm so proud to be your wife."

As he squeezed her hand, she caught the eye of Mathew Thomas, the architect of her beloved Heartseed, and Gregory Patrick, the builder, who winked.

Valentine Jellan embraced her in a tender hug. The soft-hearted man who had nursed her back to health after her abduction never failed to warm her heart.

He kissed her cheek and held her hand. "I'm glad you are finally out in the open."

"I've known about you," she said. How could I not when you disappeared in front of my eyes?"

"I'm sorry for that lapse, but I do like to introduce myself," said Val.

He patted her hand and then walked away.

Jediah shook his head. "We've never been able to squelch the imp in him."

"I wouldn't change a thing," she said.

They made their way through almost every member of their group. As they approached the final few members, Jediah touched a young man on the back. He had two females locked in animated conversation, a stunning blonde and a flawless redhead, and the apparent brunt of the anecdote, a tall muscular man, looking on. When he turned around, Alexandra's eyes flew wide open.

"Alexandra, I'd like you to meet the youngest member of our group, Gabriel Johnson," Jediah said.

She stood there, unable to speak and shaking her head. She knew a Sensate was on the Waynesburg police force, but would never have guessed the starchy officer that questioned her regarding her abduction and the blushing fellow standing in front of her could possibly be the same.

"I'm not the youngest anymore," said Gabriel. "Thank you, Ms. Saffle, for taking on that distinction. It's a pleasure to finally have you completely under our wing."

Jediah put his hand on Gabriel's shoulder. "I couldn't agree with you more, Gabe."

"Please call me Alexandra," she said. "Thank you for all you did to find me."

"You are welcome. I wish we had been the ones to save you from Magis instead of Ryeth. I would have been in a better position to guard our security."

Alexandra felt a pang of regret. "I wish that too," she said.

Jediah stepped between them and put an arm around each. "Listen here you two, I'll have no airing of regrets this evening. With that said, I now would like to introduce my lovely wife to our key resource Sensates. I now present to you three fellow Ultras, Reslyn, MacAila, and Jonathan."

"It's a pleasure to finally meet you," said Alexandra. "Thanks for your efforts in attempting to locate me during my captivity. Jediah told me how you banded together to work as one. I'll be forever grateful."

Jonathan wasted no time in responding. "It's great to put a face to the mind imprint Jediah gave us. I, for one, can't stand that part. I need to meet the imprint or it makes me feel downright clairvoyant and spooky."

The beautiful blonde shook her head. "Don't worry, you'll get over that in a hundred years or so," Reslyn said.

MacAila patted Jonathan on the shoulder. "Yeah, sooner or later you've gotta quit the kid stuff, bucko."

Jonathan hung his head in mock acquiescence. "Great, I have to sit here all evening between these two and get picked on."

Alexandra smiled. No man in his right mind could truly be unhappy sitting between the two captivating females. Nothing shy of a goddess, MacAila's long flowing red tresses framed her slightly freckled porcelain cheeks. Her haunting blue eyes shone so clearly they looked like jewels. Equally as stunning, Reslyn's silky blonde hair combined with a flawless, well-toned body and packed curves in all the right places.

The mutual trust and easy friendship that

surrounded her was almost palpable, forming a brotherhood, strong and unyielding. The Sensates wrapped her in an envelope of family love she hadn't felt since her parents passed away.

"We're the ones who are glad to finally meet you. Jediah's kept you under lock and key long enough," Reslyn said.

"Thank you," Alexandra said, and then she wondered the same thing. She turned to Jediah pointedly and asked, "Why *did* you keep me under lock and key so long?"

A slow smile spread across his lips and his eyes smoldered. "Because I wasn't ready to share you."

"Makes sense to me," said MacAila. "He waited long enough to get you."

Alexandra could feel the heat start in her chest and move upward to color her cheeks. "I guess there are no secrets in Balisier."

"Not really," said Jediah as he winked at the Ultras.

Jediah took her hand, led her to a table, and pulled out a chair for her. She gathered the folds of her gown to sit, but nearly slipped from the chair when a frantic voice entered her mind.

I know you're there. I can feel you. Answer me.

Alexandra's eyes flashed to Jediah's. He hadn't heard. She opened the connection so he could hear her as well. Although Jediah cautioned her about a possible threat, something told her she *had* to respond to the girl.

I'm here, Alexandra replied.

Alexandra sensed hopelessness mixed with excitement.

The voice said, *Are you a prisoner too? Are you like me? Can you do things with your mind?*

The oppression Alexandra felt coming from the voice zapped her strength. Her legs wobbled as she dropped into the chair. She drew in a long breath as she closed her eyes and placed her fingers on her temples. Jediah's hand never left her shoulder.

No, I'm not a prisoner.

The voice's tone turned fierce. *Then. They. Don't. Know. About… You.* The lack of hope turned to anger, then to despair. *Why are you free and I'm left to rot in this stink hole?*

Where are you? asked Alexandra. She listened for the voice and felt unimaginable desperation.

I don't know. Her voice became a whisper, trailing off, as did her thoughts.

Alexandra sensed a great loss of time, gray vacant spaces where memories should reside, and underneath it all a strong will to survive. A picture formed in Alexandra's mind, and she could see blank walls, bright lights, no windows, and a large industrial door. The door loomed foremost in the girl's mind as it grew to mammoth proportions. It swirled into a misshapen image, sometimes focusing on the hinges, and in the next split second, centering on the lock.

Jediah pulsed warmth and serenity to Alexandra, who channeled her husband's special gift to the unknown female.

Alexandra felt her transition into a state of tranquility. *The drugs.* The girl grew frantic. *I'm losing you…* Her voice trailed off.

I'm still here! Alexandra forced the concentration to great heights, and then felt Jediah's abilities combine with hers, but despite their efforts, the connection to the girl slipped away.

Alexandra met her husband's eyes. "Did you

feel her desperation?"

"Yes, it was like a lead anchor pulling her down."

She read the anguish on his face and knew her captivity and overall hopelessness had transferred to him as well.

Her fingers closed tightly on his arm. "We have to do something," she said, "we can't let this continue. Even if it is part of a trap, we can't ignore it."

"Sweet girl, I do not take this lightly. This weighs heavily on my mind, as I know it does yours. For now, let's concentrate on getting through this night, and then we can tackle it full strength on the morrow."

As always, his calming nature encircled her. It stiffened her resolve to ensure the unknown's safety.

She smiled and turned her attention to the festivities. "Tonight we enjoy all the pleasures Balisier has to offer, my husband, and revel in all that is good in this world. Tomorrow, we will look into our new dilemma."

She felt his arm tighten around her shoulders as she gave her thoughts over to the scene before her.

The secret village was so full of activity she barely noticed Jediah slip away. She took a moment to observe the crowd gathered in her honor. Alice Jane simply radiated. It was hard not to stare at her new sister-in-law as she made her way through to one group and then to another. Alice Jane's stature, though much taller, was so similar to Nancy Jane's that remorse caused her eyes to mist. Before her heart became too heavy over the loss of her mentor, Jediah reappeared with two glasses of champagne.

As she took his hand and rose to her feet, the

entire group of Sensates raised their glasses to honor the new member.

Chapter 13

Dressed impeccably in charcoal gray trousers and a black fitted silk shirt, Ryeth watched as Kimberly crossed the second floor landing, glanced around, and headed for the top of the stairs. He felt her presence the moment he entered the lobby, and knew the instant she left her room.

Even indoors, her black hair caught the subtle light and glistened. She wore a designer knee-length black dress that hugged her figure and black strappy heels. The only adornments were a pale blue diamond tennis bracelet and matching two-carat pendant around her long neck held by a delicate gold chain. She radiated confidence and exquisite taste in fashion. Her eyes looked down as she checked the time on her watch, and at precisely eight o'clock, she descended the stairs to the first floor lobby.

He chose to watch as she took each step and slowly came down to the base of the stairs. Only then, did he rise from his seat near the corner and cross the room to greet her.

"Ms. Koza, it is again my pleasure to see you."

"Thank you, and it's Kimberly, please."

"Certainly, and I will insist on Ryeth."

"As you wish," she said as she lowered her lashes with a nod.

"Would you care for a glass of wine before we are seated for supper?"

"Thank you, no. I'd prefer to wait."

Ryeth nodded and said, "Let's make our way to the dining room, shall we?"

He offered her his arm, and she slid hers through his. "The management was able to lure a chef here from a Michelin four star restaurant in New York."

"That must have taken some doing. Do you think blackmail was involved?" she said.

Ryeth grinned. "There could be a little something held over his head, but, to tell the truth, I think he wanted to relax his pace a bit."

The Maître De recognized Ryeth and sat the couple immediately at a secluded table with a view of the mountains. They placed their order, and upon Ryeth's recommendation, they ordered the chef's specialty, Chateaubriand, and a glass of wine.

"How long have you lived in this area, Ryeth?"

An easy first question, and one he'd rehearsed. "All my life," he said, "but I've traveled a bit, here and there. You deemed yourself a recent transplant from Florida earlier, why the move?"

"Change of scenery, mostly. I'm a writer and I wanted to add a bit of flavor to my next book, entitled *Intrigue*, set in the Poconos."

"You're a mystery writer?"

"Yes, but not very noteworthy." She flushed a provocative shade of pink. "I write mostly for myself, and commit to absolutely no marketing. It's more of a hobby than a profession."

Ryeth inwardly congratulated himself. The conversation seemed natural and was flowing without effort. He felt his shoulders relax. "Why did you choose the Poconos?" he asked.

As she responded, Ryeth didn't miss the light twinkling in her eyes, the way she moved her lips when she spoke, and how she centered her gaze on him. Amidst the supper crowd, he sensed an aura around them, separating them from the rest.

He had to pull himself from his dream-like state to concentrate on her answer.

"It's just far enough from New York City to have the mix of rural and urban types I need for my story: big city stock broker meets small town doctor. Plus, I wanted to be far enough north to have a nice helping of snow."

"We will be able to meet your snow criteria within a few months. The mountain's allure changes in the winter months to one of awe and wonder." He sipped his wine. "Long ago it signaled certain death for anyone unprepared to endure its harsh reality."

"I've never thought of it quite like that," she said. "Today we roam these mountains on snowmobiles and play in arctic snow suits."

He rotated the stem of the wine glass between his thumb and fingers and stared at the swirling liquid. It was hard *not* to remember the bitter winters of his youth. Struggling through six feet of snow to tend to the cow and horse in the barn flashed through his mind. He sat the wine glass down, and said, "Centuries ago early Indians and pioneers struggled daily just to survive the season. If the mountains could talk, wouldn't they have a story to tell?"

Kimberly smiled and looked at him with a devil glint in her eye. "By the way, what did your tree have to say today?"

Laughing at himself, he replied, "If you must know…" his thoughts trailed off.

"Yes?" She waited for his response like a cat who'd pinned a mouse in a corner.

He sighed, and decided to be as honest as possible. "She rarely talks anymore. She's quiet, contemplative, and perhaps gets a wee chuckle when I look the part of village idiot."

"You should be ashamed of yourself for blaming your apparent psychosis on a tree," she said, her cool blue eyes flashing with a 'gotcha' inflection.

"Then you've never spoken to a tree?" he said. "Such a shame, for the older a tree, the greater the insight. They glean a powerful amount of wisdom hanging about watching the world go by, century after century."

"Did she impart any wisdom today?" Kimberly asked.

"None that I hadn't already surmised for myself, which was to be aware of my surroundings before speaking." He nodded. "I'll remember that, so not to bait myself in the future for your pleasure."

She smiled. "Touché, but I'll warn you ahead of time - I plan to take full advantage of any lapses."

"Agreed." He smiled at the exchange, realizing how much he enjoyed her company. "So, are you looking for something to rent or to purchase?"

"I think I might purchase," she said. "Right now, the market heavily favors the buyer, and there are quite a few homes for sale that appeal to me."

"Any specific area?"

"No, I don't know enough about the area personally. I've been searching on the Internet, but I'll have to rely on the realtor for advice."

"I'd be more than willing to show you around, if you'd like." He couldn't believe he was offering his time to do something so menial, but the offer had just fallen out of his mouth without warning. Then, the thought entered his mind, what if she said 'no'? His heart raced for a mille-second that seemed like hours before he heard her reply.

"What a great offer. Perhaps you could recommend a realtor as well?"

"I have one I use exclusively, Carol Myers. She used to work for a huge government group in charge of appraisals. Now, she manages a string of clients with exacting tastes and requirements. I can introduce you, if you are interested."

"She sounds perfect. What I originally thought a chore has turned out to be quite pleasurable. Thanks for your assistance, Ryeth."

Her honest smile of appreciation warmed his heart. "No problem at all, would you like to get started tomorrow?"

"Yes, the sooner I get settled, the quicker I can get started on this book that has been festering in my mind."

Their meal complete, Ryeth escorted Kimberly back to the lobby.

"Shall I pick you up here tomorrow morning at nine?"

"If you're sure it won't be a bother, I'll be ready."

"No bother at all. Wear some sturdy shoes so you can look over the grounds if we come across anything you like."

"Okay, I'll be ready and prepared. Thanks for the lovely evening, Ryeth. You were a most charming companion." She held out her hand.

He gripped her hand in his. It was soft to the touch, yet firm. "As were you."

"I'm looking forward to tomorrow. Goodnight." She flashed him a dazzling smile. Her blue eyes sparkled.

Odd, he could have sworn that earlier in the day, her eyes had been green with gold flecks. Maybe it was the lighting in the lodge. Green or blue, no matter which, they were quite beautiful. "Goodnight."

She climbed the stairs to the second level. He couldn't take his eyes off her. When she spun at the top of the stairs and caught his gaze, he nodded, turned and walked out the lobby door without looking back.

He left the lodge with a half-smile; it had been centuries since his heart had felt so light. Far from happy, for his brooding nature seemed to lurk just beyond reach, he just might be on the edge of truly looking forward to a tomorrow. He didn't remember the last time that had happened, although he knew it was definitely before his parents' deaths.

***

As Kimberly entered the elevator, regret weighed heavy in her chest. She liked him. He was a nice guy. And she had lied to him. Who would believe she was a writer? She should have at least come up with another cover story that was plausible. She'd never written a creative paragraph in her life.

Danged if she didn't get into the stickiest situations. At least this one she initiated herself. After meeting him in the flesh while jogging, she had to admit to herself that she truly had no choice. He was one of the most enigmatic men she'd ever encountered. The ripped muscles of his arm danced beneath her fingers when he led her to dinner. His clothes fit his body so well they gave a cat-like stealth to his walk that said to women - come take your chance, and to men - get in line behind me. Ryeth's self-assurance was staggering. She'd come across strong men before, but they all paled greatly by comparison. He was eye candy, all six and a half feet of him.

Bottomless eyes. The depth of him was something she wanted, no needed, to experience. There was more to him, much more, and Kimberly was willing to take the plunge into the abyss.

The longer the evening wore on the more impact he had on her senses. Maintaining an outward appearance of cool, calm, and collected made her nerves a shambles. At one point she felt like her skin was on fire. Never before had a man caused so much emotional turmoil.

Kimberly entered her room, leaned against the door and thanked her lucky stars that she was still in one piece. As she undressed, she stopped half way through to remove the colored lenses from her eyes. She placed the blue ones in their case. Tomorrow, she would wear the brown ones flecked with gold.

The masquerade was unfortunate, but she wasn't willing to be found out just yet. Before she revealed her true self, she was determined to figure out what made that man tick. There were too many unanswered questions regarding his appearance in the woods, and as far as she was concerned, she wanted answers. Tomorrow she would continue her slow assault on him, or subject herself to his assault, until she broke through that calm exterior and knew the man from the inside out.

Satisfied with her plan, she pushed the regret for her deception to the far reaches of her mind.

Chapter 14

Alexandra and Jediah arrived at Balisier's counsel chamber before the others. His hand squeezed hers, and even though she didn't need it, she sensed Jediah's reassuring aura. The counsel room reflected the Sensates' relaxed and homey lifestyle. High-backed, cozy chairs surrounded a black walnut table, leather-bound books lined the bookshelves, and tasteful art decorated the walls.

"I still find it hard to believe we are hundreds of feet inside a mountain," she said.

"We owe Onatah our thanks for finding it," said Jediah. "Imagine the courage it took to come inside this chasm alone for the first time."

Alexandra touched the back of a chair thoughtfully. "She was quite remarkable. I can't even wrap my mind around being the first Sensate, thousands of years ago." Her voice trailed off. "I can't wait to spend more time with Hazel, our historian."

Jediah rubbed his thumb over the back of her hand. "Our history is magnificent. You'll enjoy every minute of it."

William, James and Val appeared at the same time, which startled her. Recovering quickly she said, "Did you guys plan to appear together? How did you know you wouldn't bump into each other?"

William chuckled, James grinned, and Val spoke. "Well, if you *must* know, we have bumped into each other on occasion. I even knocked James down a time or two."

"That wouldn't have happened the second time if you had paid attention when we picked our landing spaces," James said.

"Oh, I see." Alexandra jumped in. "Pre-assigned landing spots. When was someone going to tell me about that piece of trivia?"

The men looked quickly at Jediah.

"Hey, don't look at me," he said. "I thought we decided to let newbies find out on their own."

Alexandra said, "Now I understand why Jonathan was so eager to relinquish the title of newbie. How long will this indoctrination last?"

William patted her shoulder, "Only until we get a new Sensate; fifty, possibly a hundred years, tops."

She shook her head and smiled. "You gentlemen are a sorry group." Alexandra sunk into one of the chairs surrounding the table.

Jediah bent and kissed her cheek, "Yeah, but we'll grow on you." He pulled up a chair and sat next to Alexandra. "Shall we begin?"

James and Val sat, but William remained standing. He faced their small group. "First, I'd like to welcome the newest member to our counsel. Alexandra, it's a pleasure to have you. Your individual gifts will make us stronger."

"Thank you, William," she said.

William continued. "We are here today to decide on a course of action regarding Ari. What do you think we should do, Alexandra?"

She glanced quickly at Jediah, who offered no assistance, and then scanned the others. "In all honesty, I'm not sure. My first instinct was to save Ari; the second was to ensure our security. I've reconsidered, and now believe the security of our group should have been my first consideration. It will take some time for me to get used to my new responsibilities. So, before I share my thoughts, I have questions. How did she escape our net? Without knowing the inner working of our group and all the facets of daily Sensate life, I can't assess our strengths or weaknesses. To ask me what to do is premature, since I have no depth of knowledge into our group. So, a question back at you: Why didn't we know about her? And, how much time do we have before we are compromised?"

The group fell silent. She rose from her seat and walked over to William. "I'd like to hear what you think."

He gave her a half-smile. "So, you want to know what the old guy thinks?"

"My thoughts precisely." She stepped behind her husband's chair and laid her hands on his shoulders. Serenity swept over her. The men before her represented over two thousand years of Sensate ingenuity. They had carved out their niche in this mountain, and survived without compromising their honor. Surely, they could find a way to circumvent her faux pas with the police and save a captured Sensate without breaching the knowledge of their existence.

"I've been spending quite some time on a workable plan," William said while winking at her. "My first thought was for all of us to re-locate for fifty years or so and just disappear until it all blows over."

She couldn't believe her ears. Were they so cold-hearted that they could just leave the imprisoned Sensate? Granted, she didn't know if it was a trap, and she didn't know the impact it might have on their group, but the unknown female deserved consideration. Her chest rose and fell as the muscles in her neck stiffened.

James stroked his chin. "I had the same thought. I guess it's human nature to bolt and run."

"Yes, I'll have to admit the thought crossed my mind as well," said Val. "What about you, Jediah?"

What? They bandied this around like some kind of inconsequential task? This was a person in need. A person with powers. Was this unknown Sensate to be another cast-off like Ryeth? How many of these people were out there?

"Guys, give her a wee break, will you?" said Jediah. "Her nails are digging into my shoulders."

She glanced down at her hands; her knuckles were white, so she released her grip and rubbed her inflicted spouse.

William took the floor again and smiled warmly at her. "I'm sorry, Alexandra, but it is important for you to relax your emotions before discussing an important issue. Emotions can cloud your judgment."

"I'm sorry, you're right. It's just that she sounded so helpless," she said. Sensates had an honest way of getting their point across. It took a concentrated effort, but as she took a cleansing breath and exhaled, she relaxed and took a seat next to Jediah.

Leaning back in his chair, Jediah, the epitome of control, assumed his role of leader. "I know the unknown female Sensate's plight has been weighing heavily on our minds. We all want her safely within our fold, but with the heightened scrutiny from the FSB bearing down on us, we need to move conservatively, lest we *really* stir up controversy."

Jediah sighed. "We know that James, Val and I are under suspicion along with Alexandra and Alice Jane, so I deem it imperative that we five are visibly removed from any rescue operation."

"Agreed," said William. "You four will have to work behind the scenes, and Alice will be told to be on her guard."

"You're right," said James. "I think William might be best utilized to select the team for the operation." He nodded to William. "You know our abilities better than anyone."

William looked across the table at Alexandra. "I'll need to spend some time with you, my dear. We don't know the capabilities of your powers or their limits. Our unknown may have been searching for help for some time, but because we weren't within her broadcast range, no one heard her. It's a shame really; but how could we have known she was out there?"

"I'm willing to do anything to help," said Alexandra. "How does this work? Can we only sense Sensates in the northeast?"

Jediah said, "Our greatest concentration is here in Pennsylvania, so naturally we can sense Sensates out as far as our strongest ability permits. This process has worked in the past, but somehow we missed her lineage. The recessive gene that allows us to become Sensates has been tracked by our people since Onatah. We know when a child with that gene will be born. We follow the child to see if the core values warrant acceptance into our group, so in those cases, we send Sensates world-wide to watch over them."

Alexandra considered this new bit of information, then said, "Since we don't know where the unknown is, should we set up a network of

Sensates to crisscross surrounding states?"

"That's a great way to pinpoint her location," Val said. "I'll organize that part. I'd also like to be kept up-to-date on any conversations she has concerning the drugs she is given. Through our experience with Magis, we know specific drugs can render our abilities useless. If this girl has been there for years, she's developed an ability to protect herself."

"Speaking of keeping everyone up-to-date..." Jediah said. "I'd like each of you to allow Alexandra's touch to your mind. As soon as the unknown contacts her, she'll open the connection to all of us instead of just me. It will keep communications fast and efficient."

The group nodded. Alexandra's mental touch went from James, to Val, and then to William. She smiled and said, "Done."

***

William reached into his pants pocket and pulled out a worn stone, which he placed on the table. She watched as he toyed with it for a few seconds, then held it in his hand and rubbed his thumb across it. The room grew quiet as he spoke. "We need to discuss Ryeth."

Although she tried to suppress the impulse, her body jerked. Not a wince, but a full-fledge jerk that shook the table. All eyes turned to her. As she picked at her nails, blood rushed to her cheeks. Shame bore down on her with the weight of lead. She gritted her teeth, but could bear the burden no longer. Like a boiling teapot, the words escaped her like pent-up steam.

"I've been in contact with Ryeth." She looked at

the group and tried to gauge their reactions, but she met only blank stares. When her eyes came to rest on Jediah, he smiled. One eyebrow rose as if to ask a question.

She stammered. "He came to me on our honeymoon. Oh, I don't mean he was there with us, I mean he contacted me then."

Her eyes went quickly to the others, who seemed unaffected by her news. Jediah inclined his head, but still did not speak.

She felt the blood pumping in her stomach. "Oh heck, I may as well just spit it out. I didn't say anything because I wasn't sure if I should. I was concerned about the Prophecy, and I thought the group might not want anything to do with him. When he reached out to me, I couldn't turn away. I know I shouldn't have taken the risk, but I had this feeling..."

With the burden lifted, she let out a heavy sigh. "Oh, one last thing, he can hear Ari too."

"Well now," said James, "I guess that takes care of how, when, where and who should contact him."

Val's eyes lit up as he said, "Alexandra, share any pertinent information from your conversations, would you please?"

She looked from man to man then to husband as a slow smile spread over her lips. "Okay, fellas, here's the scoop..."

Chapter 15

Ryeth paced the oak planked floor of his mountain home. Waiting for the 'Sensates Proper,' as he was loathed to think of them, pricked at the back of his neck. Did they have to talk about everything before taking action? Blast it! He could grow a full beard in the time they took to make a decision.

Patience was not one of his virtues and he knew it. He tried to beckon patience forth a number of decades past, but he never seemed able to wrap his mind around waiting. Perhaps that's where he failed when rescuing Alexandra from that toxic man, Magis. Had he contemplated his action and considered the ripple effect, he might have been able to prevent Homeland Security from breathing down the Sensates' necks. Single-handed he'd opened a door that they'd protected for over two thousand years.

He didn't have the ability to reverse time; if he did, he would have already rewound it to that very day and given it a whole new spin...

But this waiting. He had to do something.

***

Alexandra's telepathic updates over the last week kept him up-to-date regarding the girl, but learning that the Ultras failed in locating the unknown Sensate chafed his ire. He wasn't used to failing, and didn't like being associated with any group that didn't meet up with his level of determination. Heck, they probably thought talking about it would make her materialize right in front of them.

When Alexandra told him that only she and he could hear the girl's voice, Ryeth quickly put two and two together. It had something to do with that darned hwihs on his and Alexandra's shoulders.

As much as Ryeth felt the Sensates were working slowly regarding Homeland Security, he had to admit that Gabriel's imprint of Agent Stoner's and Gooch's minds turned out to be the best resource, but with the Sensate group following every clue they picked up that way, it left little for Ryeth to contribute. He set his mind to task how he might help without compromising their intelligence. He discarded many notions because he knew the Sensates proper would not approve of his methods.

Then a thought so sweet it made him smile entered his mind. Heck, he might even have a bit of fun doing it. He figured out how to use his abilities to pinpoint the unknown's location. He just needed to test it. A plan solidified as a sly smile crept across his lips and twinkled in his eyes.

The unknown's pleas came approximately the same time each day. Using his vast array of memorized locations throughout the country, he positioned himself to quickly move around as he heard her cries for help.

The first day he moved through many locations in Maine, Vermont and New York, but he noted her signal came in stronger at his home in Pennsylvania.

He resumed the same process the following day and eliminated Georgia, North Carolina and Virginia. As he moved across the country from east to west, her signal grew stronger.

On the third day, he isolated the unknown's signal coming from the western portion of Ohio, near Dayton.

He immediately contacted Alexandra with the news. *Alexandra.*

Yes, Ryeth?

She's somewhere in Dayton, Ohio.

He felt her intake of breath before she replied. *This is fantastic news. How did you find her?*

Feeling comfortable with Alexandra allowed Ryeth to respond without restraint. *I hopped around like a rabbit with its tail on fire during her shouts for help.* He sensed her amusement.

If you had shared your plan, I could have helped you...

For nearly five hundred years I have catalogued locations throughout the world where I can land unnoticed. And, only you and I can hear her. It was a one-rabbit-job.

Alexandra sensed Ryeth's pleasure. *What's the exact location?* she asked.

When I got close, her signal was too saturated. I was unable to pinpoint it without going directly to her. The best I can say is that she's within ten miles of Dayton.

He sensed Alexandra's unguarded excitement. A deep breath filled his chest; satisfaction filled the rest.

Ryeth, thank you so very much. Maybe the Ultras can hear her if they're closer. I'll have William send them out to places near and around Dayton.

Her enthusiasm made him smile. She closed the conversation with a quick, *I'll be in touch* and was gone.

Chapter 16

Officer Gabriel Johnson took a deep breath and adjusted his tie before entering the conference room at the station. In all his hundred plus years, he couldn't remember a time when so much rested on his shoulders. The Sensate High Counsel would be monitoring the thoughts of every person in the conference room through him, and although he understood their need for assurance, he wished the 'connection' could take place without him.

"Ah, Officer Johnson, this here's Ray Stoner and Terry Gooch from the Fringe Science Bureau, FSB for short," Det. Mokros said, performing the introductions. "I'm certain you are as surprised as I am to find out Agent Gooch has been here, under our noses, for four years."

Hiding his shock by shaking hands, Gabriel could feel his pulse quickening. Agent Terry Gooch was Jediah's landscaper. He had interviewed him during Alexandra's abduction. *Jediah! They have been watching you for years.*

Relax, he heard in his mind, and recognized Jediah's touch. It was comforting to know he wasn't really alone. Jediah's serenity washed over him and his heartbeat slowed.

Agent Gooch gave Gabriel a hard look, then dropped his hand.

"I'm afraid I've not heard of the FSB," said Officer Johnson, "and I'm not sure I fully understand what Fringe Science is."

"Let's all take a seat and get down to business," said Det. Mokros. "I get the feeling we're in for a bit of an education."

Pouring a cup of coffee from the carafe on the table, Agent Stoner added cream, and while stirring, he began. "Let me start with a little background. The FSB is a research department. 'Fringe Science' is science that exists outside of conventional mainstream science. It's highly speculative, and open to interpretation."

Agent Stoner, whose eyes had not left his coffee cup, now looked up into those of Officer Johnson and Det. Mokros. After noting the impact of his words, he continued. "I can see you're keeping thoughts of little green men to yourself. You're not far off the mark, but if you rein in your thoughts to Earth alone, you'll be in our ballpark.

"The FSB is a division of Homeland Security and the Air Force Research Lab. It's based at Wright-Patterson Air Force Base in Dayton, Ohio. When a fringe science oddity presented itself, our group formed as part of the research lab's Sensor division. It comes as no surprise that you haven't heard of us; we are buried so deep I'm surprised we get paychecks," he finished with a grin.

"What's the connection to the Higgins-Saffle case?" asked Det. Mokros.

Agent Gooch responded. "Monitoring, for now. We're following up on the red flag in her case because she can't remember how she got home. It could be nothing, or it could be an instance of teleportation."

"Like in 'beam me up, Scotty?' You've got to be kidding me." Det. Mokros huffed.

Neither Agent Gooch nor Agent Stoner altered their dead-pan demeanor.

"You're serious, aren't you?" asked Det. Mokros.

Agent Gooch's lips pressed into a thin line before he said, "Dead serious."

Det. Mokros stood and ran his fingers through his hair. He walked around the table, looked out the window, and finally returned to stand behind his chair. "Well, you've got my attention. Assuming we believe you, that ESP or extra-sensory perception exists, how are we to proceed?"

"We'll require your assistance to monitor the activities of the parties involved: Alexandra Higgins-Saffle, Jediah Saffle, Alice Jane Saffle, James Dawson, and Dr. Valentine Jellan."

Hearing this list, Officer Johnson snapped his pencil in half and as his pulse quickened, he heard Jediah's touch to his mind. *Breathe, Gabriel. It is all as it should be.*

"A bit too much for you, Officer Johnson?" Agent Gooch said raising his eyebrows.

Gabriel felt the agent's condescension and lowered his eyes. He scanned Gooch's thoughts to ensure his cover.

"Aw, leave him alone," snapped Det. Mokros. "It's a bit much for me too." He cleared his throat and continued. "What makes you think teleportation exists?"

Agent Gooch glared at Det. Mokros. "It's not our job to question the tactics of our superiors, and it certainly isn't yours."

As far as Gabriel was concerned, if the High Counsel needed further proof the Sensates were in peril, they now had it. They were exposed. Somehow, someway, the government agency knew teleportation existed.

Gabriel chose his next words carefully. "You saw an object move from place to place? It was probably sleight of hand. The best magicians can make bridges disappear," he said.

"Look." Agent Stoner sighed audibly. "I have my reservations as much as you do, but if my boss says to clear up this issue, I will do it to the best of my ability. And if I'm told that people can fly through the air to get from one place to another, I'm going to consider it. So let's just assume, for this particular case, that teleportation exists, okay?"

Agent Stoner slapped both palms down on the table. "I'll hear no more to the contrary on this issue, got it?" He scanned the room, took a gulp of air, and continued. "Let me run through the ramifications for you. If Alexandra used teleportation to get from place to place, we might be able to uncover it by scrutinizing her travel plans. This means verifying Internet and phone purchases and checking credit cards against locations. The best way we've found to confirm it is to attach or inject a GPS tracking device."

Agent Gooch said, "We had the perfect opportunity after her return home from the abduction before she truly came around, but we couldn't get near her. Saffle and his cronies blocked us with medical and legal hoopla. We had to play nice."

"We have no proof Alexandra Saffle can teleport," said Agent Stoner, "but until we discover how she got from Point A to Point B, she's our new best friend."

Gabriel touched on each of the agents' minds as they discussed the division of surveillance duties and sent their imprints to Jediah. As he watched the two adversaries dole out the assignments, it gave him satisfaction to know Jediah and the High Counsel would implement countermeasures to safeguard the Sensates' secret.

***

Gathered around the conference table at Balisier were William, Val, James, and Jediah. Between the four, they had amassed thirteen hundred years of Sensate knowledge and history.

Although Jediah presided over the High Counsel, William, with six hundred twenty-seven years to his credit, was the oldest living Sensate. While William considered the topic at hand, he rubbed his thumb over a small piece of petrified wood, now worn smooth by many years of contemplation.

"They only have suppositions regarding Alexandra, no real proof," William said. "We'll need to monitor both Stoner and Gooch to stay one step ahead of their investigation. I'll watch Stoner; Val, you can handle Gooch."

"Sure," replied Val. "I'll ask MacAila and Jonathan to assist me."

Jediah leaned back in his chair. "That leaves Reslyn to work with me." He paused to choose his words. "I was surprised to hear they had considered inserting a GPS tracking device in Alexandra. I can't believe our good fortune in not letting them near her when she arrived home. We would never have recovered from that break in security. I can't stress enough our need for surveillance from now on. We need to stay on top of this. Reslyn and I will concentrate our efforts to circumvent any tracking mechanisms. We'll look into methods for scrambling signals and devices to detect and trace GPS signals."

James, the lawyer in him coming forth, rose from his seat and walked behind the others. "This is serious business, Jediah. You are talking about circumventing national security. Without listing all the laws we would be breaking, there's a good chance that if we're found out, we would face serious prison time or death for treason. We have always been honor bound to uphold our high standards of justice. I can't help but think we are crossing the line."

Jediah nodded. "I am aware of your concerns, but, unless we can come up with an alternative, I can't see any path forward other than this to ensure our security."

Jediah's head hurt. His temples were throbbing. His eyes narrowed and he clenched his jaw. He could feel the strain of each council member's thoughts before he said, "We have to consider the greater good."

"The greater good according to who?" asked William. "A couple of hundred Sensates versus billions... do we have that right to decide?"

The pain in his head peaked and then lessened as he came to terms with his decision. "We have existed, unknown, for over two thousand years. Our powers could topple governments and countries. If used as an advantage in a war, our powers could end up supporting the wrong side. Neutrality has been our safeguard. The knowledge we have, the powers we possess, are to be used for good. Our group needs to be circumspect."

He stood, walked around the table, shoved his

hands in his pockets, and then faced the group. "We will vote on our path forward. The result must be unanimous. By a show of hands, who is in favor of protecting Sensate secrecy at the expense of usurping national security?"

The question had been bold, clear, and concise. It didn't give rise to any other interpretation. Jediah raised his hand.

William, Val, and James raised their hands.

James looked over the group and said, "May God protect us, one and all."

Minutes went by without a spoken word. Jediah broke the thick silence. "I would also like agreement on one additional point."

He met each pair of eyes and then spoke his solemn vow. "If any one of us determines we have crossed a moral line we shall turn ourselves in to the authorities and suffer the consequences. Agreed?"

"Agreed," they said in unison.

Jediah heaved a mighty sigh. "With our moral considerations set aside, let's continue. I think it would be wise to keep this predicament limited to the Ultras, which now includes Alexandra, until we know exactly what direction it will take. The FSB's main area of focus seems to be teleportation. We don't know if they suspect other abilities. I'll watch over Gabriel as he works with the agents in case he gets overwhelmed."

William released a pent-up breath so loud that all eyes were drawn to him. As he raised his sagging head, he spoke. "Jediah, we need to discuss Alexandra. We have to move forward with her indoctrination as quickly as possible. Why didn't you invite her to this meeting?"

Jediah felt the color rise to his cheeks. "I know

I should have, but she is such an innocent. Even with the evil foisted on her by Magis, she still believes people are good inside. I didn't have the heart to let her know what we might have to do to maintain our security."

James nodded. "I understand completely. She is young and a new Sensate. But, if this is to become a showdown between our beliefs and potential exposure which includes the misuse of our abilities, we will need the support of every Sensate, and especially those with magnified powers."

"I understand," Jediah said. "I will give her a complete mind transfer of our decisions and vows. She will be up to speed the next time we meet."

"Very well then," said Val, "let's see what sense we can make of this and plan our next steps.

"Hand me the copy of that Prophecy, would you, Jediah?" William pointed to the page in front of him on the table. "Let's see if there are any implications there."

"Sure. I've been reading and re-reading it so long, I have it memorized anyway..." Jediah passed the document to William, and then rose from his seat. He ran his fingers through his hair and then rubbed the back of his neck. Sequestered for over four hours, they had yet to produce a connection between the FSB and the Prophecy.

***

"Say, Jediah," said Val, "why don't you recite it? Sometimes, a different inflection can bring about new meanings. We need to remember that this was written down many years ago and has suffered through several translations."

"We've tried everything else, why not?" Jediah shrugged his shoulders and began slowly:

"One from pain and one from strife,
Join together guarding life.
Crossing boundaries, breaking rules,
Both are marked as ancient tools."

"I think we agree on the interpretation of this part," William said. "Two Sensates who are marked with a hwihs will join forces. The path they take will require them to break rules and boundaries. We know Alexandra has a hwihs, and that it was due to the pain of losing her parents that she came to us. She is one of the duo. Since no other known Sensate has a hwihs, we must contact Ryeth to see if he is the other."

"I'll take care of that," Jediah said.

"Agreed," nodded Val. "Please continue."

"One alone and schooled in lies,
Anger, scorn, and hate the guise.
Taught by others to be cruel
Hence brought forth the timeless duel."

Jediah said, "I'll be the first to admit this verse is confusing. At first, I attributed it to Ryeth, but now, I'm not so sure."

"The 'anger, scorn and hate' seem to fit," said Val.

"Yes," Jediah said, "but the last line infers that it was due to all the hate and anger that the duel began. I just don't feel that's the case. But, if not Ryeth, then who?"

Still rubbing the piece of wood, William said,

"The term 'timeless duel' is causing me concern."

"How so?" queried Jediah.

"'Timeless duel' is typically the contest between good and evil. Puff up our egos all you want, but I still don't think the battle referenced in the Prophecy is the same one as Alexandra's slip up. I don't see a good vs. evil there. It could be as simple as an internal conflict, or as grave as World War III."

Following William's train of thought, Jediah said, "We may not have all the information required to properly interpret this part. Let's skip this for now. I'll continue."

"In the heart where all hope died,
Grows the truth from deep inside.
All required is hope and trust
Break the tide; turn hate to dust."

"I get the feeling this verse hinges on the one before. The same foreboding exists," said Val. Since no other comments were forthcoming, Jediah continued.

"None will know and none can see,
Plans of secret hold the key.
If one fails the last will fall,
One that's close could doom us all."

Pacing back and forth, Jediah sensed they were, once again, back to facing the lion without whip or chair. Their only path forward seemed to hinge on Ryeth and he was not sure Ryeth could be trusted.

Jediah closed his eyes and rubbed the bridge of his nose. "I feel like I'm banging my head against a concrete wall. These words don't make any sense. I think we need more information before we can get anywhere. I'll contact Ryeth after I've had a chance to mull this over a bit."

"He has to be the other with the hwihs. It's a darned shame we have so little knowledge of him," William responded.

"We've had centuries to predict the essence of the Prophecy," Jediah said. "A course of action on our part as a response to the FSB inquiry seems like treading over thrice-disturbed soil, which we can't really tamp down. So, we're agreed on following our original plan to monitor the FSB agents' minds for clues, and reaching out to Ryeth for information. Correct?"

Val, James, and William nodded in agreement.

Rising to leave, William said, "As always, we're just a thought away if you come up with something."

"Thanks," said Jediah. "Right now, I'm just concerned about Alexandra. It seems she's out of the frying pan only to be consumed by our fire. So much has happened to her in the past few months it's hard to believe she's kept everything in perspective," Jediah said.

"Ah, she's a strong girl," said Val. "That wife of yours will determine her path and eke forward when many would turn back." He smiled, winked, and then vanished.

William and James gave curt nods to Jediah and vanished as well.

***

Alone within the confines of Balisier, Jediah opened his mind to the power contained within the solid walls of their community. He had done much to protect the Sensates over the years, as had William and Val. Their counsel functioned well-enough with the loss of Teater's contributions, but Jediah sensed that soon there would be a need for the fibrous connectivity Teater had provided in the past.

Teater, Alexandra's great-great grandfather and Jediah's best friend, made everything look easy. Even at the tender age of sixteen, his presence could not be denied. Teater displayed an aptness for developing his senses that exceeded his Sensate guides' abilities almost from the beginning. Throughout his time in Waynesburg, Teater strengthened their fortress within the mountain and, in doing so, solidified their way of life. The fact that Balisier's deed now rested in the hands of the youngest and strongest Sensate in existence proved his commitment to their community.

The anguish Teater suffered when he left their group in Waynesburg was etched in Jediah's mind. Teater chose a solitary path away from the group to ensure his seed generated the missing link that assured Alexandra's birth. Once that link was in place, Teater walked away from his family and returned to their group.

Jediah snorted, yeah, he had returned alright, but he hadn't stayed. Teater's undeniable thirst for knowledge, and his quest to know the limits of his abilities took an unforeseen turn of events.

Why had Teater forced Jediah's vow of secrecy? Jediah was tied to this vow even though it had affected his mother, and now, Alexandra.

Although Alexandra held no grudge, his knowledge of the facts regarding Teater's 'death' was a nagging prick at the back of his neck. Jediah did not like keeping secrets, most of all from his trusting, loving wife.

Blast Teater. He needed his counsel now more than ever. He slammed his fist on the counsel table. Peace of mind would not come from looking back.

Jediah left Balisier for home and to tell his wife the details of his morning.

Chapter 17

As he walked up the steps to the lodge, Ryeth mentally kicked himself for letting his hormones take the lead. Why had he gotten involved with Kimberly? Centuries had passed without an interaction with a female. He'd stuck his nose in Alexandra's abduction and screwed that up royally, and then he'd opened a line of communication with her.

He shook his head and heaved a weary sigh. Complications had jumped on his shoulders and clung to his thinning exterior ever since he'd decided to interact with others. He shook his shoulders, but the imagined weight failed to shift or fall off. Arriving at the door, he opened it to pre-envisioned doom.

Across the lobby, he caught doom's eyes. They were molten copper today. She wore black leggings, black boots, and a multi-colored thigh-length tunic. Enticed by her allure, the weight on his shoulders lifted instantly.

He could not deny the ease as which he moved forward to greet her. "Ms. Koza, you are a pure delight this morning."

She beamed. "Thank you, Ryeth. It's good to see you too."

He reached for her large handbag and threw it over his shoulder. Offering her his arm he said, "Shall we go?"

Her scent was earthy, like wood poppies in the

spring. When she placed her hand on his arm, it sent impulses through the tiny hairs and made him catch his breath, which he quickly hid with a clearing of his throat.

"Carol Myers has several places ready for your inspection today. Perhaps one will meet with your satisfaction." He opened the car door and tossed her bag onto the back seat.

"Thanks for talking with her and setting this up. I promise not to be such a burden in the future." After hoisting herself into the Hummer's seat, her face rose to meet his gaze.

Ryeth cocked his head and said, "It's too early to tell, but I might try getting used to burdens."

He closed her door, and while walking to the driver's side, he decided he just might do that after all.

They hadn't left the entrance of the park when Alexandra's voice entered his mind. *Can you talk?*

His jaw clenched. *Your timing is very poor.*

Sorry, she said, *can't be helped.*

Alexandra flooded his mind about Ari, Homeland, and what Homeland knew about their powers. In seconds the transfer ended.

Get back to me ASAP, she said.

Will do.

Ryeth relaxed his fingers on the steering wheel. He had no wish to lie to the tempting creature beside him, but the urgency in Alexandra's touch demanded a response.

He reached into his pocket and pressed the self-text feature on his phone. Within a few seconds, his text alert went off.

As he fished his phone from his pocket he said, "I'm sorry, I'm expecting notification regarding a business deal."

He gazed at his phone, then replaced it in his pocket.

"Kimberly, I'm sorry to have to pull the plug on you so early in the day, but a situation has come up that requires my immediate attention. Carol Myers will escort you through the properties and return you to the lodge. I hope that's satisfactory."

"Wow that was fast. I guess the burden became too great?"

Her words cut, but when he searched her face, he was relieved to see she was toying with him. "Can I make it up to you later, perhaps tomorrow?" he asked.

"You have already gone above and beyond the hospitality required of a stranger. I appreciate the help you've given. I'm sure the realtor and I can take it from here."

As they arrived at the curb in front of the realtor's office, he turned and said, "I have no wish to be considered a stranger."

He exited the car and escorted her to the door. "Until tomorrow?" Ryeth took her hand and raised it to his lips. A tingle of excitement passed through him as he raised his eyes to meet hers.

"I'll be looking forward to it." Her smile etched in the forever section of his mind.

After quick introductions, he made his departure.

***

Alexandra's transfer of recent events confirmed Ryeth's worst fears. The whole threat to their society could be traced back to his intervention during Alexandra's abduction. The fault was his and his alone.

Homeland Security's Fringe Science Bureau presented considerable danger to Sensates. Although he had developed no love for the Sensate group, his lip curled knowing something might happen to Alexandra due to his interference.

Years of honing his powers helped him devise strategies as he drove back to his home. Once there, away from prying eyes, he acted quickly and without regard to the consequences of his actions.

Alexandra's earlier transfer had given him imprints of Agent Gooch and Stoner's minds. He'd left the monitoring of the agents to the Sensates, but perhaps his particular abilities could further their cause. As he slipped easily into the agent's thoughts, he was also able to enter the mind of their superior, Chief Morgan Black, something he didn't think the Sensate group had learned to do.

Ryeth relaxed into the folds of his leather couch, closed his eyes, and let the stirrings of her thoughts become his own. It wasn't long before he obtained a wealth of information.

Morgan Black was a woman who thought highly of herself, an attribute she acquired to survive in the man's world of espionage. Lovely to the eye, underneath her pleasing exterior she possessed all the endearing traits of a scorpion. The woman's audacity and lack of humanity held his interest. Had he more time, he would have studied her as a deviant, but after witnessing her daily activities first hand, he had little time to exercise the more macabre part of his own character.

Ryeth dug through Black's mind with exacting precision and located the facts required to carry out the mission.

Morgan Black re-read the bureau's mission statement:

"The Air Force Research Laboratory's Sensors Directorate mission is to ensure unequaled reconnaissance, surveillance, precision engagement, and electronic warfare capabilities for America's Air and Space Forces by developing, demonstrating and transitioning advanced sensors and sensor technologies...."

Her mouth twisted in a sardonic smile. Sensors, that's where she and her group came in to play. By stepping sideways into the odd fringes of science, her career had accelerated much quicker than it would have had she stayed with the mainstream thinkers. Her specific talents lent themselves to the peculiarities people had to offer. Plus, the lenient nature of her superiors allowed her to access extreme behavior patterns within her personality that would have gone undeveloped otherwise.

Power over others suited her.

Black also rechecked the definition of irregular warfare:

"Irregular Warfare: a violent struggle ... for legitimacy and influence over relevant populations. Irregular Warfare favors indirect and asymmetric approaches, though it may employ the full range of military and other capabilities in order to erode an adversaries power, influence, and will."

These two tenets formed the backbone of her career. Black considered the consequences of her actions for a mille-second, and then brushed them aside with confidence before beginning entering the meeting.

She felt all eyes on her as she walked to the head of a large oval table. Standing behind her chair, she scanned the group before her and counted five she knew she could trust. Of the remaining seven, three were on the fence, and the four remaining 'do-gooders' would cut her off at the knees if they knew her agenda.

The head honchos at the Air Force Research Laboratory Sensor Division hadn't coddled Black the past twenty years. While grooming her to oversee the Fringe Science Bureau, they had done their worst to ensure she could make tough decisions, no matter the cost. Her exterior was so hardened that the fiercest of men had fallen short when challenged by her convictions.

As she scanned the paltry group before her, she sneered. They had family and friends, but she had power. Life and death were hers to divvy out, and she handled that mission with the commitment expected of her position. Her career choice had cost her greatly; Black no longer recognized herself when she looked in the mirror.

"Thank you for being prompt," she said. "For those of you who have been working blind for the past seven years, I thank you for your diligent work without knowing the reason behind your tasks. Terry and Ray, because you were in the field, I kept you on a need-to-know basis due to the nature of our work. Today, you will be brought up to speed and learn how valuable your efforts have been.

"In 1954 a mother came to us with claims that her sixteen-year-old daughter showed signs of ESP, extrasensory perception. What separated this mother from thousands with similar complaints was the fear and contempt she had for her daughter. At the time, we were still wrapping up the Roswell incident from '47, so we weren't able to follow up until two years later. We put Subject 613 under surveillance in 1956, and in 1958, we remanded her into the custody of the FSB."

She touched a fingerprint security button on the wall and entered a code. A screen illuminated behind her showing a woman strapped to a gurney. A white cloth draped over her body left only her face, arms, and ankles visible. Intravenous lines fed by hanging bags entered a mixing manifold before entering her body. The woman was held down by thick leather straps at her ankles, wrists and a large one across her midsection. The unconscious female appeared unaware of their observation.

"This is Subject 613," said Black. "Don't let her apparent good looks and calm exterior fool you. 613 has something we need, and we have been tasked with obtaining it."

She scanned the reactions of the group before proceeding. Satisfied she had their attention, she continued. "Please open the dossiers in front of you."

As the group read the summary page, she noticed Terry Gooch was the first to appear shocked.

Black focused on his response. He gazed at the others before speaking, which gave her insight into his character. His nervousness showed. Finally, as if he could contain himself no longer, he spoke. "Chief, that can't be Subject 613. She'd be in her seventies by now and the woman on the gurney is a young woman."

"I assure you, Agent Gooch, this *is* Subject 613 and she *is* in her seventies."

Satisfied her presentation had left an impression, she pressed the button on the wall and closed the screen.

"Pay particular attention to the subject's history and the included test results," said Black. "I expect each of you to be up-to-date regarding the contents of the dossier tomorrow by 0800. At that time, I will assign specific duties. Are there any questions?"

Only her five staunch supporters possessed the nerve to look at her. The others lowered their heads or fidgeted with the folders until she left the room. Black held her chin high and straightened her shoulders as she walked down the long corridor and into the observation area.

Of all the subjects sequestered under her supervision, 613 was her favorite. The other subjects had not exhibited neural activity during early testing. 613 had, but as they increased drug testing, the neural patterns had lessened, then ceased altogether and remained as such for decades.

It was due to this lack of exceptional brain function that the FSB had decided to close down all the older subjects and begin with new ones. While reviewing 613's tapes before ordering her extermination, Black caught the subject smiling. The smile didn't last long, but Black could swear from that moment on, 613's demeanor had changed.

Typically defiant, she now had bouts of complacency. The change was slight, even to Black, but it was enough to hope 613's powers weren't compromised.

Black grabbed 613's chart and flipped to the medications section. The chart listed an initial dose of 10 mg ketamine followed by 8 mg supplemental to keep her at a steady state. Black authorized a ten percent reduction on the chart. If 613 had powers, she wanted to see them in action.

Due to the lack of foresight, 613 could have lapsed into mental instability years ago. By dosing her so long, the FSB could have destroyed the very military advantage they sought.

If she could rouse 613 to a level where her powers could be ascertained, and then controlled and utilized, Black could write her own ticket forward. The decision she made was risky, but, in her estimation, inevitable, and could end her career.

She brushed the negative thoughts aside and signed the order to euthanize the three subjects who had never shown increased neural activity. Unlike 613, they had aged normally, their bodies nothing more than shriveled hulls of human flesh.

Black reviewed the multitude of tests 613 endured. None indicated any abundance of hormone or any abnormal DNA characteristic that contributed to her youthful appearance. The FSB scientists ceased their battery of tests in 2000. Review notes from the project manager indicated the monies spent resulted in no findings, and suggested they abandon the project.

Black's lip curled. 613 held the secret of aging that Ponce de Leon had failed to discover. She smiled as she ran a hand over her cheek; eternal youth intrigued her - teleportation interested the FSB.

A door opened behind her. His scent reached her nostrils. Without turning she said, "Are we still on for tonight?"

His hands wrapped around her waist from behind and pulled her close. She felt his lips on the nape of her neck. "Your wish is my command," he said.

Her powerful position had lured him initially, but her theatrics in bed made him stay. In order to keep the young pup in tow, she'd performed antics that she deemed repulsive, but the man was so desirable, her will and common sense caved without reservation.

"Any news from the field, J.T?" she asked.

"None."

"Then get out of here. I'll see you later."

She turned just in time to catch his muscular body walk out the door. If she had one weakness in all her forty-two years, it was that man. After straightening her hair, she unbuttoned her suit jacket, sat down in front of the panels, and continued her observation of 613, both past and present.

***

613 heard him clearly through her mental fog. The beast she considered her jailer and the man were close enough for her to hear, but only his baritone voice with its slow rumble formed actual words in her mind. *'Your wish is my command',* he'd said.

If wishes carried any weight at all in her convoluted world, she'd have been to Timbuktu several times over by now. Depression wafted over her as reality set in. Another day, or night, or week, or month, or whatever the hell it was, was now in session. Life, or what she imagined as life, ceased to exist years ago. The world had come to a screeching halt and inhumane torture had begun.

Only by reliving her early years, minute by minute, had she been able to survive the cruelty that now mimicked life.

She knew she was different. When she looked directly at people, she heard what they were thinking. It both scared and fascinated her. Listening to people occupied so much of her time she seldom spoke.

Oftentimes, she had tried to get others to hear her

thoughts, but no one ever replied. The conversation with her mother still ached in her chest:

'Mama, I can hear what you're thinking. Can you hear what I'm thinking?' she'd asked across the supper table.

'Quit talking foolishness, child. Eat your supper.'

'But, Mama, it's true. You are always thinking of the old days before daddy died. You wish he were here instead of me.'

Her mother paled, but she continued. 'I know you took me from someone when your baby died, and that's okay, because I love you, Mama.'

Her mother's eyes bulged. Mama reached across the table and slapped her so hard she'd fallen from the chair. Mama spewed all sorts of words she had never heard before and called her a witch touched by the devil.

From that day, she never spoke of Mama's thoughts again, but she knew her mother watched her all the time.

She was sixteen the day her mother ushered men into their parlor, she read their thoughts and knew her mother had asked them to come and take her away. Mama stood in the doorway with her arms crossed over her chest and watched as the men in black suits bound her hands, put her into the black car, and took her far away. The men in black suits spoke nicely, but their thoughts never lied.

613 knew wishes were not hers to command.

Chapter 18

Ryeth acted quickly. Unlike the structured, do-gooder Sensates, he had no one to meet, help him formulate a plan, or to caution him on his actions, so his turn-around time was short.

He spent the day monitoring Chief Black and uncovering her intentions. Ryeth dug through her mind for personal information about the three to be euthanized.

Two had no living relatives and the third was a younger man who had a wife still living and grandchildren. The records indicated the three had undergone various chemical alterations of their memories. They were all self-sufficient, but they would require medical supervision upon recovery.

Next, he picked through Black's mind to retrieve in-depth information of the inner workings of the FSB, which included guards' schedules and rotations. The human mind was a well-traveled path for Ryeth, so narrowing the specific areas where memories and information were stored was a cinch. Every tidbit required for his plan was ripe for the picking in Black's unsuspecting mind.

As Ryeth prepared to leave Chief Black's mind, he located the exact points he would use later to drive his point home.

Next, he performed an Internet search for new housing for the three subjects. Once he found a place that suited his qualifications, he made a quick trip to view the facility and speak with the director of special services. Ryeth gave explicit instructions for their care. He secured the services of a physician and psychiatrist to attend to their needs.

Lastly, he arranged for their private arrival with no questions asked. After contributing a substantial donation to the top-notch facility, he went back home to recheck the final details of the operation.

The plan commenced in the wee hours of the morning. Ryeth created static on the FSB's video security camera for a split second as he snatched the subjects one by one and instantly placed them in their new home. His actions were so quick, they remained sleeping throughout the process. The only pause in his procedure was when he stopped a few additional seconds to draw the covers up over them as they slept in their new beds.

To conclude the mission, he completed one last, well-deserved detail. He re-entered Chief Black's mind, went directly to the specific area he'd located earlier and pinched several nerve endings white-knuckle tight.

***

Covered in sweat from arduous lovemaking, two exhausted bodies lay side-by-side in a luxurious king bed. Morgan Black had wanted him; but spent, she wanted him no more. Her mind had already moved on to work when his voice interrupted her thoughts.

"I guess I should go," J.T. said, his deep baritone voice going unnoticed.

She sighed. The awkward moment had arrived. "You can stay, if you want," she said.

"We both know how that plays out. It's not a

scene I wish to re-create." He sat up and reached for his trousers.

Black leaned over and traced the lines of the muscles on his back. She liked the act of sex, but not the closeness; her needs were more savage in nature.

She watched as his well-formed body gathered his things and without another word or a look back, left the room.

Her relationship with J.T. was near perfect. Three years of good sex had its plusses. As a stress-reliever, it rated high in satisfaction; as the answer to an animalistic need, it slam-dunked the competition.

J.T. was as close to an alpha male as she could stand. A true alpha would require her cowering to his dominance. She snickered. In her den, the lion might have the looks, but it was the lioness that was feared.

A few moments later, she heard the door slam. She was alone and at ease once more.

613's project entered her mind and consumed her. She grabbed her laptop from the nightstand and pulled up 613's medical history and flipped to the medications. By her calculations, she should have some positive response from the subject within a week.

She knew she was playing with fire. But lowering the doses of the drug that controlled telekinetic abilities should allow the window to open in manageable increments where 613's abilities might seep.

Black pulled up a real time video of 613. The leads attached to her skull permitted instantaneous monitoring of her neural activity. She re-checked and zoomed in on the fail-safe injector attached to 613's arm, which automatically delivered immediate sedation if her neural activity spiked.

A reduction in dosage hadn't taken place since 1984. Early in 613's imprisonment and under partial sedation, 613 had escaped the restraints and tried to flee the building. The FSB apprehended her seconds before the sedation wore off and she had use of her full powers. Agents who visually witnessed the escape reported watching as 613 phased in and out of view as she attempted to teleport from captivity.

Those in control of 613 at the time were afraid to lose her again, so they limited their experiments to her neural activity and attempted to locate the part of her brain responsible for her abilities.

Black scoffed at their feeble attempts to harness 613's powers. Patience was the key to finding a dosage with combined drugs, which would allow neural activity but prevent the use of her abilities. Electronic data gathered over the past few months coupled with the interaction of specific drugs made it possible for Black to develop a strategy that could become a game-changer in world domination. In her hands, 613 could emerge as the pivotal piece on the chessboard.

She turned off the laptop and laid it back on the nightstand. Sated, exhausted, and pleased with herself, she fell asleep planning her next move.

***

The phone woke her at 4 AM. As she rolled over to stop the blasting, piercing ring, a murderous migraine threatened to split her skull. The pain was so great she barely heard the voice on the phone.

The call alerted her to an incident at their secondary facility. Nauseated and exhibiting tunnel vision, she grabbed two pain killers, dressed, and drove with reckless abandon to the FSB.

"What the hell went on here?" she asked the guard posted outside the containment area. The blood in her head pounded with such force she screamed the words and winced at the pain they caused.

The guard jumped. "They just disappeared, ma'am." He shifted his stance. "One second they were here, and the next, they were gone. I don't know how else to explain it." Sweat beaded on the man's upper lip.

She swayed against the pain behind her eyes and put her hand on the wall to steady herself. "Did you hear anything?"

"No, ma'am."

She swallowed, choking back the bile that formed in her throat. The weakling before her represented the type of human she despised most. Underlings.

"How long have you been on duty?" she asked.

"Since eleven o'clock."

The inferior male shook visibly. Black sneered at his lack of strength as she continued questioning him.

"Did you, at any time, leave this door unattended?" She spat the words, her face contorted.

"No, ma'am; when I left on break, Agent Carson took over for me."

Filled with disgust for the trembling specimen before her she said, "Turn in your badge and gun at the Security Office; you're through here."

His eyes went wide as he spoke. "But, ma'am, I didn't do anything wrong."

Black turned on her heel and stormed down the hall to view the security tapes, refusing to acknowledge his existence one second longer.

She opened the door to the dark room lit only by the display screens that covered the wall. The brightness of the monitors pierced her eyes, causing her to nearly retch.

Jack Hanson, the head of security, turned and shook his head. "See for yourself, there's a flash of static, and one-by-one, they disappear. My men are checking the grounds and going over the rooms for fingerprints. I've viewed the agents at their stations, and at no time was the area unsecured."

As she dropped into a chair she said, "I'll expect a full report on my desk by noon. Get out."

She waited as he left the room, expecting a door slam that never came.

Unlike 613, at the secondary facility the three missing subjects spent their days in relative comfort, living out their lives in captivity, but in hotel-like accommodations. Their security level was much less than 613's, yet since their arrival, the FSB videoed, captured, catalogued, and scrutinized every movement they made.

The first run through of the videos revealed exactly what Hanson said. Rooms 2, 3, and 4 all exhibited a half second of static, after which, the occupants disappeared.

Slow motion further showed each sleeping with their covers drawn. The covers didn't move from their position, other than to drop straight down when the subjects vanished. Just as if someone let the air out of inflatable dolls, she surmised. After viewing each clip in detail numerous times, she arrived at the same conclusion as Hanson - they had disappeared.

She monitored the videos from 613 for the time of the other subjects' disappearance and noted no change. Not so much as a flicker of her eyelids had occurred.   Before Black left the secured area, she doubled the guards on 613.

A beep on her phone commanded her attention; she swallowed hard as she read the Director's name, knowing the piper had to be paid.

Chapter 19

Around 9 AM Ryeth sent a telepathic message to Alexandra, filling her in on the previous day's news plus his early morning activities. At first, he sensed shock, then an instant later, happiness. Her tone was firm when she replied.

Ryeth, we need to talk.

Aren't we talking now? Apprehension crept into his very soul.

In person, she said.

When? He raised an emotional wall.

Now. We'll come to you, she said.

We? His teeth clenched so hard he could feel the strain in his temples. This was just the sort of thing he hoped to sidestep. Why couldn't they just leave him alone?

The High Counsel of Sensates. May we come?

He clenched his fists tight. *Yeah, I guess.*

Ryeth stood to greet those who had shunned him centuries ago and swallowed hard. The muscles in his neck stiffened and the reflex action continued down his spine. His nails cut into his palms. Realizing his angst, he commanded his body to relax. A twist of his neck resulted in an audible crack.

He had time for one deep cleansing breath before the moment of reckoning arrived.

Alexandra and Jediah appeared first, closely followed by three men.

The older one blurted out. "Do you have any

idea what you have done, boy?"

His anger caught fire. "Boy?" Ryeth cocked his brow. "I haven't been called 'boy' in centuries."

The old guy continued his assault. "You acted on impulse and put others at risk, and that demotes your actions to a childish prank in my book." The older man shoved his hands in his pockets and walked away from the group.

Ryeth felt eyes on him and looked up to see Alexandra smiling. Jediah didn't look none too perturbed either, which eased his anguish a bit.

Alexandra held out her hand. "Ryeth, it's a pleasure to finally meet you."

He took her hand in his; it was warm and soft; however, it was her voice that melted away the chafe left by the old guy's remarks. "I guess the time is right," he said.

"You already know Jediah." She placed a hand on Jediah's arm, and then continued, pointing as she spoke. "I'd like you to meet James Dawson, Valentine Jellan, and the eldest of our clan, William Snyder."

"Well, grandpa," Ryeth said to William, "I guess I can overlook the 'boy' comment. Tell me, what did I do that was so horrible?"

The comment visibly raised the hackles on William once more. "You stole three people from the FSB. You can't thumb your nose at the government and not expect repercussions."

Ryeth sat down in a leather chair and leaned back. "Oh, I expect there will be repercussions, but none will soil *your* group's hands. I left no trace to be uncovered, no videos to be seen, and no witnesses to tell. Just empty rooms."

"You're too cocky." William spat.

Ryeth leaned forward. "And you're too judgmental." He shot back.

Jediah placed a hand on William's shoulder. "What's eating you, William? I've never known you to be so… so caustic."

"Caustic?" His shoulders sagged. "Well, I guess I am." He walked over to Ryeth, looked down at him and said, "The time has come for you to clear the air regarding your parents."

Ryeth's eyes narrowed to slits. His body became rigid with rage, yet he spoke with calm precision. "You think it's that easy? You think you can barge in here after nearly five hundred years and ask the question that should have been asked back then?"

He slowly stood coming to his full height, towering over William's slight build. He glared at William. "It's not happening, old man. I didn't receive the benefit of your guidance then, and I don't need it now. I'll not ask your permission to do what I think needs done, and I don't accept your reprimand."

Jediah stepped between the two. His calming aura swept through Ryeth and caught him off guard.

"Whoa," Ryeth said as he stepped back. He looked sideways at William, who seemed visibly affected as well, then back to Jediah. "You need to bottle that stuff."

Jediah raised one eyebrow and grinned.

Alexandra said to William, "If I recall correctly, I was just given a newbie lesson on controlling my emotions."

William paled. "All right, all right. I think I've exhausted my anger anyway."

Val addressed William and said, "Anger? What's going on in that mind of yours?"

William's body relaxed and he sighed. "I'm

ashamed," he said. "Ashamed we turned our backs on one of our own without knowing the whole story."

Jediah responded. "It wasn't up to you; you didn't have any say in the matter back then."

William shrugged. "Yes, that's true, but when I did gain control, when I could have done something, I didn't. I could have searched for him. I could have asked him his version of the story." He looked to Ryeth. "I'm sorry I failed you."

There it was. The apology he'd long sought, and it had come from a man who still didn't know what happened that day. William had accepted the wrong inflicted by others as his own. Humbled by one man's readiness to shoulder the blame, Ryeth's resistance waned. "Thank you, William."

Ryeth held out his hand to the senior Sensate who warmly clasped it in his own.

James cleared his throat. "I, for one, don't believe the long-standing allegations against this man, and since the testosterone has cleared, perhaps we can get down to the business at hand."

"You have no proof of my innocence," Ryeth said to James.

"Or of your guilt," said James. "But I am willing to accept Alexandra's rescue from Magis, and the mystifying removal of three innocent people sentenced to death as proof of your honor."

The others nodded.

"So what happened?" asked Jediah. "I can't wait to hear the details."

"Well, to begin with," said Ryeth, "from the impression I got from the unknown, and from the look of the facility I whisked through last night, I think all were held in a similar facility. In other words, I believe our unknown Sensate is being held by the government."

"We were thinking the same, and we are glad to have your confirmation," said Val.

"Here's another tidbit," said Ryeth, "The unknown said, 'the woman who took her' had lost a child."

"The unknown was stolen?" said Alexandra.

Ryeth nodded. "That's what it sounded like, so if you're looking for clues as to who this Sensate might be, that might help."

"We'll get the others working on this," said Jediah, "but we have no idea of the year or place. This might take some time."

All eyes were on Ryeth once again. He told them about the unknown's background, then said, "The government took her, I'm sure of it."

"How horrible for her," Alexandra said. "What a terrible thing to do to a child. And now she's strapped to a bed. All her life she's been probed and examined. I can't even imagine her sorrow."

Jediah reached for his wife. He wrapped his arms around her. To the group he said, "That could have been any one of us." His point hit home. Alexandra's face went white.

Val said, "Our situation is grave. One of our own is imprisoned; she could have been turned against us psychologically; it's possible that she's an innocent; and, the government is watching us - waiting for us to make a mistake and expose ourselves."

William, who had been listening without speaking, finally spoke. "Yes, it's clear the Prophecy has landed on us with both feet. We've sat here for decades since that girl was taken and assumed our safety. All those years the government has been working on that child. We don't know how much information they got from her. She was a youngster, she could have shown or told them anything."

"According to this Chief Black," Ryeth said, "They don't have much. Either her powers are limited, or they were so afraid to lose her, they kept her drugged the whole time. Otherwise, she would have teleported out of there."

The group stared at Ryeth. "I don't understand your stares," he said. "Can't all Sensates teleport?"

James laughed. "Yes, they can. We just didn't know *you* knew that."

Ryeth turned red at the collar. "Just because I haven't been to your hideout, doesn't mean I don't know some of your tricks or that I don't have a few tricks of my own."

William said, "You know about our hideout?"

"Don't let your testosterone surface again, William," Ryeth said. "I know it exists, nothing more."

The Counsel wanted much more from him; that was quite apparent. He sensed their caution, their curiosity, and their strength.

He turned away. Why had he traveled this endless path so long? Although he had monitored human conversations and gathered general social nuances, Ryeth now entered uncharted waters.

Mixing with others was his exception, not his rule. His first sixteen years of life with his parents, conversations with housekeepers, and more recently, those with Kimberly, were all the normalcy he had to pull the concept from to begin anew.

He turned back to face the group that watched his every move. Only one answer came to mind - isolation. He felt no comfort standing with those of his own kind.

Ryeth sensed Jediah's powers oozing beneath his calm exterior. The power of the others were equally as strong. Alexandra's powers radiated the most, but she kept them tempered. He sighed. This group would make better friends than enemies, he surmised.

He rubbed the back of his neck, gauged the overall attitude of the group, and then donned a slightly wicked smile. "I guess you'd like to know how I got those three out of there."

Chapter 20

After the meeting with the Sensate High Counsel, Ryeth sought decompression at his favorite pawcohiccora. Last years' hulls covered the ground and felt like large marbles under his feet.

He brushed aside a nice area with the toe of his boot and slid down the trunk to rest at its feet. By concentrating on the sounds of the forest, he blocked all past events from his mind. A gentle breeze rustled through the leaves; he smelled the sweet scent of Sassafras and could almost taste his mother's tea. As always, the pang of loss shot through him as he held his parents' memory close to warm his heart.

His mother's vision remained fresh and beautiful, just as she had been centuries ago. Ryeth had never seen her equal in beauty and grace. Whether she cooked by the hearth or toiled in the sun, she never lost the gracefulness of form she alone possessed. His mother kept her long black hair woven into braids. When she washed it in the cool water of the stream, she would allow it to hang free and dry in the breeze. It glistened as it caught the sunlight and reflected deep blue opalescent hues. It reminded him of... of... his eyes flew open. Kimberly's hair. They were the same.

A smile crept over his lips. His chest rose and fell with slow measured breaths. The leaves on the trees became brighter; the sun shone warmer. The air grew exponentially and swelled his chest.

Ryeth drifted into a trance where he recaptured the essence of his parents. He imagined them meeting Kimberly for the first time. His father, Juan Garmendia, with his rough plow-worn hands would grasp her soft ones in his and welcome her to their home. He, who was well-versed in honing the untamed land into useful farmland, would delight Kimberly with his conquering stories until her eyelids drooped.

In his mind's eye, he could see his mother pull Kimberly into a warm hug that ensured her comfort. Onatah would bring forth precious sweets, hoarded for just such an occasion. She'd offer soft furs to keep Kimberly warm by the fire or a cooling tea from the jug she kept deep in the well. His mother would welcome her as a daughter.

Ryeth's thoughts continued uninterrupted for hours, as he played out every possible outcome of Kimberly's introduction into their lives with each one ending in her permanent stay.

The sun sat low in the sky by the time he rose from the tree. Before he left his Eden, he envisioned Kimberly one last time dressed as his mother, in soft doeskins beaded by her own hand.

***

With a light heart, forty minutes later Ryeth appeared at the front desk of the lodge and asked the concierge to ring Kimberly Koza's room.

"I'm sorry sir. Ms. Koza checked out an hour ago."

His breathing slowed. "Did she leave any messages?"

"I'm afraid not."

Ryeth's heart slowed. Time almost stopped. "Did she leave a forwarding address?" It was his last hope. He waited for the answer he knew was coming.

"No, I'm sorry."

Ryeth turned to leave and said, "Thank you."

Ryeth reached for his phone and dialed. As he neared his car, Carol Myers answered his call.

"Carol, this is Ryeth. I was just checking on the client I sent you. Were you able to assist Ms. Koza?"

"Hello, Ryeth, she said. "It's the oddest thing. I thought things were going along nicely. But after I showed her two of the places - and she seemed taken with one of them - she abruptly told me she'd come to a decision not to purchase after all. So, I took her back to the lodge and dropped her off."

"I see. Thanks, Carol, I'm sorry I wasted your time."

"No problem at all. It's part of my job."

Ryeth shook with anger. Blood rushed through his temples and pounded in his veins. She. Was. Gone. He hadn't imprinted her mind, gotten a phone number, or gained additional information about her home in Florida.

He threw his phone across the vehicle onto the passenger seat. It hit the door and the face shattered. White knuckles gripped the steering wheel with enough force to embed his nails into the leather.

Regret coursed through his body; physical pain wrenched his gut. His hand flew to his chest where the long-ago feeling rose and squeezed until it ached. The grueling loss he suffered as a sixteen-year-old boy returned once more.

***

Ryeth scribbled a note to his housekeeper, shoved a few personal items into a bag, and then left his Pennsylvania home.

As arranged, his Swahili guide, Irele, met him at the base camp at Umbwe. He breathed in the humid scent-filled air and hungered for the crisp biting air of the peaks in the distance. The peaks of Mawenzi and Shira, although challenging in their own right, paled against Kibo, the highest peak of the great, snow-capped mountain, Kilimanjaro. The consuming task loomed before him - his answer to unrequited emotional turmoil.

They departed the village of Umbwe with four other climbers, but separated from them to scale the dwindling glacier scarps via the more treacherous western summit. Ryeth's concentration never wavered from the task of setting his foot and inching ever upward.

They stopped to rest overnight at the Crater camp near the Western Breach. Nestled underneath an overhang, they made camp in one of the many caves formed eons ago from the vents of the volcano. Survival requirements left little time for his mind to wander back to the girl with ever-changing eyes as he climbed into his sleeping bag and fell into an exhausted slumber.

Rumbling began from deep within the earth and caused Ryeth to wake with a start. Rocks crashed down on their heads. As he climbed out of the zippered bag, he frantically shouted a warning to Irele, who failed to awaken. Dodging the rubble, he hurried to his friend and guide. He grabbed as much of their gear as possible, wrapped his arms around an unresponsive Irele, and transported them away from the landslide.

Without a pre-arranged spot for landing, they arrived tumbling down the mountainside of Arrow Glacier. Both the gear and Irele flew from Ryeth's arms as shards of ice and rocks pelted him from all sides. Seconds turned into minutes as the noise deafened his ears to all else. Rocks chased him down the steep incline as he tumbled and fell with the debris from the mountainside. He smashed into a boulder, skidded off the side and finally came to a blessed halt face down in ice and rock.

Rolling onto his back, he screamed as excruciating pain shot down his arm. Nerve endings sent piercing jolts of electricity that exploded throughout his left shoulder and chest. His breaths came in gasps; his chest rose and fell as he struggled in the thin air to suck in the oxygen his body craved. He lay still until the mountain was quiet once more.

Ryeth pulled himself upright and managed to sit as his head reeled. Dizzy and disoriented, he focused on his surroundings to steady himself. He braced himself with his right arm and stood. His left arm hung limp at his side.

"Irele," he yelled. Lungs deprived of air burned in his chest. He gulped air deep into his chest and yelled louder. "Irele." Echoes bounced around the mountain tops and ended in silence.

The light from a full moon allowed Ryeth to see the damage further up the mountain. A smooth section indicated where the slide originated. His eyes followed the landslide's trail downward to where he now stood. Yards of crumbled rock surrounded him and made walking precarious.

Instead of stumbling across the unstable rubble, Ryeth fixed a position to the outside of the landslide and re-located himself there. He reached inside his jacket and pulled out the GPS tracker both he and Irele carried. The screen indicated Irele was a few hundred yards North West. His footing now secure, he used his compass to locate positions that brought him closer to Irele.

He finally spotted Irele's bright orange jacket in the distance and walked to his side. Irele's temple had a large gash. It had bled until the frigid air clotted the flow. He was breathing, but knocked out cold.

Nearby, Ryeth noted an outcropping of rock. As he made his way toward it, he steeled himself against the inevitable. He positioned himself next to the boulder's edge, took a deep breath, and with all his might, slammed his shoulder back into its socket.

A primal scream escaped his lips as he dropped to his knees. His breath came hard as once again the thin air failed to fill his lungs. Stars danced behind his eyelids as the throbbing pain peaked, and then eased.

He waited for his head to clear, unable to fathom the reasoning that placed him in his current predicament.

Soft rosy lips and deep set, long-lashed eyes found their way into his thoughts. He fought back to eradicate them from his memory, but they persisted in haunting him. Too tired to wrestle any longer, he allowed the invasion. The memory of her perfume permeated his senses until he half expected her to be standing in front of him. To find her and then to lose her made no sense. She had liked him, he was sure of it; now she was gone.

Ryeth shook his head to clear it. He walked back to Irele, gathered him in his arms, and transported them to the foothills outside of town, away from prying eyes. Wonderful life-giving air filled his lungs and revitalized his body.

The walk to town was slow and grueling, but he knew the consequences of using his powers. After depositing Irele at the infirmary, he flashed home to Pennsylvania, leaving his contrived 'story' for later.

The mirror of his bathroom reflected a large black and blue patch on his shoulder. Cuts and bruises covered his face and hands. As he lowered himself into the large sunken tub, steam filled the room, bathing his airways with moisture-rich, soothing comfort. He allowed his mind to wander back to Kimberly and the loss of her from his life. His loss of self-control had resulted in a near death situation for both Irele and himself. He chastised himself for not handling the situation better.

His mother had an amazing amount of self-control, and his father, a highborn Spaniard, had always demonstrated tremendous restraint and discipline. So where did that leave him?

Ryeth chafed as he acknowledged his lack of aplomb by running off to parts unknown, tumbling down a mountainside, and compromising Irele's life.

Trying not to be so hard on himself, he planned his next move regarding Kimberly. Before he let her out of his life, he would know the reason why she left without a word.

He spent the remainder of the day cleaning up the mess he'd left in Umbwe. Irele, though dazed and confused, remembered nothing after bedding down for the night. Once Ryeth was assured Irele would receive the best of care for his concussion, he returned home.

Somewhere between Umbwe and Pennsylvania,

Ryeth heard Ari's voice.

Chapter 21

The haze lifted slowly and filled the first few seconds of awakening with hope, which dissipated instantly as 613 recognized her surroundings. They had drugged her, and she had taken measures, once again, to assure her mental safety. Only trace amounts of the drug lingered, so she knew it was safe to release her mind from its shield.

A dull ache persisted in her temples. She closed her eyes against the sadness building up inside and shifted her hips on the uncomfortable gurney in an attempt to alleviate the soreness from lying prone so long. The restraints cut into her ankles and allowed little movement. After twisting her shoulders in one last attempt, she heaved a heavy sigh and gave up.

"Please remain calm." A monotone voice came over the speaker. "Someone will be with you shortly."

Go to Hell, you rat-faced excuse for a human. Blast you and your drugs. Her words contained the venom she felt, but were meant for her satisfaction alone. She allowed no words to escape her lips.

She opened her eyes, and without moving them, looked around the room. It was different. This one had the same cold, institutional walls without windows and barred overhead lighting, just like the last one, but it seemed larger. She didn't know how long she had slept, or if they had moved her to a new room or a new facility. Her mind raced as she gathered her thoughts. She closed her eyes and concentrated with every ounce of strength she could muster as she broadcasted her plea for help.

Are you out there? Please answer me. I thought I sensed you. I need help. Where have you been all this time? Please, please, help me. She listened for a response.

I'm here, said a calm voice.

Elation surged through her body. She had to rein in the emotions or the 'watchers' might suspect something. *Oh, my god, are you really there or am I hallucinating?*

I'm here. What do you want?

Her heart pounded in her chest and her legs twitched. What if her captors had devised a way to trick her? She tried to sense more, but only ran into a black wall. She had always been able to read their minds. This person didn't sound like her captors, nor did she hear hostility in the words. Determined not to let her one chance in an unknown number of years slip through her fingers, she took the plunge.

What do I want? Do you have any brains in your head? I've been held captive for years. I want you to get me the hell out of here. Can you do it?

Maybe. The voice was non-committal.

Maybe? Blood rushed to her cheeks as she clenched her fists. *What kind of person are you?*

A cautious one.

The person she heard probably feared capture. If so, she couldn't blame them. She had trusted her 'mother' and look where that had gotten her. But she needed assurances too. *Why should I trust you either? How do I know you aren't one of my captors?*

You don't.

Her stomach churned. Although she might be

grasping at thin air, somehow the hope of nothing seemed better than nothing at all. *Then how can we begin, and why did you even bother answering if you're not going to help me?*

I didn't say I wouldn't help, Ryeth said. *Where are you?*

I don't know.

Who are you?

It couldn't hurt to tell her name. *My name is Ari. I don't know my real last name. The woman that raised me, and turned me into the authorities, was Riggs. Roberta Riggs. Who are you?*

I can't tell you that.

Although she felt her confidence sag, she clenched her teeth and tried to remain kind. *I understand. It's enough that you are here.* Steps sounded in the hallway outside the door. *They're coming.*

Ari, this is important. Leave your thoughts open to me.

You are asking me to trust you when I have spent my life protecting my secret?

Yes. It's the only way I can help.

So many years had passed without any response to her cries for help. Euphoria mixed with caution created a heavy load on her decision making processes.

Trust me, Ari. Please.

I'll try.

She heard the door open, but she did not move her head to see which lab rat entered. The sounds of metal moving on a tray confirmed her suspicions that this particular lab rodent was there to inject yet one more drug into the never-ending list of foul attempts by her jailers to assure her acquiescence.

Ari had learned a lot about human physiology over the years. By concentrating each time a new drug entered her blood stream, she could pinpoint the exact area of her mind to shut down. After years of perfecting this technique, she had been able to fool her captors into believing that every drug worked the same on her. The drug that now sought to incapacitate her had a much higher strength than the last. Her internal sensors fought to stave off the attack. Allowing her body functions to react for their monitoring yet keeping her mind safely detached required tremendous concentration.

In order to maintain a clear mind, Ari couldn't allow her attention to veer from her primary goal. She could no longer maintain the connection regarding the other like herself. Now completely absorbed in defense, every gray matter cell became her focus. She wouldn't remember what happened next, so she focused all her energies on protecting what she deemed most valuable, her mind. As she fell into a dream-like existence, her brain filtered drugs from entering her cranial cavity.

***

Ryeth pulled every sliver of information from Ari's memories during the connection. He filtered through the disconnected bits and pieces and tried to reconstruct her life.

He opened his mind to Alexandra and shared everything he put together.

Did you hear that? he asked.

Yes, said Alexandra. *Her name is Ari. I felt it was best to not speak.*

That was probably for the best, he said. *With*

the investigation centered on you, you need to keep a low profile, and as far as she knows, she has only heard one voice. Let's keep it that way, at least until we discover if she's telling the truth. That way, if it is a trap, nothing can be traced back to you or the group.

He sensed the rapid working of Alexandra's mind before she spoke. *The person who raised her was Roberta Riggs,* she said. *We can certainly start there to find out more about her.*

Alexandra was so excited she talked a mile a minute. *I can't believe you were able to extract the make and model of the black car from Ari's memory. Ryeth, that was ingenious, and it will help narrow down the year the government took her. I'm guessing somewhere around 1956?*

Ryeth sensed Alexandra's untethered exuberance; it was catching. *That's what I'm thinking too.*

She continued. *The name of the woman who took her might help to narrow down the location.*

Yes, I agree. Speaking of locations, was your group able to pinpoint her location in Dayton? he asked.

She held her breath, then spoke. *Yes, and the news is not good. They just moved her to a more secure place. It's a government facility located within the Wright-Patterson Air Force Base.*

That's close to where I liberated the others. Isn't the main office of the FSB nearby? asked Ryeth.

Yes. We're thinking that Ari and the un-answered questions regarding my escape from Magis are somehow connected.

Ryeth sensed her sorrow. *Alexandra, if you look*

at the global picture of these events and consider the Prophecy, no matter how it came about, fate would have still arrived at this outcome. We both had a part to play. So, why don't we agree to quit blaming ourselves and use those energies to work toward a solution?

He felt her tension ease a bit. *You're right; so is Jediah. Okay, I'll try not to go down that path again.*

Alexandra's sense of commitment was strong. He asked, *What did you think of Ari?*

Alexandra relaxed. *I didn't sense any subterfuge or cunning. What I did sense was fear of losing hope and a bit of indignation that you weren't flying to her rescue.*

He smiled, for he had sensed the indignation as well. *I don't doubt that she is a Sensate, but how can that be? I thought you guys had complete control over your flock.*

That might be a question for Jediah and the High Counsel; I'm still a newbie and don't know our history in that respect yet, Alexandra said. *Are you still in contact with Ari? I can sense something, but I'm not sure what it is.*

Ryeth furrowed his brow and tried for a connection. *I can't sense her anymore.*

Why did he tell her that? Now she knew she could sense something he could not. Why did she always compel him to divulge more than he wanted to share? What hold did she have over him? He'd even sounded sappy when he tried to make her feel better. Why should he care?

His lip raised in a sneer. He didn't owe the Sensates anything. Sure, they had apologized, but that didn't change much. He was still on the outside.

They didn't invite him into their fold. They didn't trust him.

The age-old hatred started in the pit of his stomach, grew to mammoth proportions, and threatened to eviscerate him. He immediately severed the connection with Alexandra and transported himself to the top of the world, unable to control the rage building inside.

The Arctic chill blasted him full force. He sucked in the air through his nostrils until his nose hairs froze. As he stood facing the sub-zero temperature in shirtsleeves, the resentment began to subside. He was not one to 'play nice' with all the little Sensates, so what did he hope to accomplish? Alexandra's ability to relax his fortified wall was an invasion. His back stiffened and he began to shake uncontrollably. Moving quickly back home, a warm fire greeted his frosty limbs and cheeks.

Although several minutes had passed since he withdrew from the conversation with Alexandra, the sting of exposure still released acid into his stomach. They knew where he lived. Alexandra knew her powers reached farther than his. He shoved his hands into his pants pockets with such force he had to withdraw them to heist up his pants.

The suppressed emotions from untold years caused Ryeth to shake from head to toe. Unable to release the energy, he created an orb and transported himself to the bottom of Cayman Trough three miles deep in the Caribbean Sea.

Unseen by those who might judge him, Ryeth released the energy buildup. The walls of the orb expanded and then contracted as the energy surge passed through into the sea. As it sliced outward through the water, Ryeth maintained the orb's integrity. Before the wave reached damaging proportions, he called it back and softened it until nothing but a small whirlpool remained.

His shoulders relaxed and his breathing slowed. As he stood looking into the murky depths of the ocean, his eyes adjusted and, after a while, fluorescent creatures permeated the darkness.

The inability to control the rage that coursed through his veins pricked at his neck. For a man who liked to appear emotionless, the rage that surfaced caught him by surprise.

When he made the decision to interact with others, he had relaxed his vigil. His eyes closed to narrowed slits as his teeth clenched. The orb's air began to thin, so he moved to his home, and landed on his back deck.

As he released the orb, water that had entered during the expansion of the orb, splashed onto the deck. His toes wiggled and squished inside his favorite pair of Lucchese boots, which were probably ruined. His boot maker would be none too pleased to know he had treated them so carelessly.

It seemed he would never learn to control his rage. At least this time, he was able to release the emotions so that nothing was harmed.

He concentrated on Ari and tried to sense the partial connection Alexandra had mentioned.

Nothing.

Chapter 22

Alexandra shared Ryeth and Ari's conversation with the High Counsel before the actual meeting began, but she held back the wrath she sensed before Ryeth severed the connection.

His heart was good, she'd sensed that early on, so why did Ryeth have so much hatred and anger inside?

A cough from Val brought her back into the present as she looked quickly to her husband.

Jediah's brows came together. "That name, Roberta Riggs, sounds familiar to me, and I don't think it has anything to do with that tennis player. I'm sure it will come to me, it seems like it's just on the tip of my tongue."

"Hmm," said Val, "I can't place it."

Jediah brushed off the thought. "Anyway, this is great information we can build on."

"It's heart-wrenching and sick, if you ask me," said Alexandra. "To carry a child, lose it in childbirth, and then steal someone else's child to replace it is vile. Imagine what the parents of the stolen baby had to go through."

"Vile as it is," said James, "it gives us another way to track down Ari's past. If this happened when Ari was sixteen, and we know the government took her into custody in 1956, she was born about 1938."

Val scratched the back of his neck. As he shook his head he said, "The child was probably a newborn, so we can look at the records for stolen infants. Back in the thirties and early forties the recordkeeping was not what it is today. A lot of the information exists in family bibles."

"I'll hand this off to the Ultras to follow up on," said Jediah.

"Good. Let's get to the matter at hand," said James.

"Yes. We need to come to a decision," said William. "Is Ryeth to be admitted into our group or not?"

The Sensates' High Counsel members sat around the table. All eyes were on Alexandra whose back was stiff. "If you forgive him, or whatever you want to call it, then why has he not been invited to join our group?" she asked.

Jediah refused to speak out in support of his wife. He watched as varied emotions played across her lovely face.

She stood, indignant, and then he saw her calm nature take over. "Is it because you still don't have the facts? Why should he have to prove himself?"

She addressed her next words directly to James. "Unless we have skipped over the law, isn't he innocent until proven guilty?"

James smiled. "Yes, you are right, Alexandra, but we do have over two hundred people to consider. Ryeth may have your trust, and mine if that counts, but does he have the trust of every person in our group? Do we have the right to expose them?"

Valentine Jellan wore his heart on his sleeve, and his support vividly on his face. Like Alexandra, he believed wholly in the good in people. He stood, and crossed to Alexandra, then wrapped his arm over her shoulders. "We are the same, sweet girl. But I have learned to temper my beliefs with just a tad of caution."

She met his eyes and said, "We have no proof against him. He has been nothing but honorable to me, except for the very beginning when he did scare the life out of me." She looked to her husband to collaborate her words.

"I can agree that I do not feel threatened by him," Jediah said. "However, we have always been wary of any addition to our group." He glanced to Alexandra. "Although your inclusion was foretold centuries ago, we still followed our protocols before admitting you."

Her shoulders sagged. Val gave her a squeeze before returning to his seat.

"I understand," she said. "I just can't shake the notion that he needs us as much as we need him."

"Don't be so down," William said. "You have done an excellent job by breaking the silence between us. It has been far too long. Your intuition is right on target, as far as I'm concerned. I think Ryeth is going to surprise all of us in the future."

Alexandra sat down. "Okay, if we can't invite him here to discuss our fate, I suggest we meet at Heartseed in the future so we can learn what he can contribute. Balisier will not be exposed."

Jediah watched his wife, and felt her disappointment, yet beneath her logic, he sensed her firm resolve to have Ryeth admitted. "I agree," he said.

The others nodded in agreement.

Alexandra was not through. "Here we sit in judgment of him, biding our time, while he has had nearly five hundred years to formulate his opinion of us."

She put her hands on her hips, looked hard at them, Jediah included, and said, "What makes you think *he* will accept *us*?"

***

Men! Alexandra needed a woman's point of view. Between lessons with her Sensate guides, meetings with the High Counsel, a new marriage, becoming a Sensate, averting the end of the world - the Prophecy - and managing her new home, she thought her nerves might snap. In the past, she would have confided everything to Cassie, but now, because of her secret, she couldn't share with the one whose opinion meant the most.

The answer was another Sensate. James' wife, Sarah, was very sweet, but she would be motherly in her advice.

Alice! That kick-butt female just might do the trick. She attempted telekinesis.

Alice Jane, it's Alexandra.

There was no response. Maybe Alice's powers didn't reach from coast to coast. She tried again, but with more volume.

Alice, I need to talk to you. Dang, I should have gotten your cell number. I'm such an idiot. If you can hear me but can't respond, maybe you could call me. My num....

"Jediah has my number," said Alice Jane.

Alexandra spun on her heels. Alice Jane stood before her. She reached out and hugged her new sister-in-law. "What a life saver. Thank you for coming. I wasn't sure you could hear me, and I wasn't sure you could respond."

"No, I couldn't respond from that distance, but I could hear you. What's up little sister? Has my big brother been giving you trouble?"

"No, not really. It's this Sensate stuff."

Alice Jane sat on a stool at the kitchen island and said, "Make me a cup of tea, and I'm all yours."

"If that's your only criteria, I'm getting off pretty easy. I just made a pot."

She reached in the cupboard and pulled out a mug. The tea steamed as she handed it to her. She grabbed her cup, still hot, and sat next to Alice.

"I can tell it's something important," Alice said. "You seem like you're ready to pop, so let's have it."

"Drat, I may as well just spit it out. I'm worried that I might not be a very good Sensate, and I'm worried about Ryeth."

"Oh, is that all…," said Alice as she smiled. She placed her arm around Alexandra. "You're toting a pretty heavy load for a new Sensate. Has Jediah been able to help you?"

"Yes," Alexandra replied. "But mostly he lets me feel my own way."

"Ouch, he did the same to me when we were growing up," said Alice. "He came into his powers before I did, and when I went to him for help, well, let's just say he left me hanging. But, it was different for me because my parents were both Sensates. I can't even imagine what it has been like for you."

"It's so darned confining. I want to go somewhere and try everything. I want to know my limits. I want to do all and know all - all at once. The rules seem to weigh me down. To make matters worse, I understand the need for secrecy, but I don't understand the abnormal amount of caution extended to Ryeth. I don't think he has done anything wrong."

Alexandra sensed she had been ranting. She

collected her thoughts and looked directly at Alice Jane. "I miss my best friend Cassie. I used to talk over *everything* with her."

Alice Jane released a sigh. "No wonder I sensed you were about to burst. Your thoughts are going in all directions at once. Let's take one thing at a time." She sipped her tea, and then continued.

"First, when you attempt something, make sure you always tell another Sensate what you're going to do; that way, if something bad happens, we'll know what to look for or where to find you."

"Yes, I have considered those options..." said Alexandra.

Alice rubbed her shoulder and said, "I know you have powers none of us ever dreamed of, so if this is something new you wish to attempt, by all means, don't try it alone."

Alexandra placed her hand on Alice Jane's arm. "I'm not at that point yet. I know I have a lot to learn, but sometimes the energy builds up inside me and feels unmanageable. It creeps up on me, and I have to really concentrate to keep it in check. At other times, without even thinking about it, things happen. I'm afraid I'll compromise our group."

Alice Jane smiled; the kindness reached her eyes. "Believe me, we all worry about that. Many of us have come close. It's a genuine fear. In time you'll gain confidence and feel more comfortable in your new skin."

Alexandra sighed.

"Now, about your friend, Cassie...I've never really had a close girlfriend, but I used to talk things over with my mom. I feel the loss of that friendship like you must miss Cassie. The best advice I can give you is to spend as much time with her as you can. Don't wait until you have regrets for not doing so."

Her thoughts cleared. "I think you're right. My solution could be as simple as spending time with Cassie. I'm not 'rooted' here yet, at least not like I was in Wheeling."

Alexandra rubbed the rim of her cup with her thumb. "Alice, there's more." She watched Alice's face as she spoke. "I have the hwihs on my shoulder."

Alice lowered her eyes and nodded. "I thought you might," she said with a nod.

Alexandra continued to monitor Alice's reactions as she spoke her next words. "Ryeth has one too."

Alice Jane's eyes widened. "He does? So that's why you believe in him."

She nodded.

Alice spoke slowly and grew somber. "Then the Prophecy is true, and it *is* close at hand."

"Yes," she said.

"I see my big brother has been keeping some hefty information from me."

Alexandra rushed to defend Jediah. "Not just from you, from all Sensates who are not Ultras or part of the High Counsel. We thought it best to develop a plan, then present it to the masses."

"Alexandra, we've known all along that the Prophecy existed, and that it was coming soon. The fact that you're here, admitted into the group, is proof. Since we live for hundreds of years, I'll bet the majority think we have plenty of time to plan. I don't think they know it's this imminent."

Alexandra watched as Alice took time to consider the repercussions. When she spoke

Alexandra knew her words were true.

"The High Counsel is correct. It is best, when giving bad news, to offer an offensive plan at the same time. It will give a sense of security to our group." She took another sip of tea.

"That's what we thought," said Alexandra, a bit relieved that she wasn't going to run to Jediah and criticize his leadership. "Oh, speaking of thinking, I never once considered what you might have been doing when I called for you. I hope you weren't busy."

"Well, to tell you the truth, I've been a bit at odds with my job. I've been working at Lindbergh Aerospace for almost seven years. I love the company, and I've been able to advance their progress in some areas. But the work is slow, what with all the regulations and paperwork, and I think I've maxed out my time and patience there. I quit yesterday. Someone was sure to notice pretty soon that I'm not getting any older…"

Alexandra noted her smile. "I haven't had to go through that process yet," she said. "I guess being a newbie does have some advantages. If I stop to think about it in a purely vain way, I'm sure I'll love not getting older, but leaving those behind who are *not* Sensates and continuing your life somewhere else is going to cause serious pangs of regret. I'm learning that right now."

She missed Cassie more than she could say. "I couldn't talk to my best friend about any of this, and I was sorely missing a female friend." She took Alice's hand in hers. "I'm glad you're here."

"Me too. It's great to have a sister. We've never really had the chance to talk much."

Alice Jane looked closely at Alexandra and her

eyes twinkled. "So, by the way... tell me more about Ryeth."

***

Back in Seattle, a slow smile formed on Alice Jane's lips as she remembered her conversation with Alexandra. If it was true that ears turned red when someone talked about you, then Ryeth's ears should have gone red, burst into flames, and burned to a crisp. A brooding, dark man with a keen mind appealed to her. That he was a Sensate was even better.

Alice arranged to have her furniture placed in storage for the umpteenth time, settled financials, took her car to the shipper, and endured the 'goodbye' party at Lindbergh. Today, she would move her personal items to Larkspur, the family's Victorian city dwelling in Waynesburg.

The loss of her mother caused a tightness to form in her chest. She regretted not spending more time with her during her last days.

Her mother, known by all Sensates as simply 'Nancy Jane,' had been a champion of sorts to many Sensates, and most recently, to Alexandra. Alice didn't begrudge the time her mother spent nurturing Alexandra, but she wished she had been nearer when she found out her mother had decided to make her final journey. The last few days had passed so quickly that she didn't have a chance to prepare for her loss. Coming back to the house her mother loved might help to ease the pain and mend her heart.

Alice Jane texted Alexandra her travel plans. The hours spent cooped up in an airplane were not overly appealing to her, but she knew the process had to take place, especially since Homeland Security watched her every move.

An airport limo service dropped her off at the terminal and she waited in the airport security line with all the other cows heading to slaughter.

It didn't surprise her that she was selected for an in-depth security search. Her carry-on received a thorough search as did her handbag. She sensed the disappointment of the guards as they were obliged to let her go on her way. As she waited for her shoes to be returned, she texted Jediah that she was 'on my way,' which was a coded note to him that they had chosen her for the closer scrutiny.

Her phone rang. Alexandra's name displayed on the screen.

"Hello," she said.

Alexandra's voice filled with joy greeted her. "I'm so glad you're coming home. Jediah will pick you up at the airport, and after you drop your things at Larkspur, I hope you'll consider coming here for a late lunch."

She sensed Alice Jane's sincerity as she said, "Little sister that sounds perfect."

"Good. Be careful, don't let anyone hurt you, and don't let that plane fall out of the sky."

Alice shook her head and smiled. "Sometime soon I hope to get used to your thought process. Where did that caution come from?"

"It's just something my family used to say to each other," Alexandra said. "It's a reminder to be safe, always keep your guard up, and to be prepared for anything. You are my family now, so I extend the same to you."

"All right. I'll do my very best not to let this

plane fall out of the sky. I'll see you soon."

She heard Alexandra's 'bye' as she clicked off the phone.

Her shoes were returned. As she slid on the stacked heels, she considered kicking herself for selling her Cessna Citation.

Chapter 23

Alice Jane watched as the moving van pulled away. The move to the Saffle's home in Waynesburg was the first step in fulfilling her obligations as a Sensate.

She watched their gardener come around the corner of the porch. Terry had been with them for four years. She mentally prepared herself for the conversation with the undercover agent for Homeland Security.

"Hey Terry, it's good to see you again," she said, smiling.

"I was sorry to hear about your mother. She was a good woman," he said.

"Thank you. She loved this place and thought you took good care of it. Are you willing to stay on now that's she's gone?"

"I sure am," said Terry. "I love Larkspur's gardens. I'm glad you've come to manage the place."

"Me too," she said, "I feel closer to Mom here."

"I understand." Terry nodded. "Well, I'll be gettin' back to trimming that wisteria. If I let it go longer than two weeks, it turns into a jungle."

He turned, waved, and went on his way.

Her eyes narrowed to slits. She would need to be on her toes at all times. One slip-up and he would be on her like a scavenger crow, her innards exposed. She didn't like the agent this close, but she counted on her years on the 'outside' to keep her safe. Alice

Jane shook off the feeling of uneasiness as she got comfortable in the porch rocking chair.

She turned her thoughts to Larkspur. The old Victorian held warm memories, but the vacancy left by Nancy Jane mimicked the vacuum she now felt in her heart. Nancy Jane Saffle, her mother and the only person who knew her secret, had passed from this earth. Morally, she could keep her secret no longer.

Her mother had held the family together through the loss of two husbands. Even though she could call up every memory of her father, it was hard to remember him. He'd passed away while she was still young. Teater, her step-father, had left a larger imprint with his zany lust for life.

The wind blew through the honeysuckle vines and brought the sweet scent into the air. She ceased rocking, placed her legs up on the bannister, and leaned her head against the back.

Her mind wandered to the future that awaited her. Because she looked so young, people she met normally asked her what she did for a living. It was tiresome to begin again. Over the years she'd had careers in aviation, aerospace engineering, chemical research, quantum physics and many others. Heck, she had passed the bar, and even been a Pediatrician.

Time passed quickly as she played a mental game of been-there-done-that. Maybe the time had come to immerse herself in a new and upcoming field. She could play off the most recent aerospace engineering and lean toward a NASA position, but she considered the real excitement might lie in the private sector.

She smiled as a vision of Star Trek communicators turned easily into cell phones. Maybe there was more to meet the eye. Planetary travel.

Upcoming companies were developing rockets, taking over where the lunar landings had ended. Edgar Rice Burroughs' John Carter on Barsoom became an inspiration. She closed her eyes and envisioned Burroughs' Mars.

The long day turned into a beautiful dream as she became John Carter and discovered a world unimaginable. A wild world of intelligent species, new landscapes, space travel, and gravitational changes became a subconscious realm of possibilities.

"You are working way too hard," said Jediah as he woke her from the dream.

"Oh." She sat up and ran her fingers through her hair. "I'm sorry. I sat awhile and thought about Mom, then I drifted to my future, and before I knew it, I was transported elsewhere."

"Hey, don't say that too loud. We don't really transport, you know," he said.

"Oh hush. You can be a bore sometimes." She looked around, "Where's Alexandra?"

"She'll be along shortly. Have you decided what job you're going to do this time around?"

"Not yet, but I just might end up hanging out with John Carter on Mars," she said half smiling.

Jediah shifted his weight and rubbed the back of his neck. "What do you mean by that?"

"Nothing really, just pondering the choices." Her brother looked serious.

"Why? What's wrong?" she asked. "Why are you looking at me like that?"

The muscles in his jaws tightened and released. "It's nothing. Just promise me you'll let me know before you delve into anything. I just might have some brotherly advice to share."

"Sure, I'll let you know. It isn't like I haven't

changed jobs before…" Alice said.

"I know, you're a big girl, right?"

She stood, stretched her back, and walked to the door, her hand on the knob. "Holler for that wife of yours, I'm hungry."

Alice went inside. The smell of pork and sauerkraut filled the air. As she whipped the potatoes into a creamy mash, she heard Alexandra's lilting voice.

"My mouth is already watering," said Alexandra.

"Mine too," yelled Jediah from the hallway.

She dipped her finger into the bowl of mashed potatoes and then sucked the blob from her finger. Satisfied with the flavor, she placed a dab of butter on the top of the heap and sprinkled a bit of chopped parsley to finish. Turning to her family, she said, "Set the table, would you please?"

"Sure 'nuff," said Jediah as he handed dishes from the hutch to Alexandra.

Alice placed the meal on the table as they all sat down. Before they dug in she decided it was time to clear her conscience. "I want to talk to you two about something," she said. "I'm not sure how to begin…" Alice pressed her lips together.

"What's wrong?" Alexandra took her hand.

She looked at Jediah, whose face paled.

"Jediah, it's not that bad…" she said. "I've just been keeping something secret for quite a while, and since Mom's death I know that I have to share it."

"You'd better spit it out, Alice. I'm beginning to think the worst," Jediah said. His eyes narrowed.

She sensed fear growing in Jediah; it didn't make sense. He wasn't afraid of anything. Her heart leapt, but then her anger took over. She drew the napkin from her lap and threw it on the table.

As she stood she said, "What in Hades are you thinking? I've done nothing wrong."

Alexandra grabbed Jediah by the arm. "What's wrong with you?" she said. "I've never known you to be so on edge."

Alice watched as Jediah's jaw clenched and released, his eyes never leaving hers. When he finally spoke, his voice was a whisper.

"Just tell me what you have kept secret." His voice was monotone.

"Not until you tell me what's nipping you in the butt." Her eyes danced with eagerness, for if she had a secret, he had something hidden in a closet as well. She could sense it.

As quickly as his ire had risen, she now sensed it ebb. He took a bite of pork and chewed slowly and deliberately.

Alice felt Jediah's peaceful air wash over her. Her demeanor changed to calm. She sat down and replaced her napkin. Her breathing was normal as she said, "That trick of yours won't make me forget, dear brother. I know you are hiding something too, but for now, I'll let it pass."

She nodded to Jediah, who continued eating.

"First," she said, "let me give you some background. I never wanted to be different. I was not thrilled to be a Sensate. I could never find the gratification in the 'gifted' world as you did, Jediah."

Jediah straightened in his seat. "I knew you wanted a life separate from the group," he said.

"It was more than that," she said. "I wanted a real life - a normal life. When I didn't grow older, I resented that I had no choice, that I had no control. For decades, I didn't use my powers; I let them fall by the wayside. I learned to turn it all off."

Jediah leaned toward his sister. "I didn't know you felt so strongly."

"Mom knew. She always knew everything, and she knew the right thing to say to make me feel normal. She's the one who helped me block all my powers and abilities. We even found a way so that no other Sensate could tell I was a Sensate."

Jediah leaned back in his chair. "I didn't know that was possible," he said.

"It wasn't. I don't think any other Sensate is capable of this, at least Mom wasn't."

Jediah said, "Tell me how you do this."

Alice gave the mechanism to Jediah, and also to Alexandra. She watched and waited as both tried to sense her, and smiled as they both failed.

"We have always been able to sense each other," Jediah said. "So, you can make yourself undetectable by Sensates. Any other tricks up your sleeve that we should know about?"

"Well, yes. I'll remove all my blocks, and you tell me…" As she dropped her shield, she watched as Jediah and Alexandra's eyes widened.

Alexandra jumped up and hugged her. "You're an Ultra!"

She nodded, far less excited than Alexandra was. "I'm afraid so."

"How long have you known?" Jediah asked.

"It happened just a few years after you came into your full powers," she said.

He shook his head. "All these decades you never said a word."

She rose from the table. "It wasn't what I wanted. I never wanted the powers, and I never wanted this life. Mom knew, somehow, and she understood, so we worked together to find a solution."

Alice sighed. "A few years ago, when I knew Alexandra's time was near, I began to play with my powers, knowing you might need me to ward off the Prophecy."

She noted the relief on Jediah's face; she sensed his happiness.

"Is that the extent of your secret?" Jediah asked. She felt safe once more when his eyebrow raised.

"Not exactly," she said. "I've used my powers on other Sensates to see what I could do, and to find out whether or not I was detected."

"Other Sensates?" said Jediah, as he rubbed the back of his neck. He let out an enormous sigh.

"I know, I know. That honor thing. Well, I did it and it's done. I won't do it anymore, so don't go looking down your high-falootin' nose at me. I couldn't very well try things on normal people, now could I? At least Sensates are used to hearing voices in their heads." She became aware of her rambling, so she closed her mouth and sat down.

Alexandra rose, walked over to Alice and placed her hands on her shoulders. "Something tells me you're not the first Sensate to step over the line."

"Yeah, you're probably right, but they weren't *his* sister." She looked hard at Jediah. "How is it possible for you to be such a gung-ho Sensate and for me to be such an opposite?"

"Alice, we are not so different," he said. "If you ask any Sensate, I'm sure they will tell you that they struggle too. We can only do our best." He gave a half chuckle. "It isn't like we have a map to follow on how to be a Sensate."

"Boy," said Alexandra, "I could have used one of those at least a million times already."

"Then," she said, as she watched for their reaction, "it's safe to say I know everything about Ryeth?"

"Oh boy, you've been listening in?" said Jediah; he shook his head. "You really push it to the limit, don't you?"

She shrugged. "I was curious."

Alexandra looked at her with her head cocked. "Then you can hear me *and* speak to me telepathically from a far distance?"

"I'm sorry, yes," she said. "I'm sorry for the white lie. Now to be fully honest, I also know about Ari."

Jediah's shock was apparent. "But we blocked everyone…" he said, his brows drawn together.

"I am Nancy Jane's daughter," she said with a sly grin. "Do I need to say more?"

Chapter 24

The black-haired, multi-colored-eyed vixen refused to leave Ryeth's mind. Her image formed in his mind when he showered, she appeared in his dreams, and interrupted his thoughts multiple times throughout the day.

If he believed in such things, he'd say he was bewitched, for now, he considered her an obsession.

She couldn't have disappeared without a trace. He called the local cab service pretending to be an officer of the law. Later, he phoned all the limousine services.

It took no time to allocate the airport security officer's credentials and use them to search flight records.

Amtrack was easily miffed into believing he worked for the FBI and unloaded their passenger information without further questions.

Next, he scrutinized all the car rental services, but no one with the name Kimberly Koza had rented a car within fifty miles of the lodge.

The final search was of tax records for Florida. The only K Koza listed was 72 years old and male.

Ryeth became lost in his search for the elusive Kimberly. No matter how much he berated himself, he knew, down deep, she had left of her own accord.

It just made no sense. Could he have read the signals wrong? Maybe he was too much taken to realize she hadn't been 'taken' at all.

Ryeth leaned back into his leather sofa and closed his eyes. Checking in on the antics of the poisonous Morgan Black had become a daily pastime he rather enjoyed, mostly because it had taken his mind off Kimberly more than once.

As he entered Chief Black's mind, his satisfaction grew.

***

"Get out of here. I can't stand to see your face," she said.

As soon as the door closed, Black reached for the bottle of Advil in her purse. She spilled four gel-caps into her palm, threw them into the back of her mouth, and then washed them down with a swallow of lukewarm coffee.

She rested her temples in her hands as the incessant pounding grew. Never had a migraine lasted this long or been so severe. It was all she could do to get out of bed.

It couldn't have come at a worse time. She needed all the ingenuity she could muster, and as of this minute, she hadn't mustered a darned thing. She'd almost lost her job over the disappearance of the three useless subjects. Now, the higher-ups were watching her every move. Pah! If she had been one day earlier to dispose of them, no one would have been the wiser.

The disappearance of the three subjects spurred her to make some drastic changes in her plans for 613.

She prepared a new holding room for 613, with the latest in security. Heat sensors, motion detectors, high-speed broad spectrum cameras, infrared cameras, and a new device that could pick up DNA from exhaled air, would certainly foil plans for her removal.

If any of that group from Waynesburg as much as set foot on the premises, they would be hauled off immediately to join 613. Gooch, working as gardener, and Mokros had supplied the FSB with DNA samples from all five of the suspects. All she had to do was wait.

She picked up 613's chart and hesitated a split second before she lessened the dosage. Her face contorted into a scowl.

Her goal, the perfect dosage, would enable her to eliminate 613's defenses and control her abilities. Control and power loomed before her; she would learn what 613's contributions could make to the Department of Defense, and serve her up on a gold platter. *Silver* wasn't near good enough.

Ryeth heard Black's thoughts screamed in anger, *I won't be stopped. I'll figure out how to get what I want. This stupid woman will heel to my demands or live her remaining years as a vegetable.*

Before leaving Black's mind, Ryeth twisted the nerve endings once again.

***

Ryeth walked to the window of his mountain home. A group of American Chestnuts he had saved from the blight were beginning to drop their spiny burrs. He watched as anxious squirrels ran through the trees and bit off the burrs, dropping them to the ground for harvest.

Remorse filled his thoughts. He had been unable to locate Kimberly. No Kimberly Koza was found who authored books, no Kimberly in Florida matched her description, and no Kimberly came back to the lodge.

He chided himself for placing so much emphasis on their meetings. Perhaps everything she said was a lie. Maybe she did it to protect herself. Then again, he could have read too much into it.

Regrets. He hated regrets. Between those and 'if onlys' he could sum up the totality of his life. If only he had gotten Kimberly's cell number. If only he had read her mind. Why had *she* become the exception to his rule? It was a curtesy he had never extended to a female companion before.

Blast it, that's what had made the difference. He'd dallied with the others, reading their minds and knowing what they were going to say before they even said it.

That's why he had enjoyed their bantering. He hadn't known what was coming next. That, and the way she held her chin. She was proud, and confident. He also liked the way he felt when she was around. Young and alive; she was a breath of fresh air.

If only…

Chapter 25

Alice Jane sensed the flurry going through the Sensates. That one of their own had 'hidden' her talents made no sense to the majority.

The only truly uncomfortable scene had come when she had to stand before them and explain the 'why' of her decision. To her surprise, although they didn't fully understand, they accepted her choice with ease.

Explaining her eavesdropping was another thing altogether.

From the crowd came a question. "Did you listen in on all our minds?"

"No," she said, "It was mostly the High Counsel and the Ultras."

She heard gasps from the group and hurried to clarify. "At first, I just wanted to know what was going on while I was away, so I listened mostly to Jediah so I would know when the High Counsel meetings would take place. Then, when I learned the Prophecy neared, I listened to see if I could develop abilities to aid our cause."

Murmurs came from the crowd and then it fell silent.

"I am sorry I listened in. I know it was wrong and that I failed all of you by not adhering to our moral code. Please find it in your hearts to forgive me."

It was the best she could do. She removed

herself from Balisier and went back to Larkspur. They would now decide her fate.

As she placed make-up items in the bathroom, she looked into the mirror. A slender, black-haired, ivory-skinned woman looked back. She leaned into the mirror to get a closer view of her violet eyes, a trait she shared with her brother. She sniffed. That physical characteristic was the only item that signaled them as relatives.

She leaned back and made space on the second shelf. There she placed the boxes that contained specially-made contact lenses of green, blue, dark brown, topaz, and gray. A smile began at the corner of her mouth. She closed the cabinet door and turned away from her reflection.

She wasn't bad, just a little naughty. Although she knew that other Sensates had probably listened in a time or two among family members or even when they wanted to know what someone else thought of them…. Those were like little white lies, and perhaps, allowable. But what she had done was more severe. She had listened in on the High Counsel and Ultras, the governing body of their group. Her penance would be more than a slap, but less than an exile. She could only wait.

She could easily listen in now, so that she wouldn't be surprised at her punishment; they wouldn't even know. Curiosity tempted her.

Curiosity wasn't the only thing that tempted her, and *he* wasn't formally a member of the group. That was a loophole. One she intended to take full advantage of until her hands were tied.

She leaned back into the comfort of an oversized chair, drawing her knees up to snuggle into its depths. As she closed her eyes, she was able to see through his.

Ryeth was in the woods again, no not exactly in the woods, he was watching the squirrels outside his window, but what was he thinking? His mind was blank. She actually felt the vastness of space he reflected. She sensed power, great power, and she was drawn to it, and to him.

***

Alice stood before the High Counsel.

William spoke first. "What you did was invasive. The one thing we have here at Balisier is trust, which you have betrayed." He shook his head.

"Alice Jane," James said, "I still don't understand your actions. If you had come forth in the beginning, all of this could have been avoided."

"Yes, yes, James, we've gone over that," said Val. "Quit beating her up over her decision not to use her powers. You and I both know that had we known, she would probably have been a member of the counsel and privy to the information anyway."

She looked to her brother who remained passive. It was apparent he withheld himself from any decision due to his bias. She would have expected no less.

Alexandra looked down at her hands and didn't meet her eyes, but she sensed a feeling of comradery coming from her.

Her eyes dropped to the marble-tiled floor. Alice stood rigid; she could feel her legs lock in place, which caused her to sway, a bit off-balance. Their eyes on her made her feel like a criminal being judged.

Just when she opened her mouth to spill out her

anger-infused thoughts, she felt a peacefulness spread throughout her body. Her knees unlocked; her shoulders relaxed.

She looked up to see Jediah's eyes on her. His caution, in the form of serenity, closed her lips.

"We have come to a decision," said James.

"And it wasn't easy," said William, "because we disagree, something we don't normally do. I want you to know, little lady, that it is me who disagrees. In all my years…"

"Okay, William," said Val. "We get the point."

William stood and shoved his hands in his pockets. He walked away from the group and sat in a corner.

James smiled at her. "We have decided that you should become a member of the counsel."

Her shoulders fell. "But I don't want…"

James cut her off. "That's exactly why we made you part of the counsel. At least this way, we can keep an eye on you."

"And her shenanigans," yelled William from the corner.

James continued. "You will be a fully liable member of the deciding group, and as such, totally responsible for your actions. You will adhere to our values and act accordingly."

Alice Jane sighed. "I understand," she said.

James said, "Fine. I'm glad that's settled. Have a seat will you, Alice Jane? William, get back over here so we don't have to yell for you to hear us."

William stood and shuffled to his seat. "Just so you know, I'll be watching you." He pointed his finger at her.

Jediah took over control of the meeting. "It's time to make plans to bring Ari home. William, has your group fixed a position on her location."

"Yes," he said, "we know she is being held in the south wing, centrally located as a hub of sorts. Seven areas surround her room with a circular hallway access. Here's a drawing we obtained from the architect's thoughts, since no actual drawings exist." He handed out copies. "We believe the FSB destroyed the plans for security reasons."

Jediah said, "Are these red points on the drawing cameras?"

"They are," said William. "We can disable those as Ryeth did, so they're not a problem."

Alice's heart skipped a beat at the mention of his name.

"Do we know where the DNA sensors were installed?" asked Jediah.

"All are in Ari's room, but we're still working on the location of the controller. If we can find that, maybe we can circumvent the whole process," said William.

James intervened. "I think we need to draw Ryeth into our group."

Alice Jane felt the sharp intake of breath in her chest. She looked down at the table and concentrated on slowing her heartbeat. When she looked up again, she was in full control.

"We had this conversation before," said William.

James placed his hands on the table. "Yes, we did." He sighed. "But how can we expect him to trust us? I think he deserves a show of trust from us. Nothing ever changes if someone doesn't stop the circle from continuing. He's given us no reason to think he intends us harm."

"I, for one, trust him completely," said

Alexandra. "He had the opportunity to harm our group and me when he rescued me from Magis. His actions may have compromised us, but if you recall, Terry Gooch was the Saffle's gardener much longer than I was in the picture. The FSB had already set up camp in our backyard years before Ryeth's potential exposure happened."

Alice Jane met Alexandra's eyes as a vote of confidence and nodded.

"He said he already knew we had a hideout," Alice said.

Everyone in the room looked hard at her.

"What? I told you I listened in…" she said. Drat, why did her first statement as part of the group have to turn into another admission of guilt? She slid down in her chair.

Jediah broke the tension by laughing. "I suppose you did," he said. "It will just take us some time to realize how much you know. It was just a little shock to our senses, nothing more."

"Alice," said Alexandra, "being a female, like me, and knowing what we're like, did you… did you peek into Ryeth's mind to see if he intended us harm?"

Alice felt her cheeks redden. "No, I didn't."

"I'm sorry, Alice," said Alexandra, "I had to ask."

"I know you did, little sister. No harm, no foul," she said.

James called for a vote to invite Ryeth into the Sensates group. All were in favor, which surprised Alice Jane.

As she looked around the group, she smiled. Though gruff sometimes, the group was honorable. They had dealt with her fairly, even though the criteria tied her hands. They were good people.

Jediah closed the meeting. "We will have Alexandra invite Ryeth. I think he will be less abrasive with her than with any of us. My wife seems to be able to calm the savage beast." He reached over to hug Alexandra.

Speaking before thinking once again, Alice Jane said, "Do you really think he is that wild and unpredictable?"

"He has a temper," said Val. "He almost destroyed Magis' mind when he saw what he did to Alexandra."

"But he didn't," said Alexandra.

James said, "I do seem to recall in the not too distant past when a certain Sensate yelled so loud in the bowels of Balisier that rocks burst on the outside of the mountain."

"Yeah," said Jediah, "that would have been me. But I had just cause."

"Who's to say Ryeth didn't have just cause?" said Alice Jane.

"That's just it," said Jediah. "We don't know enough about him.

"Avoiding him will not make that any better," said Alice Jane.

"I guess we'll find out soon enough," said Alexandra. "He'll be grilled on the spit just like you were."

***

If Ryeth had anything to do with it, and he knew he did, Morgan Black's days were numbered. He stroked the two-day old stubble on his chin. If that she-devil could set aside normal human compassion, then so could he.

He teleported to the parking garage next to the FSB headquarters. He'd seen Black's parking space and knew her car from his mind searches. Landing in a darkened corner away from the security cameras, he focused his vision on Black's SUV. The heat trace took him directly to the motor. Concentrating on the pistons, he fused them to the housing.

He closed his eyes to see through Black's and caught her rubbing her foot. She had slipped it out of the stiletto heels and massaged it without thinking as she read over the files on her desk.

A bit of concentration on his part and the stiletto weakened at the attachment to the sole. Smiling at his work for the day, he returned home to monitor Black's day from afar.

He enjoyed the antics that would ensure a horrible day for the FSB siren. A weeks' worth of activity on his part had already caused her cat to seek revenge on its owner by using her bed as a litter box; her refrigerator to leak coolant resulting in spoiled food; and her shower to alternate between icy cold and steaming hot water. Ryeth looked forward to witnessing her rage when her SUV failed.

Each night, as she slept, he entered her mind and forced her subconscious into nightmares that would scare an ogre, always twisting nerve endings before he left to ensure the continued migraine.

One of his favorite pass times was waiting for Black to wake in the morning. The look on her face when she saw her haggard reflection in the mirror gave him untold delight. It was all he could do to contain himself.

The day finally came when valuable information

fell into his lap. He contacted Alexandra immediately.

Can you talk? he asked Alexandra.

Sure, as a matter of fact, I needed to speak to you, she said.

I think I know how to get around this DNA sensor. He sensed her excitement.

Really? That's great news. I can hardly wait to tell the others. Better yet, why don't you tell them yourself? She felt his stomach lurch.

Alexandra, I don't play well with others.

I know you are still chaffed, but you have to reach beyond that. Couldn't you please try?

His indecision reeked from every pore.

She tried again. *I'd love it if you came to Heartseed, my home on top of the mountain. I can have everyone here at seven tonight.*

Drat. He could never refuse her. With all his powers, why was it that she could just waltz right in and take control? At least she had taken the step to let him into her home as he had his. Maybe there was hope...

Fine, I'll be there, he said.

I'll meet you at the arbor. He felt her warm smile as she added, *I know you know how to get there.*

He smiled in return before he closed the connection, then immediately the bitterness set in.

Why couldn't they leave well enough alone? Couldn't they just accept his help and stay out of his life? He groaned. Apparently not.

He had three hours before he had to be at Heartseed and already he could feel the noose growing tight around his neck. Rubbing it, he mentally shook off the ill feelings.

When the hour came to prepare for his second visit to Heartseed, he looked in the mirror. The stubble would remain. His eyes narrowed as a flash of memory reminded him of his first encounter with Alexandra.

That day, he had planned his entrance with a devil-may-care attitude. Hugh Jackman's look from *Van Helsing* had been his inspiration. He had worked days to perfect the blowing of the wind through his black full-length leather coat, which turned out to be no simple feat. His intent had been to shock, terrify, and mystify the young girl. While he had success in his presentation, he had not been prepared for the girl's easy teleportation exit.

He stroked the same length of stubble. His eyes drew up into mischievous slits as he planned a similar entrance, with a twist, for the second go-'round. Combining the blowing coat with a smooth descent, one he had perfected centuries ago as a Halloween stint, should achieve the right amount of awe.

When the time arrived, he cloaked himself, and as he began his slow descent from twenty feet away, he knew he had achieved his goal. Alexandra had felt his presence and turned to see him softly gliding, his coat fluttering in the gentle breeze that he controlled, and coming to rest next to her within the arbor.

Her smile was bewitching with just the right amount of devil behind it.

"You *have* to tell me how you do that. If you had come in like this the first time, I may not have disappeared on you," she said. "What an entrance."

"I aim to please," he said with a smile.

"Thanks for coming. I know these things are

not easy for you."

"It goes against my grain," he said. "Each time, it gets easier."

He held his arm out to Alexandra. She took it and they turned toward the house. As they strolled along the stone pathway she said, "We have a new member of the High Counsel. She will be joining us tonight. She's Jediah's sister, Alice Jane."

"I didn't know Jediah had a sister," he said.

"It seems he likes to spring things on people. I didn't know he had a sister until our rehearsal dinner. You'll like her. I finally feel like I have something in common with another Sensate. She is truly the sister I never had."

Ryeth cleared his throat. Though he tried hard, his feet stiffened and his legs stopped in their path.

Alexandra turned to him. "What's wrong?" she asked. Her face paled. "Oh Ryeth, how could I have been so inconsiderate? I'm so sorry. Here I am blabbering on about having a sister, and you have been, decades, no, *centuries* without contact with other Sensates. I am so very sorry."

Why did the pain always catch him unaware? He hated showing emotions, especially to other Sensates. It wasn't so bad with Alexandra, for she seemed to be a cushion for those errant emotions. But he would be cursed to a solitary existence if he ever showed lesser emotions to others.

His infraction lasted a few seconds; by the time she finished speaking his emotional wall was once again secure.

"Forget it," he said. He patted her hand. "I'm happy for you. Shall we continue?"

"I like that coat," she said.

He sensed her delight. "Thanks. I 'borrowed' it

from Hugh Jackman when he wasn't looking, had it copied, and returned it before he knew it was missing."

Ryeth didn't miss the wide eyes as she looked at him in disbelief. "You didn't really…" she said.

"I did. I told you that I don't live by your Sensate honor code."

"I'm not appalled; I just want to know what it *felt* like. Were you scared?"

He laughed out loud. "Scared? No way, little girl. That wasn't even a crack in the veneer of my escapades. It was a whiff in the wind, nothing more. I saw the coat, wanted one like it, and took the steps required to get it."

"Do you always get what you want?" she asked.

His mind flew instantly to Kimberly. "Pretty much, until recently," he said. He looked down at Alexandra. "Until you arrived, my life contained all I ever wished for. After you, I didn't know how much I had missed."

Alexandra blushed.

As they got to the door, she looked up at him and asked, "Are you ready?"

"We'll soon see, won't we?"

He walked into the spacious foyer, noting the second floor overhang and oak staircase. As he entered the living room Jediah reached out a hand in welcome. Val, James, and William stepped forward to welcome him.

As they were exchanging pleasantries, a movement from the hallway caught Ryeth's eye. As he turned for a better view he heard Jediah's introduction.

"Ryeth, I'd like you to meet my sister, Alice Jane."

Piercing black eyes met vibrant violet ones. The shock to his senses overwhelmed him. His Kimberly stood before him, as beautiful as ever.

Jediah's sister? His thoughts turned sour. Had they been spying on him? She had played him expertly.

Anger, shame, and crushing rage surged through his veins. His eyes darkened as he spun on his heels, his coattails flapping, and vanished in an instant.

He needed to clear his mind. She was a Sensate and he hadn't known. How was that even possible? He felt the presence of all Sensates, but he hadn't felt her.

Ryeth? Alexandra called to him.

He opened the connection to let her feel his emotions, but did not respond.

"What in Hades was that?" said Jediah.

Alexandra dropped into the nearest chair. Ryeth's emotions were so thick they threatened to choke her. "He feels betrayed."

"I told you that boy was a loose cannon," said William.

"He isn't, William," Alexandra said. "I know him; he doesn't act without just cause."

All eyes turned to Alice Jane, who vanished as quickly as Ryeth did.

Chapter 26

Ryeth?

Ryeth recognized her touch. His Kimberly had deceived him. They were all laughing at him for being so naïve. Why hadn't he sensed her? No matter, he couldn't trust any of them. He should have known better.

Get out of my head and stay out. Ryeth poured seething wrath into her senses. He sensed she was stunned by the assault on her emotions, and then he felt her sorrow.

I deserve that, said Alice Jane. *The others didn't know I contacted you. They still don't know. I left as quickly as you did.*

They didn't know? That changed nothing.

Haven't you done enough? he said. *I want nothing more to do with you and your kind.*

Ryeth summoned all his power to block the witch from entering his mind.

I'm sorry; please forgive me.

How in Hades had the woman entered his mind? Her powers were strong enough to get through his barriers. A sneer crossed his face. There were other ways to get rid of her... He transported himself halfway around the globe and as far south as he could go and still be comfortable in shirtsleeves.

The voice that melted his soul entered his mind once more. *Australia won't do it, Ryeth. I can find you anywhere. I want to tell you that I'm sorry for deceiving you.*

His shoulders sagged; he couldn't believe it, she was still in his head. How did she know his location? Could she see through his eyes as he could of others? He moved to another place, but this time he closed his eyes upon arrival.

He sensed she was smiling as he heard her voice yet again.

Fine, I don't know where you are, but I can still enter your mind, so you may as well open your eyes. Aren't you old enough to put away childish games?

He fumed. *Like you? What game are you playing this time, little Sensate? What about your code of honor? I thought it was bad form to go where you weren't wanted.*

His words hurt her; he felt her pain. If he felt that, then he could enter her mind, she was open to his attack. He entered her mind with the force of a savage beast whose only thought was to stop the pain in his heart.

I can stop you, she said. *But I'm not going to. I owe you that much.*

Her willingness to accept the blame and forthcoming punishment caught him unaware. He ceased the intended carnage of her mind.

Ryeth's mind felt like a vacuum, devoid of all, empty. He was a shell of a man, nothing more. The years, the decades, the centuries of being alone crashed down on him.

The half that wanted to destroy everything was face to face with the half that wanted more. He could continue down a solitary path, the one he knew so well, or he could venture forth anew into the unknown with a vivacious creature that reached into the very core of his existence.

The path was his to choose.

His Kimb...no, his Alice Jane, was incredulous. He sensed her faith in him. She was courageous and stubborn, the perfect complement to his id - and she was offering a comradery that was unknown, yet promised a haven.

His inner smile emerged. While admitting her wrongdoing, at the same time, she challenged him. The wench actually thought she could stop him from pillaging her mind. Her confidence was incredulous.

Full of cynicism he said, *You are so very sure that you can stop me?*

Yes. Try again, she said.

He burst forth without mercy. His attack should knock her to the floor. Nothing. It was as if she didn't exist.

Satisfied? she said.

Her self-confidence oozed as he felt her smug presence in his mind once again.

Fine, you had your fun, played your game, and now it's over. Just go and leave me in peace.

Her regret filled his mind. He closed his eyes and imagined a black wall so that his mind displayed nothing.

That won't work either, she said softly.

The black wall he envisioned turned into blue eyes, then green eyes with flecks of gold, then into violet eyes. The contents in his arsenal could not defeat this foe. His weaponry was no match for the unprecedented assault.

The sense of betrayal began to fade, replaced by a form of acceptance.

Why did it have to be you? he said. Ryeth allowed his façade to drop, defeated.

Why did what *have to be me?* she asked.

The one who ruined everything... Ryeth sensed his heart vulnerable and open for the first time since his parents' deaths.

Her tenderness reached forth. *Ryeth, what did I ruin?*

His name spoken from her lips crumbled his wall to ashes; there was nothing left inside. Ryeth transported himself home, fell into the depths of his favorite leather chair, and held his head in his hands.

He tried to summon the revenge that had comforted him for nearly half a millennium; it failed to appear. When he reached for hate, he found it had fallen by the wayside. Betrayal had slipped away as well. Rage, his most confident of companions, was nowhere. No familiar emotion of great proportions abounded; he was completely alone.

***

A cool hand touched the back of his neck. Her hands dropped from behind his neck and traveled down to his chest, creating a trail of fire as they moved.

Ryeth half-turned, grabbed her by the waist, and pulled Alice Jane onto his lap. His lips were on hers without thinking. A rush of compassion, strength and love washed over him as she responded.

Emotions withheld from his past released to fill the void, as Ryeth became the Sensate Onatah had birthed. Bad memories receded into the far distant past as good ones came forth. He remembered his mother's smile and his father's strength, and now, as he held Alice Jane in his arms, he enjoyed the taste of his first real kiss.

Unfamiliar emotions poured into every inch of

his six foot six frame. Repressed sensations materialized from the dust of long ago when he wished to have the love in his live that his parents had shared. His core softened to allow an open window where pleasant wings of passions could enter and roost.

He pulled away and looked into her eyes. They narrowed with his scrutiny.

"Care to tell me why you're here?" he asked.

The creature before him was exquisite in every detail, right down to her natural violet eyes.

As she lowered her lashes and toyed with the collar of his shirt she said, "I'm quite sure it's where I belong."

Ryeth's heart surged with her words. A slight smile crossed his lips. "Confident, aren't you?"

She smiled in return. "I'm at least as confident as you."

He shook his head. "I'm sorry for you, for right now, I'm the least confident I've been in my whole life," he said. "I'm neck deep in uncharted waters."

He sensed her delight. "Then you'd better get a map, because this ship is about to set sail." She raised her chin.

Her hair brushed his cheek. The scent of her perfume wafted in the air.

"There's a strong chance the weather will not be favorable. It could be rough sailing," he said.

Ryeth pondered whether he could ever be the Sensate she deserved. His past had haunted him for centuries and was a major portion of his personality. It might be impossible for him to deny that part of his identity. Did he have the right to subject her to his atypical lifestyle?

Alice Jane placed her hand on his cheek.

Through the stubble he could feel its softness.

She shook her head side to side very slowly. "What makes you think I desire calm waters? There is much more challenge in sailing through a wicked storm than gliding across a mirrored surface."

If eyes were truly the windows to one's soul, looking in hers he became lost in depths of a violet hue.

"Ryeth, I promise never to lie to you again. I will never deceive you." She leaned forward and pressed her lips to his.

Ryeth came home. This one moment in time resounded with warmth, satisfaction and security. Forever could be centuries away, or end tomorrow, either way he would hinge his forevermore in this one moment.

His voice was a whisper. "Tell me why you assumed an alter identity."

Her answer was a promise. "I'll do better than that..."

Alice Jane flooded Ryeth's mind with antics concerning him from as far back as his first meeting with Alexandra at the arbor. Her endeavors contained no malice in her actions regarding him. Pure and simple, she was interested in him, and had pursued what interested her.

From outside the group, she had watched, waited, and selected the time of their first meeting, expecting him to pull some prank and vanish. When he hadn't, she had become entranced with finding out about the one Sensate who had escaped the grasp of the collective group.

Alice Jane was envious of his freedom and power, for although she had extreme powers over the human mind, she didn't have near the power he and

Alexandra possessed.

To protect him from making the connection between Jediah's eyes and hers, she had played a game with colored contacts.

Ryeth broke through her transmission long enough to say, "Oh, please never use those contacts again."

He looked at her with a sober expression. "I'm sure Heaven exists in the pure color of your eyes."

"I promise," she said as she snuggled softly against his chest.

Alice finished her sharing session by replaying her come-uppance with the Sensate High Counsel, where he learned they had forced her to join the High Counsel as punishment.

His girl had a bit of spitfire in her blood, which pleased him beyond measure. They were more alike than he ever would have imagined. He could learn from her, and she from him. They could enjoy each other and their powers for a *very* long time.

Although Alice Jane had not asked, Ryeth shared the answer to the Sensates' long standing question - what happened to his parents?

The replay from his mind to hers visibly shook her. He continued to share all experiences and emotions up to the point where he was tied to the stake.

"Stop!" she yelled. "They did horrible things to you. You are so good." Tears filled her eyes.

Ryeth kissed her. "That was hundreds of years ago, it's now a memory that will haunt me no longer. I wanted you to know the truth."

"It wasn't necessary to tell me," she said.

"I know," he said, his heart at peace, "and that's exactly why I did."

***

Two hours later after Ryeth and Alice Jane filled in each other's personal history, they stood at the railing of Ryeth's deck. He whispered into her soft, shining hair. "You know we have to go back."

"I know," Alice Jane said, "but I don't want to be part of their counsel. I don't want to be monitored."

"Then don't," he said. "What's the worst they can do to you? Didn't your own mother defy them in helping you hide your powers?"

"Yes." Alice smiled. "I wish you would have known her. She was strong and wise."

"So was my mother. Her name was Onatah."

Alice Jane looked at him with widened eyes and said, "Onatah, *the* Onatah? Onatah was your mother?"

A bit perplexed, Ryeth said, "You know of her?"

"Of course I do, we all do. She was the very first Sensate and praised by all as our founding mother."

Stunned, Ryeth dropped onto a nearby bench. Alice sat by his side. She flooded his mind with Onatah's history. The thought transfer took only a few seconds. His travel through the years took longer.

He shook his head in disbelief. His mother had started it all. All Sensates had been created by one. It sunk in deep as he realized his young mother had been somewhere around fifteen hundred years old when Nootau ended her life. The Sensates had known of her life, and he'd known of her death.

Onatah's story had an ending; her circle complete.

Alice Jane stood and pulled Ryeth up to her. "Ryeth Garmendia, you are indeed a treasure."

His brows furrowed. "Keep that in mind as we go back to see your brother."

Ryeth kissed her sweetly as Alice signaled their coming to the others. They arrived in Heartseed's living room hand-in-hand.

Alexandra and Jediah sat on the couch. Alexandra jabbed Jediah in the ribs and said, "I told you so."

Jediah looked at Ryeth and his sister and shook his head. "You're right again," he said to Alexandra. "How do you *know* these things?"

Alexandra jumped up, ran to Alice Jane and hugged her. She stood on tip-toes to kiss Ryeth on the cheek.

Ryeth blushed at Alexandra's display of affection.

Alexandra looked like a sneaky imp as she said, "All better now?" She looked back and forth between the two. "Can we get back to helping Ari, or do you two need to take a few more minutes to compose yourselves?"

Ryeth released Alice Jane's hand, cleared his throat and took a seat next to Jediah.

He shrugged his shoulders and said, "I don't know about Alice, but I'm fairly composed. Probably the most composed I've been in years."

Alice Jane slid into a soft chair. "I'm pretty composed too," she said. "I say we get the show on the road."

One-by-one the members of the High Counsel appeared.

James came first, took a look at the occupants,

and said, "She was right."

Val came, laughed and said, "I knew she was on to something."

Last to arrive was William who took in all the smiling faces. He shook his head and said, "I never would have believed it. I'll never doubt you again, Alexandra."

Ryeth heard Jediah groan under his breath. It was the sound of a grown man eating crow, and hard as he tried, he couldn't help but be envious.

Jediah stood. "Before anyone goes running off..." he cleared his throat, "can we at least get to the invite?"

"Yes, by all means," said James. "Ryeth, we would like you to join the Sensate group."

These were words Ryeth had waited to hear for almost five hundred years. Not only had he wanted to hear them, he had needed to hear them, but now the time had passed.

He stood, walked over to James and shook his hand. "Thanks, James, I really appreciate the offer, but I'm going to decline."

He turned to face the group. "I thought it was what I wanted, but now I see I merely wanted acknowledgment. I have no wish to join a group, any group. I have lived too long with no constraints. To be saddled by them now would make me into a grumpy old man."

He couldn't help but cast a glance at William, who laughed good-naturedly.

Jediah said, "Even though you decline the offer, you are welcome at Balisier, our 'hideout' anytime. Alice can show you the way."

"Thanks, Jediah," said Ryeth. "I appreciate the trust this entails, and I am honored by the inclusion into the ranks."

Jediah nodded and said, "Then let's get this caper started." He addressed Ryeth. "Tell us what you know."

Ryeth took a breath and exhaled slowly. "I've been visiting Chief Morgan Black from the FSB on a very frequent basis ever since I stole her three captives. I hadn't been able to get anywhere with this new DNA sensor until today when she reviewed the documents that pretty much laid out how it works."

Excitement filled the air. "Can we bypass it?" asked Val.

"Not the units themselves," Ryeth said. "They work on DNA being passed into the air when a person breathes. The deck is slightly stacked against us since they have already have DNA samples from Alexandra, Jediah, and Alice Jane, aptly provided by Jediah's landscaper/FSB agent. If they were to match any one of us to Ari's escape, we could all end up like her."

"We figured as much," said Jediah. "You must have something up your sleeve..."

"It's only a thought process so far. If that sensor can pick up DNA from our breath, it will probably pick it up from our skin and hair as well. So I think we need to be encased in something so that nothing gets out."

Ryeth watched each face as the various minds worked, before continuing. "Last year when I went deep sea diving, I wished for a re-breather of sorts to use instead of those heavy tanks. We could use something like that attached to a space suit and be fully contained. As long as there no trace elements on the outside of the suits to give us away, there would be nothing left behind to lead them back to us."

"How is this going to help us?" Alexandra asked. "Has someone invented such a suit?"

"Not that I know of, but last year, a physics organization mentioned two guys from the west coast who changed carbon dioxide into carbon and oxygen. It's been almost a year since then, so I'm sure they are further along."

Alice Jane sat upright. "I read the paper they submitted in the journal."

All heads turned to her. "I know, it sounds kinda nerdy, but I was looking for a new career." She shrugged, "Anyway, a laser shoots a beam at carbon dioxide and breaks it into components. They used VUV, a vacuum ultraviolet light. If we applied a filter to eliminate the carbon, we would end up with pure oxygen."

"Do we have the ability to do this?" asked William.

"We certainly have enough engineers," said Jediah. "If we need assistance, we can peek at the researcher's work. Later on, as compensation, we'll drop a few hints to advance their research, I don't think they'll mind."

"Alice Jane, do you remember the researchers' names?" asked Ryeth.

She smiled. "It was Suit and Parker. I thought the name Suit was odd, I think that's why I remember." She paused. "Think about it, we could be making a Parker VUV Suit."

Ryeth didn't miss her pun, and was proud of her quick thinking and resourcefulness when presenting her information. The others seemed deadpan to her pun. He winked at the delightful girl with luminous violet eyes.

"This just might work," said Jediah. "I'll assemble a team today and bring them up to speed. There's no need to re-invent the wheel; we could borrow some blue suits from the CDC."

Val cleared his throat. "You would be safe with one of their suits," he said. "Nothing gets in, nothing gets out, but they are designed to work with air supply hoses. We'll have to re-configure one, after that, it can't be returned."

William rubbed the soft stone in his hand with his thumb. "This is sounding more and more like a one-man or one-woman job. Those suits are costly and they *will* be missed. If we take two, they should come from different sources. We might even want to consider a world-wide search."

Jediah looked around the room. "Any other hitches you can think of?" He nodded. "Then we have a plan. Let's get busy."

***

Alice Jane groaned. Jediah assigned her to monitor Ari's mind at all times. His reasoning was two-fold: Alice could monitor her without Ari's knowledge, and she could look through Ari's eyes and into her mind to pick up any possible threats to the Sensates. She had to admit, it was a great use of her abilities.

Leaving her mind open to Ari at all times wasn't the best way to begin a relationship with Ryeth, but they learned to take the intrusions in stride.

She snuggled close to Ryeth on the couch and asked, "What's the nasty lady up to today?"

Ryeth raised his eyebrows. "You mean after the

smoke detector went off in Black's apartment at 3AM, or when she was called into the Director's office to explain the mass exodus of security staff due to her bad temperament?"

"Are you still giving her migraines?" she asked.

Ryeth nodded. "Every single night. And I must say, it has put a damper on her love life. That J.T. fellow hasn't been around in quite some time."

"Can't say I blame him," she said. "Imagine being treated like that. I wonder why he takes it."

"I've been studying human nature from afar for decades, and I haven't a clue," Ryeth said. "Just when I thought I had a foot-hold on how the human to human interface should work, you turned up. I wasn't prepared for you. Maybe fate is more in control than we think."

She ran her finger down his cheek, her voice low and sultry, she said, "Are you prepared for me now?"

He swept her up into a powerful kiss. Alice Jane marveled at the soft lips that demanded her surrender. The smoldering kiss left her weak and breathing hard.

His stare bored deep. "What do you think?" he said. His voice was husky and full of passion.

Talking was no longer required.

Chapter 27

Ryeth woke to the soft sound of Alice Jane's breathing. He turned his head to face her. A strand of shiny black hair laying across her perfect face moved as he lightly blew it away. She was lovely; her lashes created a smoky shadow on the ivory of her cheek.

He questioned the fate that had brought them together. Fate, in his mind, balanced everything into an even playing field. If you were good, good things happened to you. Searching throughout his many years, he could summon no memory of a deed so remarkable that such a reward should come to him. If fate intended to play a dirty trick on him and take the reward away, it would be a lethal fight, for he would never give her up.

The perfect complement to his rough exterior occupied the other half of his heart. With her, he made sense.

He took a long look at her beautiful form and rose from his iron bed. The movement woke Alice. He turned and quickly planted a kiss on her sweet lips.

"Get ready, I want to take you somewhere today," he said.

"Ummm," she murmured. "I was dreaming." She stretched, splaying her arms out wide and arching her back. A moan escaped her lips as the strained muscles filled with energy.

"Dream your cute butt out of that bed," he said. "You've got some surprises coming your way today."

Her eyes opened wide. "Surprises?" she said and then vanished from his view.

She yelled from the shower, "Join me?"

Ryeth grinned from ear to ear in anticipation of the years ahead.

***

Within the hour, Alice Jane met Ryeth on the deck. He'd prepared a plate of fresh fruit topped with yogurt and granola. A steaming cup of coffee sat waiting for her.

"Thank you for breakfast," she said as she dipped a strawberry into the yogurt and bit into it.

"Where are you taking me?" she asked.

"To some of my favorite places. I was always alone when I enjoyed them. I'd like to know what it feels like to share something you love with another."

Since they hid nothing from each other, he read her thoughts. He had touched her heart with his simple request. Her emotions were so strong, he had to turn away.

Unfamiliar feelings went through his mind and ran rampant throughout his body. He sipped his coffee in an attempt to calm the flurry coursing through his veins.

He disliked the current lack of control he had over himself. If he wasn't in control, to his way of thinking, someone else was, and when someone else was in control, the scenario never played out in his favor. The urge to raise a protective wall grew from deep inside. He felt the wall rising and pushed it back with a vengeance. Nothing or no one would ever take her away from him - not even himself.

Her touch startled him. He reeled sharply and spilled his coffee on her foot.

"Oh," she said as she looked down at the stained shoe. "You're not perfect. I don't think I can accept that."

She turned and began to walk away. Over her shoulder she said, "And I thought this was the beginning of..."

She ran smack dab into him. He'd transported himself precisely in her path.

"It *is* the beginning of..." he said. Ryeth scooped her up, created a sphere, and transported them to her bedroom at Larkspur. "I believe you wanted to change shoes?" he said as he sat her feet down on the floor.

Alice Jane said, "You didn't tell me you could make a sphere. The only one I know who can do it is Jediah."

"A man has to have *some* mystery," he said.

She changed her shoes, stood next to him and the sphere took them back to his deck.

"I wonder if your mother could make one," said Alice Jane. "Can you imagine what the early settlers would have thought if they'd see it?"

"I know what they would have *done,*" he said with a slight nod.

"Oh, I guess you would know," she said. "Nasty stuff, those memories... Do you think your mom used a sphere to get inside Alexandra's mountain?"

Ryeth's eyes lit up. "Inside the mountain? So *that's* where the hideout is..." He shook his head. "I felt a strong Sensate presence at her arbor, but never once thought it was *inside.* I never put that one together."

"Your mother feared for the group she brought forth. And she was right to do so. Think of what Ari has suffered at the hands of the FSB."

Ryeth cringed and remembered his own interactions with those who didn't understand or feared his powers. He shook off the past. "How is Ari doing?" he asked.

As Alice Jane picked up the last melon bit, she said, "She seems to be conscious more. I've been able to give Jediah a detailed picture of the inside of her room, so he knows where all the security devices are located."

She drank the remainder of her coffee. "Ari keeps asking why we haven't gotten her out of there."

"She has no idea how much technology has advanced since she was captured. The biggest thing in her era was the radio," Ryeth said.

"I can't imagine being held somewhere for so long." Alice Jane said. "I wonder if we should prepare her for the shock. I'll bring that up to Val; he was amazing with Alexandra. You'd never know she had been drugged and tortured. Her recovery was unbelievable."

Ryeth's thoughts turned dark as his mind filled with memories of the shabby boat docked behind Magis' house. Visions of the fouled floor of the cabin and Alexandra's emaciated body covered in filth clouded his mind. His breathing quickened, his eyes narrowed, and his fists and jaw clenched.

Alice came to him and placed her hand on his shoulder. "Show me," she said.

He heard her words soft as a whisper.

Ryeth began his memory with his entry into the

cabin of the boat and finding Alexandra chained to the floor. He shared his intense rage and the mind control he'd used on Magis. He shared how he held Magis in the chair and nearly burst the blood vessels in his head with rapid surging blood. Rage, anger, shame and a final sense of justice passed through the conduit to her mind as she witnessed first-hand his part in Alexandra's escape.

He ended the image.

Ryeth's thoughts filled with compassion, which transferred to Alice Jane.

"I had no idea…," she said.

Chirping birds and the scent of balsam filled the air as the two were lost in thought.

She was never alone.

Two pair of eyes met instantly.

Alice Jane's eyes widened; Ryeth's turned into mere slits. Ryeth let his sense of outrage and strength flow freely.

A field of buttercups glistening in the noonday sun filled both their minds. Smells from a fresh spring day washed over them as the clear blue sky shone above.

The vision displayed a haze in the distance that ebbed closer until it began to take human form. Just before it materialized, the form halted and remained in the unfocused state floating slightly above the yellow field.

As quickly as the vision appeared, it vanished. The connection was gone.

"What was that?" asked Alice Jane.

"Well, it didn't come from me," Ryeth said. "My mind feels like a subway station with the amount of traffic it's had lately."

He splayed his arms wide. "What's next? I've

gone centuries without so much as a peep from anyone, and now, it seems like anyone can pop in, speak their two cents worth, paint a pretty picture, and pop out again."

His torment stopped midway as he heard the lilt of Alice Jane's laughter. The tenseness left his shoulders as he looked upon her beautiful face.

"What are you doing to me, woman?" he said as he shook his head. "I can't even get a good rant going without it being cut to the quick."

He cupped her face in his hands. His thumbs brushed her cheeks. As he brought his lips down to meet hers, he felt her warm body press close to his. Her breath smelled of strawberries.

He drank in the sensations that oozed from her every pore, and as he pulled away, he watched as violet eyes smoldered with his touch.

"I enjoy you," he said.

Her eyes twinkled. "And I you," she said. "I wish I'd known you sooner. I've wasted at least a hundred years."

Ryeth smiled into her eyes. "And I would've still had to wait almost four hundred to find you."

He played with a strand of her hair, then tucked her locks behind her shoulders.

"Who do you think that was?" she asked. "It had to be a Sensate."

"Yes, and whoever it was, stood by Alexandra when she was with Magis. But who?" He shrugged. "I have no idea."

"I wasn't involved when Alexandra was abducted," said Alice Jane. "I couldn't contribute much, and Jediah didn't ask for my help, so even though I kept tabs on what they were doing to get her back, I stayed away.

"I'm going to ask Alexandra," she said. "She may not want to talk about it, but I think we should try anyway. Let's stop by Heartseed before you take me on my surprise trip, okay?"

"Sure, it isn't like we have to worry about the traffic," he said. He took her hand in his, created his sphere, and they took flight.

Chapter 28

Ryeth moved the sphere slowly, and cleared the walls so Alice could enjoy the view. They paused before entering the air space of Heartseed, while Alice Jane made contact with Alexandra.

As they came to rest in the living room, Ryeth removed the sphere.

Jediah gave Ryeth a cockeyed smile and slapped him on the back. "I see you're traveling in style these days," he said.

"That's a little unfair," said Alexandra. "I've not been able to create one yet. You don't think it's a man-thing, do you?" she said to Alice Jane.

"Let's hope not," Alice said. "I'd hate to find out that gender had anything to do with our talents. Beside, we think Onatah, Ryeth's mother, might have used an orb to enter Balisier."

Ryeth caught Alexandra's and Jediah's shock.

"It's true," he said. "Onatah was my mother." He put his arm around Alice Jane and hugged her close. "Together, we were able to finish her story."

"We never knew what happened to her," said Jediah. He lowered his eyes. "She just ceased to exist. Most of our people knew *of* her, but only by hearsay. Ryeth, you *have* to tell her story to our people; they have a right to know what happened."

"I will, in time," he said.

"That's good enough for me," said Jediah. "What a wonderful piece of news. Just imagine, she and Genotah created all of us."

"It boggles the mind," said Alexandra. Her eyes were full of wonder. "Hey, I'm forgetting my role as hostess. Can I get you two something to drink?"

"No thanks," said Alice Jane. Ryeth shook his head.

Alice Jane walked over to Alexandra and took her hands in hers. "We need to ask you something."

"Sure, anything," Alexandra replied.

"When you were abducted, did you feel a presence?"

Alexandra's face paled. She dropped her hands and went to Jediah. He placed his arm around her shoulders.

Alexandra spoke slowly. "I don't have much memory of what happened to me, and I never tried to remember anything, especially since I was told it was so horrific. I figured any memory lost was a good thing."

"Alice," Jediah said, "why are you asking?"

"Honest, Alexandra, I have no wish to pry or bring up anything unpleasant. I'm even aware that I really have no right to ask." She hung her head, and then raised it to speak again.

"I wasn't there for you when you were abducted," Alice Jane said. "I wasn't there for Jediah. But I'm here now. The reason I'm asking is because just a few minutes ago a voice came to us. We'd been talking of your ordeal. When we paused to reflect, the voice said '*She was never alone*'."

The room grew quiet as all eyes were on Alexandra.

"I don't know what to say," said Alexandra. "What was the voice like? Was it male or female?"

Alice Jane looked to Ryeth, who shrugged. "It

showed us a field of yellow flowers," she said.

Alexandra's brow furrowed, "Buttercups?"

"Yes," answered Ryeth.

Alexandra paced the room. "I know the field, but I don't know how. I've seen it too. The voice is female. When I was stressed, she whispered to me *ane'mot,* which means…"

"Breathe," said Ryeth.

Alexandra looked at Ryeth and continued. "The voice called me *memiki."*

"Butterfly," said Ryeth. His heart pounded.

"Yes," said Alexandra, her eyes wide in amazement.

"How do you know the translation?" she asked Ryeth. "What language is it?"

"It is the language of my mother," he said. "The language of her people, the Algonquians or Iroquois."

Alexandra's face softened. "I've never been fearful of this voice," she said. "She was kind, and seemed to come from all around me; from everywhere, and from nowhere. I thought it was a dream."

The thoughts racing through Ryeth's mind were confused, chaotic, and needed an outlet.

"Thanks, Alexandra," said Ryeth. He needed to get out of there. He conveyed his urgent need to leave to Alice Jane.

Alice Jane hugged Alexandra, and kissed Jediah on the cheek. "We'll get back to you later. We're sorry we bothered you."

Ryeth's thoughts ran rampant. What was an Iroquois doing talking to them? Who was it? Why hadn't it spoken to him before? Why had it come to Alexandra in a time of need?

He created the sphere and they took immediate

flight.

***

"Are you okay?" Alice Jane asked Ryeth.

The orb glided over mountain tops and came to rest at the foot of the tree where they first met.

"I'm fine," he said. "I just have some thinking to do. Care to join me?" He motioned to the base of the tree.

There they sat, unspeaking, for hours. At first, Ryeth sat contented next to his age-old tree, but then he had a growing need to share the vastness of the forest with Alice Jane. As agreed, her mind was his to share, and vice versa.

He took her to many of the events that impacted his view of life. These places and events included the Jamestown settlement and the 1616 smallpox epidemic. Alice Jane saw firsthand the ravages of the disease.

Next came the horror of the 1500 children kidnapped in England who were brought in filthy ships under inhumane conditions to America for no other reason than to increase the number of settlers in Virginia.

Among the other stories he shared was the founding of Harvard University, the Salem witch trials, and the 1694 signing of the peace treaty between the colonists and the Iroquois.

She felt his smile and candor as he treated her to one specific piece of information. The year was 1823. Ryeth had taken the pledge to become part of the Pony Express. She heard his voice in her mind as clear as it had been when the words were uttered:

"While I am the employ of A. Majors, I agree not

to use profane language, not to get drunk, not to gamble, not to treat animals cruelly and not to do anything else that is incompatible with the conduct of a gentleman. And I agree, if I violate any of the above conditions, to accept my discharge without any pay for my services."

He heard Alice laugh at the old pledge, but she sobered when he shared a vision of a young Pony Express rider as he whipped by. Ryeth had the horse ready to go, and he passed the reins off to... none other than Jediah.

Ryeth watched the expressions cross over Alice Jane's face.

She sat straight up and looked him squarely in the face. "Did you know he was a Sensate back then?" she asked. Her eyes were wide. A smile began to inch over white teeth.

"I did," he said, "and if he hadn't been so focused on his mission, or falling off the horse during the transfer, he might have sensed me too."

"You'll have to tell him," she said. "He would get a kick out of it."

"Not me," he said. "I'm telling no tales."

"You'd rather be a man of mystery?" she asked.

"Why not? No one knew I existed until a few months ago. Just because I let you see part of me doesn't mean I want to let everyone in."

"Somehow," she said while stroking his cheek, "I think I've only begun to scratch the surface."

Ryeth reached over and pulled Alice Jane into his arms. As their lips met, the sphere appeared once more and whisked them away.

Chapter 29

Ryeth awoke the following day and rolled over to hug Alice Jane as she slept. His hand came up empty. He grumbled as he remembered their agreement.

The FSB monitored Alice Jane's movements, so she needed to be visible to prove that she had moved back to Waynesburg, which meant trips to the grocery store, errands to Bed, Bath and Beyond, and normal everyday activities.

Ryeth was *not* to be part of her daytime routine. They had agreed that he wasn't be to seen with any of those marked for surveillance. If all else failed, and Ari's rescuers were caught, the Sensates needed someone standing in the shadows who was willing to do whatever it took to make things right again. Ryeth fit that bill.

He took a few moments to check in with Chief Black. He'd forgotten to give her nerve endings a twist the previous evening, so her constant migraine should have subsided. His eyes narrowed as he thought to give her another twist.

As he flung his legs over the mattress and sat up, he rose to begin the day. During his shower, he listened in on Chief Black's day.

***

Morgan Black hadn't seen the whites of her eyes for days. Today, she no longer had to squint to shield the light. That blasted migraine lasted longer and was the most severe she'd ever had. She pushed thoughts of getting to a doctor away, straightened her shoulders and sneered into the mirror in the lavatory at the FSB.

A deep-seated part of her blamed the red-haired witch in captivity for her recent headaches. What if the heathen 613 knew Black held the reins that controlled her pathetic life? The lower dosage of meds could have allowed 613 to reach out and cause the migraines.

Black went to her office and scrutinized the data that contained 613's neural activity backlog. The data presented no changes, not even the tiniest of blips.

She brushed the idea aside that 613 was involved in her migraines and attributed the onset to stress. Perhaps she was just being paranoid. For all she knew 613 could be a vegetable. Beside, the migraines had stopped.

Today, she planned to up the stakes and visit 613 personally. Up to now, she had monitored from afar controlling the strings like a puppet master. The lower doses in 613's system meant that if any neural activity remained, 613 was close to coming out of her chemical fog.

Black assembled her team. They were seated before her in the preparation room; the room closest to 613. She scrutinized their faces.

"I apologize for the short notice. I just decided this morning to step up the testing on 613. Her medications are now at a level where we can determine whether or not she can be of any use to us."

Black looked hard at her five core members.

She hand-picked them for their professionalism, skill, and ability to carry out orders without question.

The last trait, the one she deemed most valuable, proved difficult to find. She had located them among the psychological evaluation borderline rejects.

"I want all of you to remember what's at stake," she said. "The actions we take here today could initiate the beginning of a new era; one that changes the face of warfare. If we can harness the power of teleportation and perhaps telekinesis, the future will be ours to command."

Black considered those before her. Though they followed her instructions with no forethought of the consequences, she was certain they hadn't grasped the importance of their venture. The team might have a theoretical concept, but until they witnessed firsthand, they would not fully believe.

She inwardly sneered their little minds. Although they were the best in their fields, their inability to see through to the impossible hindered their efforts. Perhaps a bit more information would open their minds…

Black watched her team as she said, "613 has been held in a medicated state since 1956. At that time, she exhibited the ability to teleport. We would have lost her then if she had known her way around. She accidently teleported into the lab where she was tranquilized immediately."

The deadpan faces blinked as their eyes grew wide. Some shifted positions in their seat; another coughed and looked around.

Black knew she was re-stating the obvious, but, for the record, she continued. "We can *not* let her escape. It isn't just my career on the line, but each of yours as well."

Her eyes narrowed into slits as she bore into those of her team. "If any of you fail me in this mission, be prepared to collect garbage for the remainder of your years, for you will never work in a high level position again."

Not one of the team members moved an inch. Satisfied she had their full attention and that they were all on the same page, Black assigned each their areas of responsibilities.

***

Ryeth shot the High Counsel a message that contained Black's intentions. Alice Jane appeared at his side.

"What's Ari's current status?" he asked, as she led him to Balisier.

When they arrived at Balisier, instead of speaking, Alice shared her connection to Ari telepathically with him and the members of the High Counsel.

Ryeth took a quick look at those in the room. "What's your take on this, Jediah?" he asked.

"Ari is definitely at risk. As for us, if she becomes alert, she might compromise our position even more," said Jediah.

Val said, "Alice Jane, take a seat here next to me." He motioned for her to come. "I want you to monitor her vital signs, what she sees and feels, and share them with me."

Alice did as requested.

"Ryeth, please take a seat on the opposite side here." He patted the couch. "I want you to enter Ari's mind and talk to her without stopping. You indicated earlier that she said she would leave her mind open to you. It is my hope that if she *does* regain consciousness, you can access her first."

Val addressed the remainder of the group. "Without knowing what the FSB has in mind, it is hard to predict her responses. We might be flying by the seat of our pants here. If a critical situation occurs, the first to react should not be held responsible if things go awry. Agreed?"

The others gave quick nods.

"Alexandra," said Val, "please monitor the complete process and keep the rest of the group updated."

Alexandra chose a seat apart from the others.

"Jediah, this is important," said Val, "I want you to connect to Alexandra and keep a constant sense of serenity flowing through to Ari. The combination of both your strengths should be enough to keep her somewhat under control. We can not have her startled in any way if she regains conscious."

"Val, it's a great plan," said Jediah. He turned toward Ryeth. "Ryeth, that leaves you to 'see' and interpret everything through Chief Black and share with us."

"Will do," said Ryeth.

Jediah looked around the room and received nods from all. "Let's get underway."

James and William moved to the opposite side of the room. Jediah took a seat next to Alexandra. All minds were open to each other to monitor the situation at hand. The scene formed in all their minds as Ryeth began by entering Black's mind.

***

Black led the group into 613's room. They filed in one by one and surrounded her gurney.

The physician pulled his cart next to Ari and withdrew a syringe and needle. He screwed the needle onto the syringe, uncapped the top of a bottle and filled the syringe. Lifting the IV port, he inserted a needle into the port and slowly injected some of the contents. He stepped back to monitor 613's vital signs displayed on the wall monitor and then nodded to Black.

The neurologist pulled back the lid of 613's eye, checked the readings on the printout for neural activity and shook his head.

A soft silky voice came from Black's mouth. It was so foreign to the team that that all eyes were drawn to her instantly.

Feeling their eyes on her, she glared at them in return, yet the soft silky voice continued.

"You are safe. No one can harm you. You can relax now, there is nothing to fear."

Black continued her soft chant. "Arizona, you are safe. I can help you."

Black motioned to the physician. He reached for the syringe and administered a second dose. Again, he stepped back.

"Arizona, wake from your dream," said the cooing Black. "No one will harm you." Her voice coaxed gently, like that of a mother. "I will protect you. Wake up, Arizona. You don't have to worry anymore."

Black glared at the neurologist. He shrugged and then reached to check for pupil dilation again. He jumped and pulled his hand away as 613's eyes opened wide.

"We are here to help you," Black said in a

comforting voice."

613 looked at Black and stared, and then slowly closed her eyes.

Black motioned to the doctor to administer another dose. He complied, but 613 failed to rouse.

Knowing three doses were the limit without compromising 613's life, Black spun around and stormed out the door.

She entered her office and slammed the door. Failure cut to the quick and enraged her. 613 had roused from the drugs. The creature even had the audacity to stare at her. What had happened? Did the witch will herself back to an unconscious state? If she could do that, why didn't she attempt something more to escape? Or had Black underestimated 613 altogether? Had she ruined 613's mind?

Black watched the live feed from 613's room. Her team stood alongside 613 and appeared lost without direction. She punched a button on her desk.

Her voice came over the loud speaker in 613's room. "None of you is to leave her side until you are sure she is safely back under the effects of the drugs. I hold each of you personally responsible if anything happens." She punched the button to turn off her microphone.

Once 613 was stable, she'd try again.

Chapter 30

Ari, they're gone now, said Ryeth.

I saw her, said Ari. Ryeth sensed her loathing. *She thought to fool me with her sickening sweet voice.*

Ryeth was quick to caution Ari. *Don't think about her, your emotions will show on their readouts. Keep your mind clear.*

I will, she said. Ryeth felt Ari's hope. *Are you going to get me out of here?* she asked.

Yes. Ryeth pushed confidence and patience to Ari.

I will wait. The machines are moving again. I have to protect... her voice trailed off.

Ryeth closed the connection.

"That was close," said Jediah. He looked at Ryeth. "If you hadn't been on top of Black, today's activities could have meant disaster for us."

Jediah spun around to address the group, grinning from ear to ear. "What a wonderful team effort. It was like having a fine oiled machine at our fingertips."

Jediah walked over to Val and shook his hand. "Doc, you nailed that one."

Val shook his head. "I can't believe the power in this room. We never faltered once. Ryeth and Alice Jane - what a tremendous addition you two are to our group."

"If ever there was a time for us to join our powers together it was today," said Jediah. "We thwarted Black's attempt. Now, Ari knows their intentions and she won't be fooled into believing them."

Ryeth spoke. "I think she trusted us because we called her Ari. We had no idea of her real name, Arizona. She recognized us as friends. She listened to us first."

"It's a good thing that happened," said Alexandra. "That Black was like a snake charmer. She knew exactly what to say to make Ari feel at ease. What a slime ball."

Jediah poked fun at his wife. "A slime ball?"

Alexandra turned red. "It was the nicest thing I could think to call her."

Jediah smiled. "Since we are all here, we can finalize our plans for the rescue."

James broke in. "It's not a good time for me. I have to get back to the office; I left a client sitting there," he said just before vanishing.

"I have to get back to Wal~Mart," said Alice Jane. The FSB tracked me there and I ducked into the bathroom so I could come here. In order to make this bathroom break work, I might have to buy some Kaopectate."

Her dilemma caused Alexandra and the others to laugh.

Alice Jane rolled her eyes, "The things we have to do to keep up appearances..." The lovely girl with violet eyes left.

Ryeth's face was skewed. "What's K O Pectate?"

William guffawed. "You're gonna have to look that one up yourself, sonny."

"Fine," said Jediah. "If no other emergency takes place, let's meet at four."

***

Safely back home, Ryeth went straight to his computer and typed in K O Pectate. Somewhat miffed at the results, his face broadened into a smile at Alice Jane's resourcefulness. She played the game well.

Never sick a day in his life, and with keeping his distance from non-Sensates, he'd never had to resort to any ruse to appear normal. When he looked in his medicine chest, it never occurred to him that antiseptic ointments, aspirin, cold tablets, allergy pills, or even spray powders for jock itch should reside there.

He glanced down at his arm; the scar from the wild boar was barely visible. By all accounts, it should have gotten infected.

The Sensates covered their existence well. So what had triggered the FSB in the first place? Did the UFO sightings in the forties cause people to become scared of each other? Was there more?

Something didn't sit well.

The group met at four as planned. Ryeth was impressed with their resourcefulness. He knew how big business operated. Endless meetings with the forward progress of a snail. No so with the Sensates proper. Never before had he witnessed such teamwork and follow-through.

He suffered a pang of regret for not seeking them out earlier.

After the meeting, Ryeth propped his feet up on the rail of his deck. He was impressed with the team's progress on the blue suit. The retrofit of the temperature stabilizer was pretty darned ingenious.

They had even adjusted the mechanism to auto adjust to ambient temperatures on the fly.

The last step to complete was the addition of the VUV module. The actual unit was so small it fit in his hand. Granted, his hand was larger than most, but it was still a credit to their ingenuity.

They required another week for testing, but after that, the team would select the individual who would wear the suit and extract Ari from the FSB facility. The process would involve the creation of an orb. If he had assessed the Sensates correctly, only he and Jediah had that ability.

As he considered the options, he arrived at the conclusion that he was the most logical choice, because *he* was an unknown. The FSB didn't have his fingerprints, nor did they have his DNA. If a miniscule particle managed to escape their blue suit, it could not be traced back to him or them.

Heck, even if the FSB did figure out it was him, what did he care? No cell could hold him. In any volatile situation, he could surround himself with his orb and escape unnoticed.

He doubted Jediah knew how to shield himself by using it. Over the years, Ryeth tested his orb against bullets, fire, and lasers. If he was confident of one thing, it was his mind.

They would never control him like Ari. In her defense, she was young and inexperienced when they took her. Maybe he was giving himself too much credit; he did recall a certain Sensate tied to a stake...

He smiled as pictures of Black stomping around filled his mind; he closed his eyes to see her more clearly.

***

"You mean to tell me that when she opened her eyes we didn't pick up so much as an inkling in our data?" asked Black.

The small group assembled in her office. The doctor and neurologist both confirmed flat lines in their data. 613's heart rate hadn't wavered one beat.

"How is that even possible?" she said.

The neurologist was the first to speak. From his demeanor, she knew he was afraid to say too much. "She could have come into consciousness and immediately controlled her reactions," he said. "It's possible that she's been conscious for a while, controlling her reactions, and making us think she was still affected by the medications."

"If that's so," said Black, "we might already be playing with fire."

"That's what I was thinking," he said.

She looked at the two men sitting before her. They shifted in their seats. Why hadn't they warned her of this potential outcome? Still, they were the best she could find. She gritted her teeth and hissed. "Leave me."

They rose to go.

She raised the level of her voice and said, "And don't come back until you can tell me how we can be assured of her neural state."

Ryeth forwarded this last bit of news to Jediah. Black might be on to Ari.

Chapter 31

Alexandra slid onto the porch swing next to Jediah. She recognized the furrow of his brow easy enough to know he was deep in thought, so she leaned in close.

He leaned back and placed his arm around her shoulders. "I've been playing out different scenarios in my mind. Each time, I try to figure out what happens if the person extracting Ari is caught."

He heaved a mighty sigh. "No matter what, it comes down to the same person wearing the suit," he said.

"It's Ryeth, isn't it?" she said.

"Yes." His shoulders sagged. "What right do we have to ask him to take on this responsibility?"

Jediah rose and paced. "The best plan I have so far is for all the 'known' DNA people to be highly visible as the operation goes down. That's easy enough to organize. It could be a welcome-to-town for Alice Jane and held at Larkspur. Terry Gooch, would be front and center. As far as he knows, he's still just the gardener. We could stay within his sight the whole time. It's a perfect cover."

"It's a good plan, Jediah," she said. "I understand why you don't want to involve Ryeth in such a risky venture, especially since he owes us nothing."

She stood and placed her hand on Jediah's shoulder. "When you were my Angel of Light, he took on the job of darkness. It's his way. He knows what's at stake; he knows his abilities through and through, and he has a hwihs on his shoulder. Ryeth is supposed to be a strong part of our Sensate community. He's essential to the Prophecy."

She spoke her last words as a plea. "He may want the opportunity to prove himself to others."

He smiled down at her. She felt his arm slide lower as he pulled her close. "I forget your wisdom," he said. "Like Ryeth you have a part to play if we are to survive. We have a few days to decide, but I'll keep your words in mind. I intend for the High Council to have the final say in the matter. It should be more than one person's decision."

"The timing is important too," said Alexandra. "People are in and out of Ari's room all the time. They come in to bathe her, feed her, fix her hair; and there's that physical therapist that comes in twice a day to keep her muscles from atrophying. She even gets Ari up and forces her to put weight on her legs and back muscles. Ari is drugged out of her mind. If it weren't for the therapist's two helpers, I'd worry for her safety."

"So you're thinking of an evening house warming party for Alice Jane?" asked Jediah.

She nodded. "But you knew that, didn't you? And you let me rattle on and on. Your sister was right, you are a brute."

"Ah, I do love to hear you rattle," he said.

She toyed with a lock of his hair. As the thought struck her, she said, "If we're having a party, I'm inviting Cassie."

"It's not a *real* party. Do you think we should involve her?" he asked.

A bit miffed, she said, "If someone is watching

me, and I'm giving a party, wouldn't they think it odd that I didn't invite my best friend?" She studied Jediah. Would he impose more guidelines for her to follow? If he did, he was going to have one fired up Sensate to deal with.

"You're probably right, it shouldn't just be the people the FSB are watching; that would be too perfect," he said.

His answer didn't give her any satisfaction. He only gave in because it was the right thing to do; not because he recognized she missed her best friend.

Dang, this Sensate business festered inside. Only a few short months ago her life was carefree. She could come and go as she pleased, daydream without transporting to the site of her daydream, and confide in Cassie one hundred percent. Her life had certainly taken on a new direction, and no matter how hard she tried, she begrudged the rules and precautions that had entered her life without her permission.

She pushed her aggravation aside. It had been a whole month since she'd laid eyes on the brown haired, brown-eyed moppet - she couldn't really count the slip up that ended her in Cassie's bedroom.

The excitement of seeing her confidant started to ebb its way into her mind and pushed the annoyance to the back of her mind. She knew she would have to be on her best behavior throughout the party, but no matter how it ended, she knew it would be a joyous reunion.

***

The High Counsel met once the testing on the blue suit was complete. It was undergoing intensive outside cleaning to remove any trace elements from the exterior, interior and mechanics.

Ryeth watched the members as they gathered around the table. He listened while each offered their plan for the extraction; now it was his turn to speak.

He stood to address the group. "All of your ideas have merit. That you each selected yourself for the job attests to your honor and commitment. The only difference between your ideas and mine is that deep down, you know it has to be either Jediah or myself. And," he straightened his shoulders, "if we dig even further down, we all know I am the right person for the job."

No one said a word. "Look guys," Ryeth said "why don't we quit wasting time in deciding *who* and get on with the actual *how*?"

"I don't like it," said William.

Ryeth paced, the hair rising at the nape of his neck. "What could *you* possibly have against my going? I thought you'd clap a hand on my back and say 'good riddance'", he said.

"And that's exactly why you shouldn't go," yelled William. "You don't know all you think you know. For all your years you're like a cocky young pup. If you think they aren't planning on us making a move, you're wrong. Whoever goes has to have a good head on his shoulders. I just don't know if that's you."

Ryeth's ire rose. "First I'm a boy, and now a young pup. Listen here, old man, I've been in more scrapes than you can shake your cane at, and I have survived just fine. You don't see me worried that the FSB is hot on *my* trail, do you?"

Ryeth felt Jediah's serenity begin to wash over him. He spun on a dime and said, "Stop your interference, Jediah. I don't like being controlled."

He no longer felt Jediah's calming effects. The room grew quiet. Ryeth scanned the members, his gaze came to rest on Alice Jane's face.

His face softened. "William, what is it that has you so against me?"

"You're a loose cannon," said William. "We don't know you well enough to figure out what you'd do in a given situation. I can't place my trust in an unknown. I'd have the same misgivings about any new Sensate."

"That's where you're wrong, William," said Ryeth. "I'm not a *new* Sensate, I'm just new to you. I'm seasoned, and I fly under the radar. Believe me, one time tied to the stake was enough. I learned early on to take care of number one."

"So," said William, "we're back to that again."

Ryeth threw his hands up. "I'm stating facts. You had each other; I never had that luxury," he said. "I'm standing here today as living proof that there are different ways to achieve a goal. I offer a solution, nothing more."

He ran his fingers through his hair. Before he sat, he turned to Jediah, "I'm sorry I bit your head off."

"No problem, Ryeth," he said. "We needed to know if you would stand and fight, or if you would take yourself to parts unknown if you met with conflict."

Ryeth's face fell. "This was a test?" he said. He glared at William. "You baited me?"

William shrugged, leaned back in his chair and then rubbed a stone with his thumb. "I was the logical choice," he said.

Alexandra said, "They did the same thing to me,

Ryeth. I was always leaping without thinking, and I let emotions play a major part in my decision making. I now leave my emotions behind when I enter this room."

"Ryeth," said Jediah, "as much as we hate it, we agree that you're our best candidate. But, I want you to know that our reservations had nothing to do with your capabilities. It had to do with responsibility. We felt you shouldn't *have* to save our respective butts."

Chapter 32

A Lear jet landed at Pittsburg International Airport in the early morning and taxied to a stop at an exclusive hanger. John Ryan gathered his briefcase and carry-on. As he stepped off the plane he reached into his pocket for the keys to the black SUV parked nearby.

The flight had been an easy one; use of the company jet was always an added advantage. He smiled. He like his job for the most part. The perks were great even though some subtle parts of his business were nearly unpalatable. Most people could probably say the same. No job was one hundred percent enjoyable.

After depositing his carry-on in the rear storage area of the SUV, he got behind the wheel, started the engine and read the dials. The tank was full. Sitting on the passenger's seat was a box, gift-wrapped, with a beautiful bow. Attention to detail.

He dropped off his briefcase and luggage at his apartment and then pointed the SUV toward Wheeling. In a little over an hour he reached his destination.

As he pulled in the driveway, he noticed the drapes flutter in the second story bedroom window. He reached to turn off the engine. By the time he opened the door, Cassie was already racing down the front walkway of the picturesque colonial to greet him. Her hair moved in luxurious bouncy waves as she met him halfway up the walkway and slid into his arms.

"I could get used to this type of homecoming," he said as he hugged her. He kissed her smiling lips.

"I'm so glad you could make it for Alice Jane's housewarming," she said as he placed his arm around her waist and they strolled arm-in-arm up the walkway. "I was afraid you wouldn't make it back in time from your trip."

He stopped and mocked a stern look. "You did tell me your mom was making homemade waffles and sausage this morning, didn't you?"

"Yep, just for you," she said.

He opened the front door and held it for Cassie to enter. The smell of warm maple syrup and the vanilla scent from a steaming waffle iron welcomed him. The recipe passed down from generations was, by far, the best he'd ever tasted.

"Cassie, my love, if you can cook like your mother, I just might steal you away forever," John said.

As they walked into the kitchen, the Hudson's welcomed the man who had become an integral part of their family with friendship.

"You're timing is perfect, John," said Mrs. Hudson. "Pull up a chair, we're just about to dig in."

The group sat family style around the kitchen table instead of eating in the more formal dining room. For John, the atmosphere was bittersweet.

John imagined a family exactly like this one many years ago when he huddled for warmth against the winter elements in an abandoned car. Those years were tough, but living on the streets taught him survival of the fittest and gave him keen insights into the baser instincts of man.

When a street-wise cop caught his talent for survival by the scruff of the neck, John envisioned a loftier, law-abiding goal.

This family, their acceptance and warmth, was all he ever wanted. His thoughts were interrupted by Mr. Hudson.

"John," said Mr. Hudson, "tell us all about your trip."

Within an hour, and sated by two helpings of Grandma's Waffles, he was back on the road with Cassie by his side, headed for an enjoyable day in Waynesburg.

He had come to care for the Saffles. Alexandra had so much warmth, and Jediah was a pillar of the community. His feelings for the Saffles, however, couldn't compare to what he felt for the lively girl sitting next to him. He hadn't planned on falling for her, but she'd captivated him with her openness and zest for life.

Chapter 33

All hands were busy readying Larkspur for the house warming as John and Cassie pulled their SUV around the circle drive of Larkspur.

Alexandra spied the car and ran to greet Cassie and John.

"I haven't seen you in a coon's age," said Alexandra. She hugged her friend.

"I know," said Cassie. "It feels like forever."

Jediah came up alongside them. He held out his hand to John. "Good to see you again, John," said Jediah.

Alexandra leaned over and kissed John on the cheek. "I'm so glad you could make it," she said.

"Me too," said Jediah, "I could use some help setting up."

John smiled. "Point me to the work and I'll get started." He looked over his shoulder for Cassie, but she was already walking and talking with Alexandra. They disappeared around the corner of the house.

Jediah slapped his back. "You can try and get a word in edgewise today, but I doubt you'll succeed," he said to John.

John shook his head, "What do they have to talk about?" he asked.

"Everything, they talk about everything," said Jediah. "I gave up wondering about the content, it took too much of my time."

When they turned the corner and John saw the bustle of activity, Jediah explained that they planned to keep the party small out of respect for Nancy Jane's passing, but threw out the idea knowing how much Nancy loved a party.

Jediah and John carried bags of ice to the refrigerator in the garage and Alice Jane setup tables in the rear yard.

Alexandra commandeered the kitchen with Cassie and in a short time all caught the wafted scents of their labors. Taking a quick break, they served a light lunch for the group at a table in the yard.

As they sat, Val and James came through the hedge.

"We're glad to see you have everything under control," said James. "Val and I were just walking by and smelled cookies. You *do* have cookies, don't you Alexandra?"

"I can see through you guys," said Alice Jane. "You had no intention of helping, did you? You just wanted food."

Val poked James in the ribs. "I told you they'd never fall for that 'walking by' ploy. Now that we've been caught, we'll *have* to help."

"Okay." James sighed. "What do you need done?"

"Sit down and have brunch first," said Alexandra, "then you can bring the chairs out from the garage."

James poked Val as they sat down. "I told you we'd get to eat," he said.

As the group ate and joked, Jediah didn't miss the watchful eye coming from the tool shed's window. He sensed Terry Gooch's presence early in the day and shared the FSB's surveillance of their activities with the other Sensates.

He's taking quite a gamble that we don't need anything from the shed, said Jediah to all.

Jediah sensed Alexandra's indignation as she said, *I wonder how many times he used that ploy in the past?*

I supposed quite a few, said Jediah. *He's been spying on us for at least four years. I wonder why they started watching Larkspur in the first place?*

Val elbowed Jediah. *You're just now wondering that?* he asked. *It's been sticking in my craw for days now. What the devil tipped them off?*

Jediah rubbed his chin. *I have no idea,* he said. *I just thank my lucky stars that even though we were within our home, Mom always demanded we maintain a circumspect household. Anything Sensate related was always handled telepathically. I'm quite certain Terry didn't learn anything from his observations.*

Well, no sense letting your gardener be too comfortable, said James, *we'll keep someone within sight of the tool shed door. Let's see how long his bladder lasts.*

***

Jonathan met Ryeth in the counsel room to take him to the prep area.

"Welcome to Balisier," said Jonathan as he held out his hand.

Taking his hand, Ryeth sensed Jonathan's awe at their first meeting. He lowered his eyes and cleared his throat. "Thanks."

"Sorry," said Jonathan, dropping his hand, "it's just that you've become the talk of the town, and I got to meet you first."

The slight puffing of Jonathan's chest caught his eye causing irritation to rise within. He would need to keep his wayward emotions in check to complete the task at hand. The unexpected petulance with less-than-useful reactions could be an ongoing nuisance.

As they left the room, he couldn't believe his eyes. It was true that he had seen unimaginable sights throughout his life, but Balisier inspired awe. Looking back over his shoulder, he realized they had been in a third floor room.

The outside hallway consisted of a wide ledge with a stone railing that overlooked a meticulous courtyard brimming with luscious plants. Wisteria draped an arbor with a swing; a stone pathway twisted and turned around shrubbery, flowers and trees dotted the internal landscape. That this habitat resided within a mountain was unbelievable.

Jonathan led him around the side of the building where the walkway ended at the top of a granite stairway. The Sensates in their stroke of genius had carved the structures from the mountain itself. Had Alice Jane not shared the creation of their village in great detail, he might have been stunned. As it was, his feet stopped moving in order to study the marvel before him.

What courage it must have taken for Onatah, his mother, to follow the roar of the great river and go inside the mountain where desire carried her within to a massive waterfall that emptied into a bottomless chasm. Balisier was born that day out of a need for a safe harbor for people of her kind. Pride burst in his chest. His mother's fortitude was responsible for the grandeur that lay before his eyes.

As Jonathan led him to the prep area, Ryeth pictured initial crude structures honed over the centuries by the Sensates' engineering expertise into the remarkable facility he saw today. The lighting alone was hard to fathom, for the internal village had the appearance of a summer day.

When Alice Jane told him of Balisier, she'd held back actual visions and failed to convey its splendor. He couldn't blame her; he lacked the words to describe it himself.

After strolling through a quaint park and passing a variety of shops, they arrived at their destination.

Jonathan held open the door of a quaint limestone building for him to enter. He was dumbfounded at the interior. The latest in technology stood before him. It took him a few minutes to appreciate the complete process.

The space deemed the 'prep room' was, in reality, a mini state-of-the-art facility, which would make the Center for Disease Control drool.

Individual rooms set up for each person's expertise lined the right-hand wall. The left side contained an array of mechanical devices, including a six-foot 3D printer and the assorted materials required to fabricate essential parts. CAD drawings were spread out on a large table in the center of the room that also served as an open conference area.

The back of the space contained glass walls that separated the clean room dressing area, the pressure lock, and the fully-equipped clean room, which now held the no-questions-asked blue suits.

Jonathan's voice broke into his thoughts. "Ryeth, would you like to meet the additional Ultras who are overseeing the project?"

"By all means," he said. "I can't help but marvel at the speed in which this was implemented. You guys are phenomenal."

"Thanks, it's nice to be appreciated," said Jonathan.

"Before the introductions, could you explain exactly what an 'Ultra' is?"

Jonathan seemed a bit amused. "Oh, I assumed Alice Jane filled you in on that one."

Ryeth raised his eyebrows. "Nope," he said. "Guess she assumed I knew as well."

"Well then," said Jonathan, "Ultras have a higher power strength than the normal, if you can call us 'normal,' Sensate. There are only a few of us: Jediah, Alexandra, Alice Jane, Reslyn, MacAila, you, and me." Jonathan gave a small chuckle. "Until the last few months, we were three less. We've grown quite a bit."

Nodding his head, Ryeth said, "If the Prophecy is, indeed, upon us, the greater the power of our core, the better off we will be."

"Your point is well taken," said Jonathan.

Ryeth's eye caught movement. He turned his head to see two very striking women coming toward them.

"Ryeth, I'd like you to meet a gorgeous redhead, MacAila," Jonathan said, "and a striking blonde bombshell, Reslyn."

"He never stops," said Reslyn to Ryeth.

"Yeah," said MacAila, "always with the grand, flowery introductions. You can tell he's not married."

Reslyn placed her hand on Jonathan's shoulder, "We love him," she said, "even though he's still coming on strong after 25 years of the same old stuff."

"It's good to have you with us, Ryeth," said MacAila, tossing her long red hair back over her shoulder.

"Sure is," said Reslyn. "We will be getting you ready to snatch Ari. You can get started with MacAila."

MacAila led him to the dressing area.

The technique for putting on the blue suit was elaborate. The three Ultras used the second suit to instruct him in the process.

MacAila, was in charge of ensuring Ryeth understood the helmet closure. If he nipped the material during the process, he could compromise the suit and their venture. Ryeth practiced several times until he had it perfected.

Next, he moved to Jonathan's station where he learned the precise method for sealing the boots and gloves, which had been retrofitted to his size. The closures were similar to the helmet's, so they were easy to master.

Last, he met with Reslyn who instructed him in the complete operation of the suit. The VUV controls, which were pre-set to automatic, required no action unless the suit was punctured. One switch turned on all the additional functions.

Once he became proficient at every task, the group set up a gurney and placed MacAila on it. Ryeth concentrated on the task at hand. A sparkling red orb with dark gray edges appeared that encased MacAila, himself, and the gurney. He smiled and gave the team the thumbs up.

As he started moving the sphere, it wobbled. The sides fluctuated back and forth until he was able to maintain the proper proportions. He floated the orb containing himself, MacAila, and the gurney to the High Counsel's meeting room, set them down and dissolved the sphere. He reversed the operation and moved her back to the prep room.

"Let's do it a few more times," said Jonathan, "and this time, make the orb invisible."

"Roger that," said Ryeth.

He made the proper mental changes to the method and completed the procedure several times without a flaw.

"That was a sight to see," Reslyn said. "We were told you had powers, but that sphere was impressive. One minute Mac and the gurney were there; the next, poof, they were gone."

"It was a bit sketchy in the beginning," Ryeth said, turning to MacAila. "I'm glad I didn't drop you."

"You were worried you'd drop me?" said MacAila. "I'm glad you didn't tell me that before. I was nervous enough already. Flying through the air in an orb is certainly not the same as teleporting."

Ryeth explained. "It uses another process. Would you like to try?"

The question was answered with resounding yesses from the three.

Ryeth gave them the mechanism, but without the innate ability, none could achieve the orb.

"I'm sorry," he said. "The sphere is one of my favorite abilities. I've wondered for decades if anyone else had experimented as much as I have with its possibilities."

"Only Jediah can help you with that one," said Jonathan.

Ryeth rubbed his chin, his eyebrows raised, "I guess I'll have to wait. We're not at the bosom buddy stage yet."

Reslyn smiled and cleared her throat. "So, do you feel comfortable with the process?" she said.

"Yes, I think so. The last few times it felt really smooth. The grab and snatch should come off without a hitch, if we stick to the plan," said Ryeth. "Just be prepared for anything."

"We've added a bit of negative pressure to the suit's capabilities, just in case there's a puncture," said Jonathan. "The suit will suck in for five seconds before it reaches equilibrium and begin to leak. If anything weird happens, you have those seconds to make a decision."

"It sounds like you've covered everything," said Ryeth. "I'll meet you back here at four. Go time is four thirty-seven. Everyone should be seated for Alexandra's meal by then."

"Sounds great," said MacAila. "If you think of anything between now and then, just give us a holler."

"Will do," said Ryeth. He created a sphere and transported himself to Larkspur to check on the activity.

***

On arrival at Larkspur, he kept the sphere invisible and floated around the property. When he spied Alice Jane he said, *Meet me upstairs, away from prying eyes.*

I'm on my way, came the reply.

He watched as she laid down the table cloths and walked into the house. She used the balcony stairs that led to the upstairs library. On her way up, she paused at the landing to look over the yard preparations.

Ryeth's orb came to a halt in the library and then vanished. Alice Jane was soon by his side away from the windows.

He kissed her long and hard as his arms held her tight. When he felt her legs sag, he pulled away. Half-lidded smoky eyes stared back at him. Her lips, red with passion, said, "Is everything all right?"

"Yes, I just wanted to check in on you. Is everything okay here?" he asked.

"We're putting on the show. Our audience is in the tool shed." She walked over to the window and pulled the drapery aside just enough to peer through. "See? It's that building at the back of the lot."

"He's got a good view," he said.

"After Terry arrived, we set the tables so we'd all be visible," she said.

"How many are coming," he asked.

Alice Jane released the drape. "I think about twenty-five or so. The known Sensate DNAers plus a few more from our group; Alexandra's close friend Cassie and her boyfriend, John; and some non-Sensate friends from Waynesburg. Just enough people to give credence to the affair," she said.

"Good." He gave her a squeeze.

"Do you think the plan will work?" she asked.

"If anything goes wrong it won't be for lack of planning," he said with a lop-sided smile.

"Be careful, okay?" she said. "If it looks too risky, drop it and we'll try again later."

Ryeth murmured deep in his chest. The audible sound was a deep purr. "No one has worried over me in a *very* long time."

He leaned down and kissed her once more. Firm and commanding lips met soft and pliable ones. Mid-kiss he transported home, leaving, he hoped, a damsel who hungered for more.

After a few minutes at home, Ryeth's thoughts went to Terry Gooch's spying from the shed. He considered transporting a skunk to the shed to keep him company, but didn't want to cause a stink. He grinned at his pun; it wasn't often he felt this lighthearted.

His brows came together fast as he shook off the unfamiliar feeling. His jaw clenched. He could assume the role of contentment *maybe*, but happy? That wasn't in his emotional repertoire.

A man, Sensate or not, doesn't develop 'happy' as a normal emotion when he's lived Ryeth's life. Too many years of solitude, filled with loathing for others like himself had hardened him. He liked the man he'd become; he could stop the most macho man with merely a look. He liked the confidence and power he exuded.

He knew he had a softer side. He felt it when he visited the age-old pawcohiccora in his woods, and he felt it with Alice Jane.

Alexandra was different. Her aura punctured his outer shell and hit him directly in his soft spot. Irritation caught in his throat. Even though she used no powers to accomplish the feat, it was as intrusive as Jediah's serenity. His lip curled.

He used no powers on the Sensates to accomplish his goals, and that's the way he preferred it. Tricks to prove a point, the games they played... No. He liked the simple straight-forward approach, and if feathers got ruffled, so be it.   He had to be part of the Prophecy, but part of them? Never.

Chapter 34

At four o'clock on the button, Ryeth transported to the prep area at Balisier.

He entered the dressing area where he removed all of his clothing except for a pair of form-fitting briefs. It took him twenty minutes to enter the clean room and get into the blue suit. The Ultras were there to assist.

After the suit was on, he added the gloves and helmet. As he switched on the VUV apparatus, he glanced at the prep team and gave them the 'thumbs-up.'

Well, it looks like everything is all set, he said to the team.

Jonathan checked the readout on his screen and said, *Everything looks A-OK from this end.*

As one last precaution, he entered Chief Black's mind to ensure she was not on site. She wasn't at the FSB, but she was involved in some sort of meeting involving trace elements.

Leaving now, Ryeth said to the Ultras and High Counsel.

After one last look over his shoulder at the team, he began his two hundred-fifty-mile journey from Waynesburg to Dayton in his invisible orb. He arrived outside the FSB facility within a minute or two. The orb moved through the exterior walls without notice, so he continued forward until he found the area where Ari was held.

Ryeth entered the outside of her detention area and checked the circle hallway surrounding Ari's room. A guard was posted outside her door.

Okay so far, he communicated to Jediah, who nodded to the others sitting around the tables at Larkspur.

He concentrated on the task at hand as he passed through the door and into Ari's room. The impact of her captivity hit him full in the face. Unlike the others he had rescued, Ari was strapped down. Instruments were attached to her wrists, ankles and head. A shelf of vials, intravenous equipment and needles hung above a stainless steel counter that contained gauze and alcohol pads.

Bile formed in his stomach as his anger rose. Thoughts of Alexandra's rescue passed through his mind. He detested those who persecuted others; in his mind, their punishment should equal their crime. None of this easy prison stuff would ever suffice.

He positioned his orb next to Ari. Scanning the equipment, he considered the easiest way to sever her from the attachments would be to take all that was inside the orb and leave the cut ends behind.

Before severing Ari from the IVs he contacted Val, the Sensates primary physician, who assured him that removing her from the IVs would not cause Ari any harm.

Ari's beauty mesmerized him. He's seen *through* her eyes to her surroundings, nothing more. This was the first time he saw her face, and she was truly beautiful. Her wavy red hair was combed out in a circle of sorts around her flawless, but pale ivory face. Delicate fingers looked out of place next to the cruel needles inserted in her hands.

Ryeth expanded his sphere to include her and the

gurney. Once he was sure the orb was stable, he severed the leads to the instruments and IVs, and whisked them away from the FSB.

As they passed through the walls of the facility, he saw lights flashing and heard alarms going off.

***

Within a few seconds, Ari awoke. Her eyes popped and she began to struggle violently. Held only by the straps at her waist and ankles, she could move about freely from the waist up. She wriggled and thrashed about. Her arms flew about inside the sphere and the trailing edges of the wires and tubing slapped the blue suit and hit the sides of the orb.

When the wires and tubing reached the outer rim of the sphere, the integrity of the sphere became compromised.

Ryeth struggled with the concentration required to maintain the orb's ever changing dimensions and calm the girl at the same time.

"Lie still or you'll kill us both," he yelled.

Her eyes popped even larger as she turned her face away from Ryeth and saw scenery pass before her eyes. She pushed herself halfway off the gurney and reached to touch the sphere.

The sides buckled in, but Ryeth used his mind to push it back out. It wobbled in the opposite direction. It dropped in altitude.

"Hold still, I tell you," said Ryeth as his heart raced. "I can't hold us much longer."

He reached for Ari with the gloved fingers of the blue suit and latched onto her arms to force her back to the gurney.

"Ari," he yelled, "if you are in there somewhere,

287

stop thrashing around."

His words fell on deaf ears. He could feel her slipping yet dared not hold her any tighter for fear of hurting her. The blasted gloves of the suit worked against him and prevented him from gaining a proper hold. She flung her head back and forth and kicked at the leg restraints.

Ari slipped from his grasp. He reached to grab her once again as his concentration on the orb wavered. The orb's outer edges fluctuated like a huge bubble about to burst. His breathing quickened as he fought to hold her down. With his concentration ebbing, he knew he couldn't maintain the orb much longer.

Ryeth thought to contact Jediah for help, but didn't want any actions to coincide with the timing of the escape. He was on his own. The wobbling sides grew and shrunk; the gurney and Ryeth flew from side to side. Ari fought like a wild cat. Travel became jerky.

Ari's arms broke free once more. Each time her arms neared the outer rim, the fluctuations in power swayed the orb's boundaries. She pushed against him once more and reached for the rim of the orb.

Time was critical; he had to land. As he grabbed her flailing arms, he laid his body across her to hold her down. The end had come; the concentration required to maintain the orb clashed with the attention to control it resulted in the inability to maintain the orb's outer shell.

Ryeth looked around and realized his location. He made a quick adjustment. The sphere became unstable and broke just as he touched down inside the library of a home he maintained in eastern Ohio.

Her legs wrestled against the bindings, cutting

into her flesh. Ryeth clenched his teeth. The danger had passed but the flailing uncontrollable woman continued to fight to escape.

Ari, I'm a friend, he yelled into her mind. *We have rescued you. You're no longer a prisoner. Please stop fighting me!*

She stopped struggling; her breathing was labored as she gasped for breath. Ryeth wasn't sure whether she'd heard him or she just wore herself out. Her chest heaved to suck in the air her body so desperately needed. She turned her head to face Ryeth and peered through the face mask into his eyes.

I am like you, he said. *I wish you no harm.*

She turned her head and craned her neck to look around, her breaths still coming in deep gasps.

Ryeth loosened his hold on her and waited to see if she resumed fighting. She laid still. He released her arms.

Ari's hands moved at a snail's pace up to her face. Her fingertips felt eyebrows, cheeks, and then spread to pass through her hair. She pulled a lock of her hair around and studied it.

Ryeth watched as she tugged at the tight neck of the hospital gown. Her arms dropped. She stared at him, her eyes wide and blinking.

Will you hold still so I can get out of this suit?

She gave a slow nod.

Ryeth took off his gloves and then the helmet. As he removed the suit from his body, he became a bit self-conscious of the scant clothing he wore underneath. All through the painstaking process he kept his eyes on Ari.

He came back to her side.

You're still on the gurney, so don't move. I don't want you to fall.

Ari's eyes flew wide as her hands grasped the IVs in her hands. She started to jerk them out.

Ryeth placed his hands over hers to calm her. *The tubes are cut off,* he said. *Nothing is going into your bloodstream anymore.*

She sighed, closed her eyes and then reopened them. Her fingertips continued to explore her body. Hands searched her neck, chest, and waist, where she encountered the restraint. She pulled at it, her breathing becoming more rapid.

Ryeth patted her arm. She turned to look at him.

"I'm going to remove the straps, okay?" he asked.

"Yeah," she said and nodded. Her voice was strained and scratchy.

He smiled at her, released the strap around her waist, and then undid the ones at her ankles.

She moved her legs and twisted her body.

"Do you think you can sit up?" he asked.

She nodded.

He put his arm around her back and helped her to a sitting position. She swayed and her head fell backward. Her arm reached out in instinct. Ryeth steadied her until the dizziness subsided.

Ari's breathing was labored; Ryeth sensed she couldn't catch her breath.

Her hands went to her legs. She rubbed them and flexed her toes. She gave a long sigh as her eyes closed. Her head dropped.

As she rested, Ryeth looked around the room, still holding onto her. He spied a comfortable chair in the corner.

"I'm going to move you to the chair over there," he gestured toward the chair. "Is that okay?"

Her nod was slight.

He placed his arm around her back, and the other beneath her knees as he lifted her off the gurney.

Blue gas sprayed from beneath the bed and, in an instant, filled the room. Ryeth managed one step before he staggered and fell backward with Ari landing on top of him. The room went black.

Chapter 35

The welcome home party ended. Alice Jane tried to contact Ryeth.

Ryeth? Is everything okay? She listened. No answer.

Jediah, Ryeth's not responding.

Alice Jane handed dishes to Alexandra and said, "This is the worst part of having a party."

"It's times like this I wish I was Cassie," said Alexandra. "She got into the car all starry-eyed and drove away."

"We could have hired someone to do everything," said Alice, "but what's the fun in that?"

"Yeah, right," said Alexandra as she scraped the plates. "We should be done in a few minutes."

After I take this load to the kitchen, I'm slipping over to Ryeth's house, Alice Jane said to Jediah.

Okay, make it quick, he said.

"I'm going to load the dishwasher," she said to Alexandra. "Would you bring in the rest?"

"Sure," said Alexandra as she left the kitchen to gather the remaining dishes from the back yard.

Alice Jane dropped the dishes off in the kitchen and transported to Ryeth's house.

"Ryeth!" she yelled. "Are you here?" She couldn't sense him anywhere. She tried searching using the full extent of her powers, but couldn't locate him.

She transported back to Larkspur and started to

load the dishwasher.

He wasn't there. I can't sense him anywhere, she said. *What's happened?* she asked Jediah and Alexandra. Her hands shook. She dropped a plate. The sound of the ceramic plate hitting the tile floor echoed through the kitchen. She stared at the plate as it stopped and came to rest without breaking.

I'm going to see if the others can contact him, said Jediah, *but somehow, I think it won't do any good this time either.*

Alice Jane grabbed the dish from the floor. Appearances at this point meant everything. They had to continue their roles. Terry was still in the tool shed, and for all they knew, waiting for them to slip up.

Ryeth's resourceful, said Alexandra, *and highly capable. He must have run into a snag. We have to continue as if nothing happened.*

This isn't easy, said Alice Jane.

Jediah brought in the last load of dishes. He returned to the yard to stack the tables and chairs and dropped his shoulders.

"Hey, Alice," he called from the yard. "Is it okay if we put these tables and chairs back tomorrow?"

"Sure," she called from the doorway. "It's supposed to be clear tonight. I've just finished the dishes. If you go to the front porch I'll bring some wine. We can relax a bit in the rocking chairs."

"Wait for me," yelled Alexandra as she dashed to Jediah's side. "I'll walk around with you."

Alice Jane opened a bottle of merlot, grabbed three glasses and made her way to the front porch just as Jediah and Alexandra entered the stairs.

Jediah dropped his wife's hand and took the steps two at a time. He held the glasses while Alice Jane poured the red liquid.

What did the counsel think? she asked Jediah.

Jediah raised his glass to the ladies, who toasted him in return.

We all think Ryeth can handle himself. We'll monitor the situation, but give him until the morning before we take any action, said Jediah.

Alice Jane sat in a rocker and put her feet up on the bannister. Jediah and Alexandra followed suit.

"Umm, this is good, Alexandra," said Alice Jane. "Where'd you get it?"

"It's local," she said. "*Whisperly Wineries* had a very good year. I think the bouquet is nice, and the taste isn't too dry or too sweet. I'll bring some more the next time we visit. I bought a case."

Just got some news, said Jediah. *The Ultras were monitoring the extraction from Dayton. As soon as Ryeth took off, the Ultras moved to just outside the FSB. Ryeth and Ari definitely got away, but they never made it back to Ryeth's. The Ultras will remain in Dayton for a few days taking turns to monitor the situation.*

"It's just good to relax after a full day," said Alice Jane. "Thanks for doing all the cooking, Alexandra, it was never my forte."

"It was my pleasure," Alexandra said. "Cassie helped - Jediah too."

"I meant to mention that," said Alice Jane. "I never knew Jediah was so handy in the kitchen."

Jediah smiled at Alice Jane. "That's because you never stayed here long enough to find out."

"I'm rectifying that now, dear brother. Mom said it would never be too late to come home."

Silence engulfed the three. Thoughts of Nancy Jane were never far away. They sipped their wine and stared off into the stars.

My insides are jumping up and down, said Alice Jane, *sitting here is driving me crazy.*

A few more minutes. We can't just drink and run, said Alexandra.

Alice Jane couldn't handle much more. *As soon as you two leave, I'm going to Ryeth's to wait this out.*

Don't forget to play the game, said Jediah.

I won't, she said. *I'll lock the doors, turn off the lights and retire to my room to read like a good little Sensate... at least that's what I'll convey.*

Good girl, he said.

After what seemed an eternity, Jediah rose and took Alexandra's hand.

"It's time we headed up the hill," he said.

Alexandra got up and stretched. "Yes. I'm ready," she said.

"The party was lovely, Alexandra," said Alice Jane. "Thank you for hosting it. I can't back out on living here now... I'd be crucified."

"If it takes guilt to keep you here, I'm all for it," said Alexandra.

Alice Jane hugged Alexandra and Jediah, and waved to them as they walked to their car.

***

Terry shifted from his seat atop a large concrete flowerpot inside the tool shed. What a stroke of luck. One of their own had been in attendance. He wouldn't be sorry to see this case crack wide open. Playing the mild-mannered gardener for four years had put a definite dent in his professional techniques.

He waited for the lights to go out in the upstairs

rooms before leaving the security of the tool shed. Man, he needed a bathroom.

His legs ached and his back hurt from sitting in one position for so long. And, he was hungry. All that food, and he'd had the dried up sandwich from the vending machine at the Seven Eleven.

As he walked down the street to his car, he pulled out his cell phone and called Chief Black. It went to voicemail, so he left a message to let her know the outcome of the surveillance.

Chapter 36

The alarm went off. Black whipped her head to the left to watch the monitor in the Director's office. Her face fell when she saw it was her section. Without thinking, her hand went to her chest. As she sucked in a gulp of air, she cast a quick glance at the Director and said, "I'll see to that right away, sir."

She stood and fumbled with her suit jacket button.

"Black, you're on borrowed time," he said.

"Yes sir, I'm aware of that."

"Then get moving!" he said with narrowed eyes.

Her feet couldn't move fast enough to get out of that blowhard's office. Men in power disgusted her; always lording their power over some female. His day would come. She wouldn't *always* be a subordinate.

Black flew down the steps to the detainment area. She opened the door at the bottom, and though she was twenty-some feet away from the entrance to her section, she bellowed to the guard, "Get that door open *now*."

As her stride continued past the guard, she saw the reason for the alarm. 613's door was wide open. The alarm blared in her ears. The lights in the hallway flashed. A huge red light blinked over 613's door.

Four guards at the entrance spoke, their arms flailing, but they hushed as she grew closer. They stepped aside so she could enter.

What met her eyes made no sense. Not only was 613 gone, but so was her gurney. The IV tubing hung to the floor dripping the contents of the bags into puddles. The wires to the monitors were severed.

Black noted the time the lead went flat on the EKG machine: 16:43. She checked her watch: 16:45.

She turned to the four guards, "Speak," she said.

Three turned to look at the one who was on duty. He straightened his shoulders and raised his head. "The alarm went off, I opened the door; that," he said pointing in the room, "is what I saw."

Black scrutinized the guard. She'd seen him around. "Did you hear anything before the alarm went off?"

"No, Ma'am," he said.

"Did any of you three hear or notice anything abnormal prior to the alarm?"

A chorus of 'no ma'am's filled her ears.

"Block off this area. Allow no one to enter without my consent." She turned to leave, but called over her shoulder. "I'll be bringing a forensics detail by later to go over the area."

Doom descended on her like a tsunami, fierce and without regard for the consequences. Although she knew the video would confirm the guard's story, she went to the security room to view the tape.

Just like the three who vanished, so did 613. Although she'd taken every precaution, her efforts fell flat.

She completed the report for the Director and placed it in his electronic review folder on their company program. It was the last step she'd take before the hammer nailed her coffin shut.

At 1710, she walked the distance to the

Director's office. The door was ajar. He looked up and said, "Come in, Black, and close the door behind you."

She did as instructed.

***

Morgan Black maintained her composure throughout the complete interview with the Director. Two guards met her as she followed through with the forensics team and cleaned out her office. She placed the boxes containing her personal items on the cart outside her office door to be checked to ensure she wasn't taking any proprietary documents or information from the FSB.

The two guards searched her and then escorted her out of the building.

Not once did she bellow about the unfair treatment, or scream that it could have happened to anyone. She kept her shoulders straight and her lips sealed as she walked to her car in the parking garage.

She maintained that same composure as she exited her car, walked to her luxury apartment and unlocked the door.

As she closed the door behind her, she hissed. Her blood pumped fast and hammered in her ears. She gritted her teeth so hard her jaw popped. In one quick movement, she flung her briefcase across the room. It crashed into a wrought iron table and smashed the glass top into miniscule pieces. The vase with fresh flowers dropped to the floor and spilled green water onto the plush silk rug.

Hands clenched and released at her side. She could feel the keys in her right hand as they cut into her flesh. Seething, she let the keys fall. The blood dripped from her hand onto the floor.

Demoted. Not fired. She would have to answer to yet *another* man. 613 and her freak friends would rue the day they messed with her career. She could still keep an eye on the investigation, but her position was a yes-sir position where she didn't get to hold the reins.

Fifteen years of tip-toeing around all the big wigs to obtain the position at the FSB, and only six months to lose it.

She reached into her suit jacket and pulled out her cell phone. The activity that would erase the stench of the day off her warmed her from within. She punched the number for her favorite booty call and awaited the deep male voice.

The call went to voice mail.

She threw the phone against the tiled fireplace. It shattered. Glaring at the pieces, she grabbed her keys and went out the door.

A dark pub down on Third Avenue would have what she needed...

***

The Ultras monitored the whole escape and even tagged along with Black as she hit the bar on Third Avenue. They listened as the forensics team came up empty. The DNA monitor, heat sensors and weight distribution sensors remained a flat line throughout.

They reported back to the counsel the initial success of the mission, stating they would remain there as a follow-up until things settled down.

Chapter 37

As soon as Jediah and Alexandra left the driveway, Alice Jane picked up the wine glasses and empty bottle and headed indoors.

Ryeth? Where are you?

She received no answer and could not track his location.

After locking up downstairs, she went upstairs, set the timer on the light in her bedroom and transported to Ryeth's home in the mountains.

The house seemed lonely. She walked onto the deck, which hung over the steep incline of the ridge. It would do her no good to physically search for him. If her abilities failed to reach him, something prevented it from happening. He would contact her if he could.

Dusk turned into darkness as she waited. An owl hooted woohoo, hoo, hoo and sounded as lonely as she felt. A breeze brought forth the cool mountain air. She shivered and wrapped her arms tightly around her legs as she snuggled into the cushion's warmth.

Woohoo, hoo, hoo echoed in the night.

She watched the moon rise above the tops of the pines that circled his home. A cloud passed by that was so thin the moon beams broke through. And still, she listened.

She listened for his heart beat, which she knew as well as her own. She sniffed for his scent, strong and musky. She remembered his touch, confident and sure, and she could still feel his lips from the afternoon's searing kiss.

Ryeth...

As the night grew darker, and the moon hid behind a cloud, Alice Jane went to the kitchen. She placed a kettle on the stove, and watched until its shrill voice pierced the air.

With numbing stillness, she poured the boiling water over the tea bag in her mug and watched the color change to a deep amber.

She cupped the mug between her hands as the warmth spread through her fingertips. In the living room, she took up space amid the depths of the cushions in a reading chair she'd dubbed as her own. Lowering the light on the end table, she prepared herself for the long wait until morning.

She mentally called to him every few minutes, but kept her mind open for any stirrings of his mind, no matter how little.

As the minutes grew into hours she forced her hope to hold strong. After the all-night vigil, the dark of the night receded and the dawn of a new day arrived. The forest came alive. Chirping birds flew from tree to tree, squirrels chattered as they flew from one tip of a pine tree to the next, but their antics failed to waver her concentration.

The sun rose turning long shadows into shorter ones. Leaves spun to catch the rays.

Ryeth? she called again. She listened.

It was a movement.

Ryeth! She stood and nearly fell because her legs had gone numb.

Ryeth? Are you there? He moaned. It wasn't clear, but it was enough for her to latch onto.

She transported herself to his side, ready to touch him and get him out of wherever it was.

What she found was Ryeth lying on the floor, almost naked, rubbing his head. A woman with red hair lay prone across his body.

***

Alice Jane touched his cheek. "Are you all right?" she asked.

Ryeth didn't answer. He rolled his head and squeezed his eyes shut.

Alice Jane sent out an SOS to the High Council with an imprint of the location. Val arrived first, followed by Jediah. They lifted Ari off Ryeth.

The doctor checked Ryeth's pulse, then Ari's. He gave Ryeth the once over and stated, "He's been knocked out; Ari too."

"Let's get them to Ryeth's where we've set up the room for Ari," said Val.

Val transported Ari; Jediah and Alice Jane took Ryeth.

At Ryeth's house, they placed Ari on the bed in her prepared room. Alexandra arrived to assist Val.

Jediah helped a semi-conscious Ryeth to the couch. "That was some snooze you took," Jediah said. He helped him lay down and tucked a pillow beneath his head. He pulled a throw over his body.

Ryeth's head spun around. "Alice!" he yelled.

"I'm here," she yelled from across the room. "Just getting you some coffee."

"Good," he mumbled and relaxed. His eyes closed again.

Jediah sat in a chair opposite the couch and spoke in soft tones. "Val said you'd been knocked out."

Ryeth tried to open his eyes, gave up and said with a slur, "Yeah."

Alice Jane came to his side. "Leave him alone, Jediah. At least give him time to wake up."

Ryeth tried to prop himself up on his elbow, but fell back. "Blue gas." His words came out slurred so he resorted to telepathy.

Blue gas sprayed out from under the gurney when I lifted Ari off. We hit the floor.

Jediah sent a fast message to the Ultras.

"Why didn't you come here as planned?" asked Jediah.

Alice shot her always-in-charge brother a scathing look. "Quit pestering him," she said. "Give him some time."

She knelt by Ryeth's side and ran her fingers through his silken black locks.

Women! said Ryeth to Jediah. *When they are riled up nothing can settle them.*

Jediah grinned and then his eyes widened. *Is that what happened? Ari woke up?* he asked.

That crazy woman almost dropped us both out of the sky. If she had her way and broken loose from my grasp, I wouldn't have been able to save her with that blasted blue suit on.

Ryeth pushed his arms against the cushions, swung his legs over the side, sat upright, and took a swig of the thick black coffee Alice Jane offered.

"I feel like I've been kicked in the head by a mule," he said. He rubbed his eyes and shook his head to clear it, looked around and took another sip.

"How's Ari?" he asked.

"Val's checking her out," said Jediah. "Alexandra's with her."

"How goes it with the FSB?" he asked.

Jediah leaned back into the chair. "So far, so good," he said. "Nothing has been picked up yet regarding our involvement. The Ultras stayed behind to watch Black."

Val came into the room. "Jediah, Ari is going to need some recuperative help. Alexandra wants to take her to Heartseed. We have some physical therapists within our group who will be able to help Ari along. If it's okay with you, you'll need to go with Alexandra and get Ari situated."

"Thanks, Val," said Jediah. "Of course it's fine for her to come to Heartseed." He stood and nodded toward Ryeth. "Let me know how the big fella checks out, will you?"

Ryeth shot Jediah a wry smile.

"I will," said Val.

Jediah turned and went down the hallway.

Val stepped close to Ryeth. He checked his pulse and looked in his eyes. "You said the gas was blue?"

"Yeah, light blue," said Ryeth.

"It might have been a rare Xenon 132 isotope. It's a great anesthetic, but not typically used due to the high cost to manufacture. I wouldn't put it past the government to use it because it's fast-acting. You shouldn't have any lasting side effects. But if you notice anything odd, give me a shout."

Val stood to leave. "My pharmacological team will go over the gurney in detail just to make sure we don't miss anything."

"Thanks, Doc," said Ryeth. "You're the best doctor I've ever had."

Val smiled. "I'm probably the *only* doctor you've ever had." He left as he had entered.

Alice Jane mentally checked the house; they

were alone. "I missed you," she said.

Ryeth ran his hands though his hair and rubbed his temples. "How long was I gone?"

"About seventeen hours. All through the night," she said as she snuggled next to him. "Are you sure you're okay?"

He smiled. She cared. He liked that she cared. He liked it a whole lot. Ryeth rose from the couch and swayed; the throw dropped from his body. Holding out his hand to help her up, he watched as she stood, drinking in every move her body made.

When he spoke, passion made his voice husky. "Wanna check out how 'okay' I really am?"

He pulled her close into a warm embrace.

She slid her arms around his neck. Alice raised her lips to his, and he met them lightly before he pulled back just enough to watch her eyes change from vibrant to smoky.

It was then he began his slow assault on her senses. At the moment when her knees bent and her body rested next to his, he swept her up in his arms, carried her to his room and kicked the door shut.

He tossed her onto his bed, then stood back with his hands on his hips.

He looked into Alice's eyes, now filled with excitement. She giggled, then squealed as she realized his intent. Ryeth bounded through the air.

Alice transported at the last minute to just outside his reach, but rolled close after he landed.

He pulled her near wrapping his arms around her.

"Tell me what happened at the FSB," she said.

"Ummm… after," he said as he nuzzled her neck.

"After?" Her voice was soft as a whisper.

"Yea… after."

Alexandra sat by Ari's bedside, not wanting to leave her alone. She had yet to wake from the effects of the blue gas.

Val took blood samples to establish the best way to flush the drugs from her system and to aid in her identity. He was concerned that Ari could've come from a new Sensate gene pool, or that they missed her birth. Never before had a Sensate slipped through their net. Her DNA would answer many questions.

Ari was older than Alexandra, she was certain, but beyond that, there was no way of guessing her age from her appearance alone. Her red hair contained strands of blonde, deep auburn, brown, and platinum. The wavy curls were thick and luxurious. The thought that struck Alexandra, was: 'why didn't they cut it'? Someone who provided the daily care of Ari at the FSB had taken great pains to assure her locks received the greatest of care.

She also had great skin; but all the Sensates had perfect health and great skin. Ari's skin was different, it seemed to have been carved from porcelain. She was heavenly.

Ari stirred.

Alexandra leaned near. *My name is Alexandra,* she telecommunicated to the girl. *You are safe, Ari. There is no need to be afraid.*

Ari's breathing changed. She took Ari's hand in hers. *Ari, I am Alexandra. You are free and have nothing to fear.*

Ari's hand closed around hers. Alexandra watched as her lids fluttered and then opened. Brilliant ice blue eyes came awake and stared into

Alexandra's.

"Hi," said Alexandra. "Welcome to Heartseed, my home. You're safe here."

Ari's eyes moved from Alexandra and looked around. She removed her hand from Alexandra's and held it close to her chest.

"Our group put together a plan and rescued you from the Fringe Science Bureau of Homeland Security. You were being held against your will for a very long time. The people who held you hoped to learn your abilities, your powers, and use them to their advantage."

Can you hear me? said Ari.

Alexandra smiled. *Yes, I can hear you*, she said. *Now that you are closer to us, others can hear you too. You will need to learn how to use your powers, so that you don't compromise our group.*

Alexandra switched to normal speech. "We abide by a handful of rules so that we can live somewhat normal lives."

"I understand," said Ari, her voice rough. "Where am I?"

"You're at my home in Waynesburg, Pennsylvania. My husband, Jediah, is the leader of the Sensates, which is what we call people like you and me who can talk to each other without speaking."

"Is he the man with the blue skin that carried me through the air in a balloon?" she asked. Her eyes were startled and intense.

"No, that was another member of our group. We have various abilities. He's the only one who could make an orb large enough to get you out of there," said Alexandra. "He wore a special suit to keep from being recognized by the people who held

308

you."

"Yes, he took the skin off. I remember now." Ari looked thoughtful.

Alexandra prepared herself for Ari's lack of updated knowledge. She didn't want to flood Ari with too much information all at once, so in an attempt to keep things light she asked, "How are you feeling?"

"I'm weak," said Ari.

"That's to be expected. Our doctor will stop by later today. His name is Valentine Jellan, but we all call him Val. You'll like him. He is the sweetest person you'll ever meet."

Ari's eyebrows drew into a scowl. "What's he going to do to me?" she asked.

Alexandra was quick to calm her fears. "Nothing you don't want done," she said. "He wants to flush the drugs from your system as quickly as possible so you can get started in your new life."

"What new life? I don't want a new life. I want my old one, the one that was stolen from me," said Ari.

Alexandra saw the sadness and anger in Ari's eyes and sensed a void in her soul. Her heart ached for the beautiful girl with luminous eyes.

"I know, Ari, I know," she said.

She watched as a myriad of expressions passed over Ari's face. The girl sighed. Her remarkable eyes fluttered, closed, blinked, and then closed one last time.

Drifting in and out was normal, Val explained to her earlier. Ari had endured a long and inhumane captivity and her body would take time to recover. Muscles would need to be rebuilt, and real food introduced into her stomach. The Sensates would

309

supply her with information to bring her up-to-date with the outside world. Ari would set the pace, and they would give her what she needed to become an active part of society.

Alexandra drew a light blanket over her charge. With soft footing, she crept from the room and closed the door behind her.

You have done well, memiki.

Alexandra smiled at the now-familiar touch to her mind. *Thank you*, she said, then added as an afterthought, *are you watching me?*

I do not watch. I watch over.

Kayè? Alexandra asked. Her response had come without thinking. Kayè meant Grandmother.

Yes, child, the voice said.

You were with me when Magis took me.

I have always been with you.

Kayè was gone, but the warm feeling she left in her heart was not.

What was Kayè? Spirit? Guardian? Where did she come from? Why had she come?

Alexandra smiled. For now, she didn't need to know the answers. It was enough to know that someone or something watched over her and that they would never be alone.

Epilogue

A smile broke across Ryeth's face as he played with Alice Jane's dark, luxurious hair. They sat silent, each unable to put feelings into words. He watched as various emotions passed over her beautiful face until she yawned, closed her eyes, and her breathing became slow and regular.

Ryeth pulled Alice Jane close. She'd maintained a vigil and come to his side without fear of danger. Pride in his woman swelled from within. She possessed a strong character, matched his basic attitude, and above all, had lips that begged to be kissed from dusk 'til dawn. In slumber, her inner fire hid beneath long lashes that lay across her perfect cheek. He brushed her chin with his thumb. Some women were worth keeping.

His life before knowing true love became inconsequential. The revenge on the Sensates who left him to fend on his own dissipated and blew away with the late summer breeze. Years of his solitary existence came to a crashing halt by the gentle machinations of the sleeping beauty he held in his arms. He would spend the remainder of his years making up for wasting half a millennia.

My beautiful son.

Ryeth's breath caught in his chest. Warmth spread throughout his body like a long-awaited caress. *Ma, how can it be?*

Your heart has softened and now allows me

access. I have missed you, Ryeth.

Onatah's voice was exactly as he remembered. It filled his head with melodious tones.

His eyes glistened. *Oh, Ma...*

Her essence filled every cell of his body as the shattered boy inside disappeared, leaving a complete man in its stead. The bars that contained his powers expanded, shifted, and finally snapped. His spirit floated outside his body and hung in mid-air. Ryeth was, instantly, at one with everything that surrounded him. The hair on his head mingled with the wind as he realized individual strands were now the leaves on the trees that surrounded his home. Arms that were once attached to his body reached miles in all directions as his senses stretched far and wide. He became acutely aware of all living things down to the cellular level.

His mother's senses co-mingled with his as they became one with the universe. She shared the last months of her existence with her son as he grasped the love she and his father shared. He learned of their hopes for his future, their knowledge of his powers, and sensed his mother's suffering during the centuries of inability to reach out to him when he chose rage and despair as his companions upon their deaths.

Rushing by those emotions she ended his years of longing by transferring all the love and dreams she'd stored throughout their separation to her son.

Slowly, Onatah's essence ebbed.

I have so many questions, he said.

All in good time, my son, she said. *You must help prepare our group for the oncoming siege. All that we are will soon be at risk of discovery.*

He sensed her strength waning. With one last

touch to his heart, she was gone.

Ryeth breathed air into his lungs and held it as he felt it circulate throughout his body. He released the breath slowly as his thoughts became clear. No more would he restrict the power that surged within. He had the ability to pinpoint the power, use as much or as little as he desired, and had full confidence in his ability to cause no harm should the occasion arise.

Peace filled his conscience as he realized his part in the Prophecy. Regret for the lost years tried to enter his mind, but he tossed it aside as a lesson learned.

Sure of his future, he was brought back to the present as his fingers rubbed the softness of Alice Jane's curls. His heart nearly burst as love for his woman surged through his being. There would be time to delve into the intricacies of their relationship; time that he would relish and savor. For now, he was content to be her pillow.

As Alice Jane lay sleeping, Ryeth took the opportunity to check in with Chief Black. A satisfied smile crept across his lips. He'd missed her initial reaction to Ari's departure, which he would obtain from the Ultras later, but right now, he wanted to know how much Ari's loss would set them back or if it would crush the FSB's desire for knowledge of the Sensates. Black held that key. Her removal from the investigation would work as a minimum; the cherry would be her dismissal from the unit.

What he learned from probing her mind was something in-between. Black had been reduced in rank, had no real authority, but still maintained input into the on-going investigation. It was a win for the Sensates because they were able to get Ari out before

Black used her.

The true battle loomed ahead in the not-too-distant future. The Prophecy was clear - Sensate abilities must remain secret. The government's knowledge and use of their powers would change the face of the world forever. The rivalry between the FSB and the Sensates was imminent; the battle had begun.